THE DARKEST RIDDLE

"Suppose you were a wizard restless with power, drawn to Lungold by the powers of Ohm and his promises of great skill and knowledge. You placed your name in his mind; with your trust in his skill, you did without question whatever he asked of you, and in return he channeled your own energies into powers you scarcely dreamed you had.

"And then suppose, one day you realized that this wizard, whose mind could control yours so skillfully, was false to his teachings, false to you, false to every man, king, scholar, farmer that he had ever served. What would you do if you found that he had dangerous plans and terrible purposes ... that the very foundations of his teachings were a lie? What would you do?"

Morgon watched his hands close on the table into fists, as though they belonged to someone else. He whispered, "Ohm." Then he said, "I would run. I would run until no one —man or wizard—could find me. And then I would begin to think ...

"Morgon emerges as a character in high relief, with the others melding solidly into place against an intricate plot accented by distinctive writing and evocative imagery."
—*ALA Booklist*

"McKillip has created powerful images of a haunting silence, a universe full of secret purposes and terrible possibilities."
—*The National Observer*

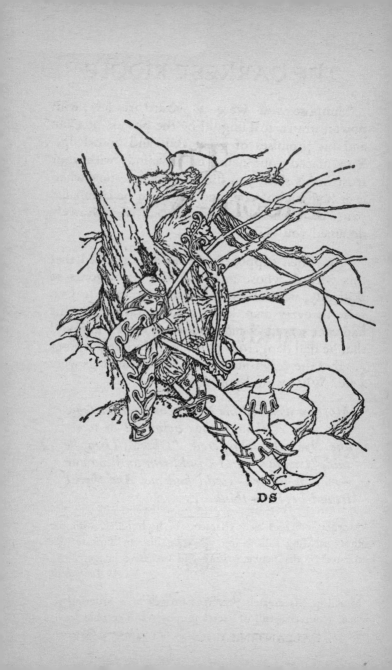

The
Riddle-Master
of Hed

patricia A. McKillip

A Del Rey Book

BALLANTINE BOOKS • NEW YORK

A Del Rey Book
Published by Ballantine Books

Copyright © 1976 by Patricia A. McKillip

Library of Congress Catalog Card Number: 76-5492

ISBN 0-345-33104-4

This edition published by arrangement with Atheneum

Printed in Canada

First Ballantine Books Edition: February 1978
Nineteenth Printing: September 1991

First Canadian Printing: March 1978
Fourth Canadian Printing: February 1980

Cover Art and frontispiece by Darrell K. Sweet

FOR CAROL
the first eleven chapters

MAP BY KATHY MC KILLIP

Notes on people and places may be found on page 223.

1

MORGON OF HED MET THE HIGH ONE'S HARPIST one autumn day when the trade-ships docked at Tol for the season's exchange of goods. A small boy caught sight of the round-hulled ships with their billowing sails striped red and blue and green, picking their way among the tiny fishing boats in the distance, and ran up the coast from Tol to Akren, the house of Morgon, Prince of Hed. There he disrupted an argument, gave his message, and sat down at the long, nearly deserted tables to forage whatever was left of breakfast. The Prince of Hed, who was recovering slowly from the effects of loading two carts of beer for trading the evening before, ran a reddened eye over the tables and shouted for his sister.

"But, Morgon," said Harl Stone, one of his farmers, who had a shock of hair grey as a grindstone and a body like a sack of grain. "What about the white bull from An you said you wanted? The wine can wait——"

"What," Morgon said, "about the grain still in Wyndon Amory's storage barn in east Hed? Someone has to bring it to Tol for the traders. Why doesn't anything ever get done around here?"

"We loaded the beer," his brother Eliard, clear-eyed and malicious reminded him.

1

"Thank you. Where is Tristan? Tristan!"

"What!" Tristan of Hed said irritably behind him, holding the ends of her dark, unfinished braids in her fists.

"Get the wine now and the bull next spring," Cannon Master, who had grown up with Morgon, suggested briskly. "We're sadly low on Herun wine; we've barely enough to make it through winter."

Eliard broke in, gazing at Tristan. "I wish I had nothing better to do than sit around all morning braiding my hair and washing my face in buttermilk."

"At least I wash. You smell like beer. You all do. And who tracked mud all over the floor?"

They looked down at their feet. A year ago Tristan had been a thin, brown reed of a girl, prone to walking field walls barefoot and whistling through her front teeth. Now she spent much of her time scowling at her face in mirrors and at anyone in range beyond them. She transferred her scowl from Eliard to Morgon.

"What were you bellowing at me for?"

The Prince of Hed closed his eyes. "I'm sorry. I didn't mean to bellow. I simply want you to clear the tables, lay the cloths, reset them, fill pitchers of milk and wine, have them fix platters of meat, cheese, fruit and vegetables in the kitchen, braid your hair, put your shoes on and get the mud off the floor. The traders are coming."

"Oh, Morgon . . ." Tristan wailed. Morgon turned to Eliard.

"And you ride to east Hed and tell Wyndon to get his grain to Tol."

"Oh, Morgon. That's a day's ride!"

"I know. So go."

They stood unmoving, their faces flushed, while Morgon's farmers looked on in unabashed amusement. They were not alike, the three children of Athol of Hed and Spring Oakland. Tristan, with her flighty black hair and small, triangular face, favored their mother. Eliard, two years younger than Morgon, had Athol's

2

broad shoulders and big bones, and his fair, feathery hair. Morgon, with his hair and eyes the color of light beer, bore the stamp of their grandmother, whom the old men remembered as a slender, proud woman from south Hed: Lathe Wold's daughter. She had had a trick of looking at people the way Morgon was gazing at Eliard, remotely, like a fox glancing up from a pile of chicken feathers. Eliard puffed his cheeks like a bellows and sighed.

"If I had a horse from An, I could be there and back again by supper."

"I'll go," said Cannon Master. There was a touch of color in his face.

"I'll go," Eliard said.

"No. I want . . . I haven't seen Arin Amory for a while. I'll go." He glanced at Morgon.

"I don't care," Morgon said. "Just don't forget why you're going. Eliard, you help with the loading at Tol. Grim, I'll need you with me to barter—the last time I did it alone, I nearly traded three plow horses for a harp with no strings."

"If you get a harp," Eliard interrupted, "I want a horse from An."

"And I have to have some cloth from Herun," Tristan said. "Morgon, I have to have it. Orange cloth. Also I need thin needles and a pair of shoes from Isig, and some silver buttons, and—"

"What," Morgon demanded, "do you think grows in our fields?"

"I know what grows in our fields. I also know what I've been sweeping around under your bed for six months. I think you should either wear it or sell it. The dust is so thick on it you can't even see the colors of the jewels."

There was silence, brief and unexpected, in the hall. Tristan stood with her arms folded, the ends of her braids coming undone. Her chin was raised challengingly, but there was a hint of uncertainty in her eyes as

3

she faced Morgon. Eliard's mouth was open. He closed it with a click of teeth.

"What jewels?"

"It's a crown," Tristan said. "I saw one in a picture in a book of Morgon's. Kings wear them."

"I know what a crown is." He looked at Morgon, awed. "What on earth did you trade for that? Half of Hed?"

"I never knew you wanted a crown," Cannon Master said wonderingly. "Your father never had one. Your grandfather never had one. Your——"

"Cannon," Morgon said. He raised his hands, dropped the heels of them over his eyes. The blood was high in his face. "Kern had one."

"Who?"

"Kern of Hed. He would be our great-great-great-great-great-great-great-great-great-grandfather. No. One more great. It was made of silver, with a green jewel in it shaped like a cabbage. He traded it one day for twenty barrels of Herun wine, thereby instigating——"

"Don't change the subject," Eliard said sharply. "Where did you get it? Did you trade for it? Or did you . . ." He stopped. Morgon lifted his hands from his eyes.

"Did I what?"

"Nothing. Stop looking at me like that. You're trying to change the subject again. You traded for it, or you stole it, or you murdered someone for it——"

"Now, then——" Grim Oakland, Morgon's portly overseer, said placatingly.

"Or you just found it laying in the corncrib one day, like a dead rat. Which?"

"I did not murder anyone!" Morgon shouted. The clink of pots from the kitchen stopped abruptly. He lowered his voice, went on tartly, "What are you accusing me of?"

"I didn't——"

"I did not harm anyone to get that crown; I did not

4

trade anything that doesn't belong to me for it; I did not steal it—"

"I wasn't—"

"It belongs to me by right. What right, you have not touched on yet. You asked a riddle and tried to answer it; you are wrong four times. If I bumbled through riddles like that, I wouldn't be here talking to you now. I am going down to welcome the traders at Tol. When you decide to do some work this morning, you might join me."

He turned. He got as far as the front steps when Eliard, the blood mounting to his face, broke away from the transfixed group, moved across the room with a speed belied by his size, threw his arms around Morgon and brought him off the steps face down in the dirt.

The chickens and geese scattered, squawking indignantly. The farmers, the small boy from Tol, the woman who cooked, and the girl who washed pots jammed the door at once, clucking.

Morgon, groping for the breath the smack of the earth had knocked out of him, lay still while Eliard said between his teeth, "Can't you answer a simple question? What do you mean you wouldn't be talking to me now? Morgon, what did you do for that crown? Where did you get it? What did you do? I swear I'll—"

Morgon lifted his head dizzily. "I got it in a tower." He twisted suddenly, throwing Eliard off balance into one of Tristan's rosebushes.

The battle was brief and engrossing. Morgon's farmers, who until the previous spring had been under Athol's placid, efficient rule, stared half-shocked, half-grinning as the Prince of Hed was sent rolling across a mud puddle, staggered to his feet, and, head lowered like a bull, launched himself at his brother. Eliard shook himself free and countered with a swing of his fist that, connecting, sounded in the still air like the distant thunk of ax into wood. Morgon dropped like a sack of grain.

Then Eliard fell to his knees beside the prone body and said, aghast, "I'm sorry. I'm sorry. Morgon, did I hurt you?"

And Tristan, mute and furious, dumped a bucket of milk over their heads.

There was an odd explosion of whimpering from the porch as Cannon Master sat down on a step and buried his face in his knees. Eliard looked down at his muddy, sodden tunic. He brushed futilely at it.

"Now look what you did," he said plaintively. "Morgon?"

"You squashed my rosebush," Tristan said. "Look what you did to Morgon in front of everybody." She sat down beside Morgon on the wet ground. Her face had lost its habitual scowl. She wiped Morgon's face with her apron. Morgon blinked dazedly, his eyelashes beaded with milk. Eliard sat back on his haunches.

"Morgon, I'm sorry. But don't think you can evade the issue this way."

Morgon moved a hand cautiously after a moment, touched his mouth. "What's—? What was the issue?" he asked huskily.

"Never mind," Tristan said. "It's hardly something to brawl about."

"What is this all over me?"

"Milk."

"I'm sorry," Eliard said again. He put a coaxing hand under Morgon's shoulder, but Morgon shook his head.

"Just let me lie here for a moment. Why did you hit me like that? First you accuse me of murder and then you hit me and pour milk all over me. It's sour. Sour milk. You poured sour milk all over—"

"I did," Tristan said. "It was milk for the pigs. You threw Eliard into my rosebush." She touched Morgon's mouth again with her apron. "In front of everyone. I'm so humiliated."

"What did I do?" Morgon said. Eliard sighed, nursing a tender spot over his ribs.

"You made me lose my temper, speaking to me like that. You're slippery as a fish, but I grasped one thing. Last spring you got a crown you shouldn't have. You said that if you answered riddles as badly as I do, you wouldn't be here now. I want to know why. Why?"

Morgon was silent. He sat up after a moment, drawing his knees up, and dropped his head against them.

"Tristan, why did you pick today of all days to bring that up?"

"Go ahead, blame me," Tristan said without rancor. "Here I am running around with patches at my elbows, and you with pearls and jewels under your bed."

"You wouldn't have patches if you'd tell Narly Stone to make you some clothes that fit. You're growing, that's all—"

"Will you stop changing the subject!"

Morgon lifted his head. "Stop shouting." He glanced over Eliard's shoulder at the row of motionless, fascinated figures, and sighed. He slid his hands over his face, up through his hair. "I won that crown in a riddle-game I played in An with a ghost."

"Oh." Eliard's voice rose again sharply. "A what?"

"The wraith of Peven, Lord of Aum. That crown under my bed is the crown of the Kings of Aum. They were conquered by Oen of An six hundred years ago. Peven is five hundred years old. He lives bound in his tower by Oen and the Kings of An."

"What did he look like?" Tristan asked. Her voice was hushed. Morgon shrugged slightly; his eyes were hidden from them.

"An old man. An old lord with the answers to a thousand riddles in his eyes. He had a standing wager going that no one could win a riddle-game with him. So I sailed over with the traders and challenged him. He said great lords of Aum, An and Hel—the three portions of An—and even riddle-masters from Caithnard had challenged him to a game, but never a farmer from Hed. I told him I read a lot. Then we played the game. And I won. So I brought the crown home and put it

7

under my bed until I could decide what to do with it. Now, was that worth all the shouting?"

"He forfeited his crown to you when he lost," Eliard said evenly. "What would you have forfeited if you had lost?"

Morgon felt his split mouth gingerly. His eyes strayed to the fields beyond Eliard's back. "Well," he said finally. "You see, I had to win."

Eliard stood up abruptly. He took two strides away from Morgon, his hands clenched. Then he turned around and came back and squatted down again.

"You fool."

"Don't start another fight," Tristan begged.

"I'm not a fool," Morgon said. "I won the game, didn't I?" His face was still, his eyes distant, steady on Eliard's face. "Kern of Hed, the Prince with the cabbage on his crown—"

"Don't change—"

"I'm not. Kern of Hed, in addition to being the only Prince of Hed besides me to own a crown, had the dubious fortune of being pursued one day by a Thing without a name. Perhaps it was the effects of Herun wine. The Thing called his name over and over. He ran from it, going into his house of seven rooms and seven doors, and locking each door behind him until he came to the inmost chamber, where he could run no farther. And he heard the sound of one door after another being torn open, and his name called each time. He counted six doors opened, his name called six times. Then, outside the seventh door, his name was called again; but the Thing did not touch the door. He waited in despair for it to enter, but it did not. Then he grew impatient, longing for it to enter, but it did not. Finally he reached out, opened the door himself. The Thing was gone. And he was left to wonder, all the days of his life, what it was that had called out to him."

He stopped. Eliard said in spite of himself, "Well, what was it?"

"Kern didn't open the door. That is the only riddle to

come out of Hed. The stricture, according to the Riddle-Masters at Caithnard is this: Answer the unanswered riddle. So I do."

"It's not your business! Your business is farming, not risking your life in a stupid riddle-game with a ghost for a crown that's worthless because you keep it hidden under your bed. Did you think of us, then? Did you go before or after they died? Before or after?"

"After," Tristan said.

Eliard's fist splashed down in a pool of milk. "I knew it."

"I came back."

"Suppose you hadn't?"

"I came back! Why can't you try to understand, instead of thinking as though your brains are made of oak. Athol's son, with his hair and eyes and vision—"

"No!" Tristan said sharply. Eliard's fist, raised and knotted, halted in midair. Morgon dropped his face again against his knees. Eliard shut his eyes.

"Why do you think I'm so angry?" he whispered.

"I know."

"Do you? Even—even after six months, I still expect to hear her voice unexpectedly, or see him coming out of the barn, or in from the fields at dusk. And you? How will I know, now, that when you leave Hed, you'll come back? You could have died in that tower for the sake of a stupid crown and left us watching for the ghost of you, too. Swear you'll never do anything like that again."

"I can't."

"You can."

Morgon raised his head, looked at Eliard. "How can I make one promise to you and another to myself? But I swear this: I will always come back."

"How can you—"

"I swear it."

Eliard stared down at the mud. "It's because he let you go to that college. That's where your priorities were confused."

9

"I suppose so," Morgon said wearily. He glanced up at the sun. "Half the morning gone, and here we sit in the muck with sour milk drying in our hair. Why did you wait so long to ask me about the crown?" he asked Tristan. "That's not like you."

She shrugged a little, her face averted. "I saw your face, the day you came back with it. What are you going to do with it?"

He moved a strand of hair out of her eyes. "I don't know. I suppose I should do something with it."

"Well, I have a few suggestions."

"I thought you might." He stood up stiffly and caught sight of Cannon sitting on the porch. "I thought you were going to east Hed," he said pointedly.

"I'm going. I'm going." Cannon said cheerfully. "Wyndon Amory would never have forgiven me if I hadn't seen the end of this. Have you still got all your teeth?"

"I think so." The group at the doorway began shifting, breaking up under his gaze. He reached down, pulled Eliard to his feet. "What's the matter?"

"Nothing that isn't ordinarily the matter when you roll over a rosebush. I don't know if I have a clean tunic."

"You do," Tristan said. "I washed your clothes yesterday. The house is a mess; you—we're a mess, and the traders are coming, which means all the women will be coming over to look at their wares in our dirty hall. I'll die of shame."

"You never used to care," Eliard commented. "Now you're always complaining. You used to run around with mud on your feet and dog hair all over your skirt."

"That," Tristan said icily, "was when there was someone to take care of the house. Now there isn't. I do try." She whirled away, the hens fluttering out of her path. Eliard felt at his stiff hair, sighing.

"My brains are made of oak. If you pump for me, I'll pump for you."

They stripped and washed behind the house. Then

Eliard went to Grim Oakland's farm to help load the grain in his storage barn onto carts, and Morgon walked through the stubbled fields to the shore road that led to Tol.

The three trade-ships, their sails furled, had just docked. A ramp boomed down from one of them as Morgon stepped onto the wharf; he watched a horse being led down by a sailor, a beautiful, long-legged mare bred in An, jet black, with a bridle that flashed minute flecks of jewels in the sun. Then traders hailed him from the prow of a ship, and he went to meet them as they disembarked.

They were a vivid group, some dressed in the long, thin, orange and red coats from Herun, others in full robes from An, or the close-fitting, lavishly embroidered tunics from Ymris. They wore rings and chains from Isig, fur-lined caps from Osterland, which they gave away, together with bone-handled knives and copper brooches, to the children clustering shyly to watch. The ships carried, among other things, iron from Isig and Herun wine.

Grim Oakland came a few minutes later, as Morgon was inspecting the wine.

"I'd need a drink, too, after that," he commented. Morgon started to smile and changed his mind.

"Is the grain loaded?"

"Nearly. Harl Stone is bringing the wool and skins down from your barn. You'd be wise to take all the metal they carry."

Morgon nodded, his eyes straying again to the black horse tethered to the dock rail. A sailor lugged a saddle down from the ship, balanced it on the rail next to the horse. Morgon gestured with his cup.

"Who owns that mare? It looks like someone came with the traders. Or else Eliard traded Akren for her secretly."

"I don't know," Grim said, his red-grey brows peaked. "Lad, it's none of my business, but you shouldn't let your private inclinations interfere with the duty you were born to."

Morgon sipped wine. "They don't interfere."

"It would be a grave interference if you were dead."

He shrugged. "There's Eliard."

Grim heaved a sigh. "I told your father not to send you to that school. It addled your thinking. But no. He wouldn't listen. I told him it was wrong to let you go away from Hed so long; it's never been done, no good would come of it. And I was right. No good has come. You running off to a strange land, playing riddle-games with—with a man who should have the decency to stay put once he's dead and buried in the earth. It's not good. It's not—it's not the way a land-ruler of Hed should want to behave. It's not done."

Morgon held the cool metal of the cup against his cracked mouth. "Peven couldn't help wandering around after he was dead. He killed seven of his sons with misused wizardry, and then himself out of sorrow and shame. He couldn't rest in the ground. He told me that after so many years he had a hard time remembering all his sons' names. That worried him. I learned their names at Caithnard, so I could tell him. It cheered him up."

Grim's face was red as a turkey wattle. "It's indecent," he snapped. He moved away, lifted the lid on a chest full of bars of iron, and slammed it shut again. A trader spoke at Morgon's elbow.

"You are pleased with the wine, Lord?"

Morgon turned, nodding. The trader ported a thin, leaf-green coat from Herun, a cap of white mink, and a harp of black wood slung by a strap of white leather over one shoulder. Morgon said, "Whose horse? Where did you get that harp?"

The trader grinned, sliding it from his shoulder. "Remembering how your lordship likes harps, I found this one for you in An. It was the harp of the harpist of Lord Col of Hel. It is quite old, but see how beautifully preserved."

Morgon slid his hands down the fine, carved pieces. He brushed the strings with his fingers, then plucked one softly. "What would I do with all those strings?" he murmured. "There must be over thirty."

"Do you like it? Keep it with you awhile; play it."

"I can't possibly . . ."

The trader silenced him with a flick of hand. "How can you set a value to such a harp? Take it, become acquainted with it; there is no need to make a decision now." He slipped the strap over Morgon's head. "If you like it, no doubt we can come to a satisfactory arrangement . . ."

"No doubt." He caught Grim Oakland's eye and blushed.

He carried the harp with him to the trade-hall at Tol, where the traders inspected his beer, grain and wool, ate cheese and fruit, and bartered for an hour with him while Grim Oakland stood watchfully at his elbow. Empty carts were brought to the dock then, to load metal, casks of wine, and blocks of salt from the beds above Caithnard. Plow horses to be taken to Herun and An were penned near the dock for loading; the traders began to tally the grain sacks and kegs of beer. Wyndon Amory's carts lumbered down the coast road, unexpectedly, near noon.

Cannon Master, riding in the back of one, leaped down and said to Morgon, "Wyndon sent them out yesterday; one of them lost a wheel so the drivers fixed it at Sil Wold's farm and stayed the night. I met them coming. Did they talk you into a harp?"

"Almost. Listen to it."

"Morgon, you know I'm as musical as a tin bucket. Your mouth looks like a squashed plum."

"Don't make me laugh," Morgon pleaded. "Will you and Eliard take the traders to Akren? They're about finished here."

"What are you going to do?"

"Buy a horse. And a pair of shoes."

Cannon's brows rose. "And a harp?"

13

"Maybe. Yes."

He chuckled. "Good. I'll take Eliard away for you."

Morgon wandered down into the belly of a ship where half a dozen horses from An were stabled for the journey. He studied them while men stacked sacks of grain beyond him in the shadowy hold. A trader found him there; they talked awhile, Morgon running his fingers down the sleek neck of a stallion the color of polished wood. He emerged finally, drawing deep breaths of clean air. Most of the carts were gone; the sailors were drifting toward the trade-hall to eat. The sea nuzzled the ships, swirled white around the massive trunks of pine supporting the docks. He went to the end of the pier and sat down. In the distance, the fishing boats from Tol rose and dipped like ducks in the water; far beyond them, a dark thread along the horizon, lay the vast, sprawling mainland, the realm of the High One.

He set the harp on his knee and played a harvest-song whose brisk, even rhythm kept time to the sweep of a scythe. A fragment of a Ymris ballad teased his memory; he was picking it out haltingly from the strings when a shadow fell over his hands. He looked up.

A man he had never seen before, neither trader nor sailor, stood beside him. He was quietly dressed; the fine cloth and color of his blue-black tunic, the heavy chain of linked, stamped squares of silver on his breast were bewildering. His face was lean, fine-boned, neither young nor old; his hair was a loose cap of silver.

"Morgon of Hed?"

"Yes."

"I am Deth, the High One's harpist."

Morgon swallowed. He shifted to rise, but the harpist forestalled him, squatting down to look at the harp.

"Uon," he said, showing Morgon a name half-hidden in a whorl of design. "He was a harpmaker in Hel three centuries ago. There are only five of his harps in existence."

"The trader said it belonged to the harpist of Lord Col. Did you come—? You must have come with them. Is that your horse? Why didn't you tell me before that you were here?"

"You were busy; I preferred to wait. The High One instructed me last spring to come to Hed, to express his sorrow over the deaths of Athol and Spring. But I was trapped in Isig by a stubborn winter, delayed in Ymris by a seige of Caerweddin, and requested, just as I was about to embark from Caithnard, in an urgent message from Mathom of An, to get to Anuin. I'm sorry to have come so late."

"I remember your name," Morgon said slowly. "My father used to say Deth played at his wedding." He stopped, listening to his words; a shudder weltered out of him unexpectedly. "I'm sorry. He thought it was funny. He loved your harping. I would like to hear you play."

The harpist settled himself on the pier and picked up Uon's harp. "What would you like to hear?"

Morgon felt his mouth pulled awry in spite of himself by a smile. "Play . . . let me think. Would you play what I was trying to play?"

" 'The Lament for Belu and Bilo.' " Deth tuned a string softly and began the ancient ballad.

> *Belu so fair was born with the dark*
> *Bilo, the dark; death bound them also.*
> *Mourn Belu, fine ladies,*
> *Mourn Bilo.*

His fingers drew the tale faultlessly from the flashing, close-set strings. Morgon listened motionlessly, his eyes on the smooth, detached face. The skilled hands, the fine voice worn to precision, traced the path of Bilo, helpless in its turbulence, the death he left in his wake, the death that trailed him, that rode behind Belu on his horse, ran at his horse's side like a hound.

Belu so fair followed the dark
Bilo; death followed them so;
Death cried to Bilo out of Belu's voice,
to Belu, out of Bilo . . .

The long, surfeited sigh of the tide broke the silence of their deaths. Morgon stirred. He put his hand on the dark, carved face of the harp.

"If I could make that sound come out of that harp, I would sell my name for it and go nameless."

Deth smiled. "That's too high a price to pay even for one of Uon's harps. What are the traders asking for it?"

He shrugged. "They'll take what I'm offering for it."

"You want it that badly?"

Morgon looked at him. "I would sell my name for it, but not the grain my farmers have scorched their backs harvesting, or the horses they have raised and gentled. What I will offer belongs only to me."

"There's no need to justify yourself to me," the harpist said mildly. Morgon's mouth crooked; he touched it absently.

"I'm sorry. I spent half the morning justifying myself."

"For what?"

His eyes dropped to the rough, iron-bound planks of the pier; he answered the quiet, skilled stranger impulsively. "Do you know how my parents died?"

"Yes."

"My mother wanted to see Caithnard. My father had come two or three times to visit me while I was at the College of Riddle-Masters at Caithnard. That sounds simple, but it was a very courageous thing for him to do: leave Hed, go to a great, strange city. The Princes of Hed are rooted to Hed. When I came home a year ago, after spending three years there, I found my father full of stories about what he had seen—the trade-shops, the people from different lands—and when he mentioned a shop with bolts of cloth and furs

and dyes from five kingdoms, my mother couldn't resist
going. She loved the feel and colors of fine cloth. So
last spring they sailed over with the traders when the
spring trading was done. And they never came back.
The return ship was lost. They never came back." He
touched a nailhead, traced a circle around it. "There
was something I had been wanting to do for a long
time. I did it, then. My brother Eliard found out about
it this morning. I didn't tell him at the time because I
knew he would be upset. I just told him that I was going to west Hed for a few days, not that I was going
across the sea to An."

"To An? Why did you—" He stopped. His voice
went suddenly thin as a lath. "Morgon of Hed, did you
win Peven's crown?"

Morgon's head rose sharply. He said after a moment, "Yes. How—? Yes."

"You didn't tell the King of An—"

"I didn't tell anyone. I didn't want to talk about it."

"Auber of Aum, one of the descendents of Peven,
went to that tower to try to win back the crown of
Aum from the dead lord and found the crown gone
and Peven pleading to be set free to leave the tower.
Auber demanded in vain the name of the man who had
taken the crown; Peven said only that he would answer no more riddles. Auber told Mathom, and
Mathom, faced with the news that someone had slipped
quietly into his land, won a riddle-game men have lost
their lives over for centuries, and left as quietly, sum-
moned me from Caithnard and asked me to find that
crown. Hed is the last place I expected it to be."

"It's been under my bed," Morgon said blankly.
"The only private place in Akren. I don't understand.
Does Mathom want it back? I don't need it. I haven't
even looked at it since I brought it home. But I
thought Mathom of all people would understand—"

"The crown is yours by right. Mathom would be the
last to contest that." He paused; there was an expression in his eyes that puzzled Morgon. He added gently,

"And yours, if you choose, is Mathom's daughter, Raederle."

Morgon swallowed. He found himself on his feet, looking down at the harpist, and he knelt down, seeing suddenly, instead of the harpist, a pale, high-boned face full of unexpected expressions, shaking itself free of a long, fine mass of red hair.

He whispered, "Raederle. I know her. Mathom's son Rood was at the college with me; we were good friends. She used to visit him there. . . . I don't understand."

"The King made a vow at her birth to give her only to the man who took the crown of Aum from Peven."

"He made a . . . What a stupid thing for him to do, promising Raederle to any man with enough brains to outwit Peven. He could have been anyone—" He stopped, the blood receding a little beneath his tan. "It was me."

"Yes."

"But I can't . . . She can't marry a farmer. Mathom will never consent."

"Mathom follows his own inclinations. I suggest you ask him."

Morgon gazed at him. "You mean cross the sea to Anuin, to the king's court, walk into his great hall in cold blood and ask him?"

"You walked into Peven's tower."

"That was different. I didn't have lords from the three portions of An watching me, then."

"Morgon, Mathom bound himself to his vow with his own name, and the lords of An, who have lost ancestors, brothers, even sons in that tower, will give you nothing less than honor for your courage and wit. The only question you have to consider at this moment is: Do you want to marry Raederle?"

He stood up again, desperate with uncertainty, ran his hands through his hair, and the wind, roused from the sea, whipped it straight back from his face. "Raederle." A pattern of stars high above one brow flamed vividly against his skin. He saw her face again, at a distance, turned back to look at him. "Raederle."

He saw the harpist's face go suddenly still, as if the wind had snatched in passing its expression and breath. The uncertainty ended in him like a song's ending.

"Yes."

2

H E SAT ON A KEG OF BEER ON THE DECK OF A
trade-ship the next morning, watching the wake
widen and measure Hed like a compass. At the
foot of the keg lay a pack of clothes Tristan had put
together for him, talking all the while so that neither
of them was sure what was in it besides the crown. It
bulged oddly, as though she had put everything she
touched into it, talking. Eliard had said very little. He
had left Morgon's room after a while; Morgon had
found him in the shed, pounding out a horseshoe.

He had said, remembering, "I was going to get you a
chestnut stallion from An with the crown."

And Eliard threw the tongs and heated shoe into the
water, and, gripping Morgon's shoulders, had borne
him back against the wall, saying, "Don't think you can
bribe me with a horse," which made no sense to Morgon, or, after a moment, to Eliard. He let go of Morgon, his face falling into easier, perplexed lines.

"I'm sorry. It just frightens me when you leave, now.
Will she like it here?"

"I wish I knew."

Tristan, following him with his cloak over her arm as
he prepared to leave, stopped in the middle of the
hall, her face strange to him in its sudden vulnerability.

21

She looked around at the plain, polished walls, pulled a chair straight at a table. "Morgon, I hope she can laugh," she whispered.

The ship scuttled before the wind; Hed grew small, blurred in the distance. The High One's harpist had come to stand at the railing; his grey cloak snapped behind him like a banner. Morgon's eyes wandered to his face, unlined, untouched by the sun. A sense of incongruity nudged his mind, of a riddle shaping the silver-white hair, the fine curve of bone.

The harpist turned his head, met Morgon's eyes.

Morgon asked curiously, "What land are you from?"

"No land. I was born in Lungold."

"The wizards' city? Who taught you to harp?"

"Many people. I took my name from the Morgol Cron's harpist Tirunedeth, who taught me the songs of Herun. I asked him for it before he died."

"Cron," Morgon said. "Ylcorcronlth?"

"Yes.'

"He ruled Herun six hundred years ago."

"I was born," the harpist said tranquilly, "not long after the founding of Lungold, a thousand years ago."

Morgon was motionless save for the sway of his body to the sea's rhythm. Little threads of light wove and broke on the sea beyond the sunlit, detached face. He whispered, "No wonder you harp like that. You've had a thousand years to learn the harp-songs of the High One's realm. You don't look old. My father looked older when he died. Are you a wizard's son?" He looked down at his hands then, linked around his knees, and said apologetically, "Forgive me. It's none of my business. I was just—"

"Curious?" The harpist smiled. "You have an inordinate curiosity for a Prince of Hed."

"I know. That's why my father finally sent me to Caithnard—I kept asking questions. He didn't know how to account for it. But, being a wise, gentle man, he let me go." He stopped again, rather abruptly, his mouth twitching slightly.

The harpist said, his eyes on the approaching land, "I never knew my own father. I was born without a name in the back streets of Lungold at a time when wizards, kings, even the High One himself passed through the city. Since I have no land-instinct and no gifts for wizardry, I gave up long ago trying to guess who my father was."

Morgon's head lifted again. He said speculatively, "Danan Isig was ancient as a tree even then, and Har of Osterland. No one knows when the wizards were born, but if you're a wizard's son, there's no one to claim you now."

"It's not important. The wizards are gone; I owe nothing to any living ruler but the High One. In his service I have a name, a place, a freedom of movement and judgment. I am responsible only to him; he values me for my harping and my discretion, both of which are improved by age." He bent to pick up his harp, slid it over his shoulder. "We'll dock in a few moments."

Morgon joined him at the rail. The trade-city Caithnard, with its port, inns and shops, sprawled in a crescent of land between two lands. Ships, their sails bellying the orange and gold colors of Herun traders, were flocking from the north to its docks like birds. On a thrust of cliff forming one horn of the moon-shaped bay stood a dark block of a building whose stone walls and small chambers Morgon knew well. An image of the spare, mocking face of Raederle's brother rose in his mind; his hands tightened on the rail.

"Rood. I'll have to tell him. I wonder if he's at the college. I haven't seen him for a year."

"I talked with him two nights ago when I stayed at the college before crossing to Hed. He had just taken the Gold Robe of Intermediate Mastery."

"Perhaps he's gone home for a while, then." The ship took the last roll and wash of wave as it entered the harbor, then slackened speed, the sailors shouting to one another as they took in sail. Morgon's voice thinned. "I wonder what he'll say . . ."

The sea birds above the still water wove like shuttles in the wind. The docks sliding past them were littered with goods being loaded, unloaded: bolts of cloth, chests, timber, wine, fur, animals. The sailors hailed friends on the dock; traders called to one another.

"Lyle Orn's ship will leave for Anuin with the tide this evening," a trader told Deth and Morgon before they disembarked. "You'll know it by its red and yellow sails. Do you want your horse, Lord?"

"I'll walk," Deth said. He added to Morgon, as the gangplank slid down before them. "There is an unanswered riddle on the lists of the Masters at the college: Who won the riddle-game with Peven of Aum?"

Morgon slung his pack to his shoulder. He nodded. "I'll tell them. Are you going up to the college?"

"In a while."

"At evening-tide, then, Lords," the trader reminded them as they descended. They separated on the cobbled street facing the dock, and Morgon, turning left, retraced a path he had known for years. The narrow streets of the city were crowded in the high noon with traders, sailors ashore from different lands, wandering musicians, trappers, students in the bright, voluminous robes of their ranks, richly dressed men and women from An, Ymris, Herun. Morgon, his pack over one shoulder, moved through them without seeing them, oblivious to noise and jostling. The back streets quieted; the road he took wound out of the city, left tavern and trade-shop behind, rose upward above the brilliant sea.

Occasional students passed him, going toward the city, their voices, wrestling with riddles, cheerful, assured. The road angled sharply, then at the end the ground levelled, and the ancient college, built of rough dark stones, massive as a piece of broken cliff itself, stood placidly among the tall, wind-twisted trees.

He knocked at the familiar double doors of thick oak. The porter, a freckled young man in the White Robe of Beginning Mastery opened them, cast a glance over Morgon and his pack, and said portentiously, "Ask and it shall be answered here. If you have some seeking knowledge, you shall be received. The Masters are examining a candidate for the Red of Apprenticeship, and they must not be disturbed except by death or doom. Abandon your name to me."

"Morgon, Prince of Hed."

"Oh." The porter dabbed at the top of his head and smiled. "Come in. I'll get Master Tel."

"No, don't interrupt them." He stepped in. "Is Rood of An here?"

"Yes; he's on the third floor, across from the library. I'll take you."

"I know the way."

The darkness of the low arched corridors was broken at each end only by wide leaded windows set in walls of stone a foot thick. Rows of closed doors ran down each side of the hall. Morgon found Rood's name on one, on a wood slat, a crow delicately etched beneath it. He knocked, received an unintelligible answer, and opened the door.

Rood's bed, taking up a quarter of the small stone room, was piled with clothes, books, and the prince of An. He sat cross-legged in a cloud of newly acquired gold robe, reading a letter, a cup of fragile dyed glass in one hand half-full of wine. He looked up, and at the abrupt, arrogant lift of his head, Morgon felt suddenly, stepping across the threshold, as though he had stepped backward into a memory.

"Morgon." Rood heaved himself up, walked off the bed, trailing a wake of books behind him. He hugged Morgon, the cup in one hand, the letter in the other. "Join me. I'm celebrating. You are a stranger without your robe. But I forget: you're a farmer now. Is that why you're in Caithnard? Did you come over with your grain or wine or something?"

"Beer. We can't make good wine."

"How sad." He gazed at Morgon like a curious crow, his eyes red-rimmed, blurred. "I heard about your parents. The traders were full of it. It made me angry."

"Why?"

"Because it trapped you in Hed, made a farmer out of you, full of thoughts of eggs and pigs, beer and weather. You'll never come back here, and I miss you."

Morgon shifted his pack to the floor. The crown lay hidden in it like a guilty deed. He said softly, "I came . . . I have something to tell you, and I don't know how to tell you."

Rood loosed Morgon abruptly, turned away. "I don't want to hear it." He poured a second cup for Morgon and refilled his own. "I took the Gold two days ago."

"I know. Congratulations. How long have you been celebrating?"

"I don't remember." He held out the cup to Morgon, wine splashing down over his fingers. "I'm one of Mathom's children, descended from Kale and Oen by way of the witch Madir. Only one man has ever taken the Gold in less time than I have. And he went home to farm."

"Rood—"

"Have you forgotten everything you learned by now? You used to open riddles like nuts. You should have become a Master. You have a brother, you could have let him take the land-rule."

"Rood," Morgon said patiently. "You know that's impossible. And you know I didn't come here to take the Black. I never wanted it. What would I have done with it? Prune trees in it?" Rood's voice snapped back at him with a violence that startled him.

"Answer riddles! You had the gift for it; you had the eyes! You said once you wanted to win that game. Why didn't you keep your word? You went home to make beer instead, and some man without a name or a face won the two great treasures of An." He crumpled the letter, held it locked in his fist like a heart. "Who knows what she's waiting for? A man like Raith of

26

Hel with a face beaten out of gold and a heart like a rotten tooth? Or Thistin of Aum, who's soft as a baby and too old to climb into bed without help? If she is forced to marry a man like that, I'll never forgive you or my father. Him because he made such a vow in the first place, and you because you made a promise in this room you did not keep. Ever since you left this place, I made a vow to myself to win that game with Peven, to free Raederle from that fate my father set for her. But I had no chance. I never had even a chance."

Morgon sat down on a chair beside Rood's desk. "Stop shouting. Please. Listen—"

"Listen to what? You could not even be faithful to the one rule you held true above all others." He dropped the letter, reached out abruptly, drew the hair back from Morgon's brow. "Answer the unanswered riddle."

Morgon pulled away from him. "Rood! Will you stop babbling and listen to me? It's hard enough for me to tell you this without you squawking like a drunk crow. Do you think Raederle will mind living on a farm? I have to know."

"Don't profane crows; some of my ancestors were crows. Of course Raederle can't live on a farm. She is the second most beautiful woman in the three portions of An; she can't live among pigs and—" He stopped abruptly, still in the middle of the room, his shadow motionless across the stones. Under the weight of his lightless gaze a word jumped in the back of Morgon's throat. Rood whispered, "Why?"

Morgon bent to his pack, his fingers shaking faintly on the ties. As he drew out the crown, the great center stone, colorless itself, groping wildly at all the colors in the room, snared the gold of Rood's robe and blazed like a sun. Transfixed in its liquid glare, Rood caught his breath sharply and shouted.

Morgon dropped the crown. He put his face against his knees, his hands over his ears. The wine glass on the desk snapped; the flagon on a tiny table shattered, spilling wine onto the stones. The iron lock on a massive book sprang open; the chamber door slammed shut with a boom.

Cries of outrage down the long corridors followed like an echo. Morgon, the blood pounding in his head, straightened. He whispered, his fingers sliding over his eyes, "It wasn't necessary to shout. You take the crown to Mathom. I'm going home." He stood up, and Rood caught his wrist in a grip that drove to the bone.

"You."

He stopped. Rood's hold eased; he reached behind Morgon and turned the key in the door against the indignant pounding on it. His face looked strange, as though the shout had cleared his mind of all but an essential wonder.

He said, his voice catching a little, "Sit down. I can't. Morgon, why didn't . . . why didn't you tell me you were going to challenge Peven?"

"I did. I told you two years ago when we had sat up all night asking each other riddles, studying for the Blue of Partial Beginning."

"But what did you do—leave Hed without telling anyone, leave Caithnard without telling me, move unobtrusively as a doom through my father's land to face death in that dark tower that stinks in an east wind? You didn't even tell me that you had won. You could have done that. Any lord of An would have brought it to Anuin with a flourish of shouts and trumpets."

"I didn't mean to worry Raederle. I simply didn't know about your father's vow. You never told me."

"Well, what did you expect me to do? I have seen great lords leave Anuin to go to that tower for her sake and never return. Do you think I wanted to give you that kind of incentive? Why did you do it, if not for her, or for the honor of walking into the court at Anuin with that crown? It couldn't have been pride in your knowledge—you didn't even tell the Masters."

Morgon picked up the crown, turned it in his hands.

The center stone faced him, striped with the dust and green of his tunic. "Because I had to do it. For no other reason than that. And I didn't tell anyone simply because it was such a private thing . . . and because I didn't know, coming alive out of that tower at dawn, if I were a great riddle-master or a very great fool." He looked at Rood. "What will Raederle say?"

The corner of Rood's mouth crooked up suddenly. "I have no idea. Morgon, you caused an uproar in An the like of which has not been experienced since Madir stole the pigherds of Hel and set them loose in the cornfields of Aum. Raederle wrote to me that Raith of Hel promised to abduct her and marry her secretly at her word; that Duac, who has always been as close to our father as his shadow, is furious about the vow and has scarcely spoken three words to him all summer; that the lords of the three portions are angry with him, insisting he break his vow. But it is easier to change the wind with your breath than our father's incomprehensible mind. Raederle said she has been having terrible dreams about some huge, faceless, nameless stranger riding to Anuin with the crown of Aum on his head, claiming her and taking her away to some rich, loveless land inside some mountain or beneath the sea. My father has sent men all over An searching for the man who took that crown; he sent messengers here to the college; he has asked the traders to ask wherever in the High One's realm they go. He didn't think of asking in Hed. I didn't either. I should have. I should have known it would not be some powerful, nightmarish figure—it would be something even more unexpected. We have been expecting anyone but you."

Morgon traced a pearl, milky as a child's tooth, with one finger. "I'll love her," he said. "Will that matter?"

"What do you think?"

Morgon reached for his pack restlessly. "I don't know, and neither do you. I am terrified of the look that will be on her face when she sees the crown of Aum carried into Anuin by me. She'll have to live at

Akren. She'll have to . . . she'll have to get used to my pigherder, Snog Nutt. He comes for breakfast every morning. Rood, she won't like it. She was born to the wealth of An, and she'll be horrified. So will your father."

"I doubt it," Rood said calmly. "The lords of An may be, but it would take the doom of the world to horrify my father. For all I know, he saw you seventeen years ago when he made that vow. He has a mind like a morass, no one, not even Duac, knows how deep it is. I don't know what Raederle will think. I only know that I would not miss seeing this if my death were waiting for me at Anuin. I'm going home for a while; my father is sending a ship for me. Come with me."

"I'm expected on a trade-ship sailing this evening; I'll have to tell them. Deth is with me."

Rood quirked a brow. "He found you. That man could find a pinhole in a mist." There was a pound at his door; he raised his voice irritably. "Go away! Whatever I broke, I'm sorry!"

"Rood!" It was the frail voice of the Master Tel, raised in unaccustomed severity. "You have broken the locks to Nun's books of wizardry!"

Rood rose with a sigh and flung open the door. A crowd of angry students behind the old Master raised voices like a cacophony of crows at the sight of him. Rood's voice battered against them helplessly.

"I know the Great Shout is forbidden, but it's a thing of impulse rather than premeditation, and I was overwhelmed by impulse. Please shut up!"

They shut up abruptly. Morgon, coming to stand beside Rood with the crown of Aum in his hands, its center stone black as the robe of Mastery Tel wore, met the gaze of the Master without speaking.

Master Tel, the annoyance in his sparse, parchment-colored face melting into astonishment, gathered his voice again, set a riddle to the strain of silence, "Who won the riddle-game with Peven of Aum?"

"I did," said Morgon.

He told them the tale sitting in the Masters' library, with its vast ancient collection of books running the length and breadth of the walls. The eight Masters listened quietly, Rood in his gold robe making a brilliant splash among their black robes. No one spoke until he finished, and then Master Tel shifted in his chair and murmured wonderingly, "Kern of Hed."

"How did you know?" Rood said. "How did you know to ask that one riddle?"

"I didn't," Morgon said. "I just asked it once when I was so tired I couldn't think of anything else to ask. I thought everyone knew that riddle. But when Peven shouted 'There are no riddles of Hed!' I knew I had won the game. It wasn't a Great Shout, but I will hear it in my mind until I die."

"Kern." Rood's mouth twisted into a thin smile. "Since spring the lords of An have been asking two questions only: who is Raederle to marry, and what was the one riddle Peven couldn't answer? Hagis King of An, my father's grandfather, died in Peven's tower for lack of that riddle. The lords of An should have paid more attention to that small island. They will now."

"Indeed," Master Ohm, a lean, quiet man whose even voice never changed, said thoughtfully. "Perhaps in the history of the realm too little attention has been paid to Hed. There is still a riddle without an answer. If Peven of Aum had asked you that, with all your great knowledge you might not be here today."

Morgon met his eyes. They were mist-colored, calm as his voice. He said, "Without an answer and a stricture, it would have been disqualified."

"And if Peven had held the answer?"

"How could he? Master Ohm, you helped us search a whole winter the first year I came here for an answer to that riddle. Peven took his knowledge from books of wizardry that had belonged to Madir, and before that to the Lungold wizards. And in all their writings, which you have here, no mention is made of three stars. I

don't know where to look for an answer. And I don't
. . . it's far from my mind these days."

Rood stirred. "And this is the man who put his life
in the balance with his knowledge. Beware the unanswered riddle."

"It is that: unanswered, and for all I know it may not
need an answer."

Rood's hand cut the air, his sleeve fluttering.
"Every riddle has an answer. Hide behind the closed
doors in your mind, you stubborn farmer. A hundred
years from now students in the White of Beginning
Mastery will be scratching their heads trying to remember the name of an obscure Prince of Hed who, like
another obscure Prince of Hed, ignored the first and
last rule of riddle-mastery. I thought you had more
sense."

"All I want," Morgon said succinctly, "is to go to
Anuin, marry Raederle, and then go home and plant
grain and make beer and read books. Is that so hard to
understand?"

"Yes! Why are you being so obtuse? You of all
people?"

"Rood," Master Tel said in his gentle voice, "you
know an answer to the stars on his face was sought and
never found. What more do you suggest he do?"

"I suggest," Rood said, "he ask the High One."

There was a little silence. The Master Ohm broke it
with a rustle of cloth as he shifted. "The High One
would indeed know. However I suspect you will have
to provide Morgon with more incentive than pure
knowledge before he would make such a long, harsh
journey away from his land."

"I don't have to. Sooner or later, he'll be driven
there."

Morgon sighed. "I wish you would be reasonable. I
want to go to Anuin, not Erlenstar Mountain. I don't
want to ask any more riddles; spending a night from
twilight to dawn in a tower rotten with cloth and

bone, racking my brain for every riddle I ever learned, gave me a distaste for riddle-games."

Rood leaned forward, every trace of mockery gone from his face. "You will take honor from this place, and Master Tel has said you will take the Black today for doing what even the Master Laern died attempting. You will go to Anuin, and the lords of An, and my father and Raederle will give you at least the respect due to you for your knowledge and your courage. But if you accept the Black, it will be a lie; and if you offer the peace of Hed to Raederle, that also will be a lie, a promise you will not keep because there is a question you will not answer, and you will find, like Peven, that it is the one riddle you do not know, not the thousand you do know, that will destroy you."

"Rood!" Morgon checked, his mouth tight, his hands tight on the arms of his chair. "What are you trying to make of me? What is it you are trying to make of me?"

"A Master—for your own sake. How can you be so blind? How can you so stubbornly, so flagrantly, ignore everything you know is true? How can you let them call you a Master? How can you accept from them the Black of Mastery while you turn a blind eye at truth?"

Morgon felt the blood well into his face. He said tautly, Rood's face suddenly the only face in the still room, "I never wanted the Black. But I do claim some choice in my life. What those stars on my face are, I do not know; and I don't want to know. Is that what you want me to admit? You take the eyes that your father, and Madir, and the shape-changer Ylon gave you and probe your own cold, fearless way into truth, and when you take the Black, I will come and celebrate with you. But all I want is peace."

"Peace," Master Tel said mildly, "was never one of your habits, Rood. We can only judge Morgon according to our standards, and by those he has earned the Black. How else can we honor him?"

Rood stood up. He undid his robe, let it slide to

the floor, stood half-naked in the startled gaze of the Masters. "If you give him the Black, I will never wear any robe of Mastery again."

A muscle in Morgon's rigid face jumped. He leaned back in his chair, his stiff fingers opening, and said icily, "Put your clothes back on, Rood. I have said I didn't want the Black, and I won't take it. It's not the business of a farmer of Hed to master riddles. Besides, what honor would it give me to wear the same robe Laern wore and lost in that tower, and that Peven wears now?"

Rood gathered his robe in one hand, walked to Morgon's chair. He leaned over it, his hands on the arms. His face loomed above Morgon's, spare, blood-less. He whispered, "Please. Think."

He held Morgon's eyes, held the silence in the room with the motionless, taut set of his body until he moved, turned to leave. Then Morgon's own body loosened as though the black gaze had drained out of it. He heard the door close and dropped his face in one hand.

"I'm sorry," he whispered. "I didn't mean to say that about Laern. I lost my temper."

"Truth," the Master Ohm murmured, "needs no apology." His mist-colored eyes, unwavering on Mor-gon's face, held a gleam of curiosity. "Not even a Mas-ter assumes he knows everything—except in rare cases, such as Laern's. Will you accept the Black? You surely deserve it, and as Tel says, it is all we have to honor you."

Morgon shook his head. "I want it. I do want it. But Rood wants it more than I do; he'll make better use of it than I will, and I would rather he take it. I'm sorry we argued here—I don't know how it got started."

"I'll talk to him," Tel promised. "He was being rather unreasonable, and unnecessarily harsh."

"He has his father's vision," Ohm said. Morgon's eyes moved to him after a moment.

"You think he was right?"

"In essence. So do you, although you have chosen not to act—as is, according to your rather confused standards, your right. But I suspect a journey to the High One will not be as useless as you think."

"But I want to get married. And why should I trouble whatever destiny Rood thinks I have until it troubles me? I'm not going out hunting a destiny like a strayed cow."

The corner of Master Ohm's lean mouth twitched. "Who was Ilon of Yrye?"

Morgon sighed noiselessly. "Ilon was a harpist at the court of Har of Osterland, who offended Har with a song so terribly that he fled from Har out of fear of death. He went alone to the mountains, taking nothing but his harp, and lived quietly, far from all men, farming and playing his harp. So great was his harping in his loneliness, that it became his voice, and it spoke as he could not, to the animals living around him. Word of it spread from creature to creature until it came one day to the ears of the Wolf of Osterland, Har, as he prowled in that shape through his land. He was drawn by curiosity to the far reaches of his kingdom, and there he found Ilon, playing at the edge of the world. The wolf sat and listened. And Ilon, finishing his song and raising his eyes, found the terror he had run from standing on his threshold."

"And the stricture?"

"The man running from death must run first from himself. But I don't see what that has to do with me. I'm not running: I'm simply not interested."

The Master's elusive smile deepened faintly. "Then I wish you the peace of your disinterest, Morgon of Hed," he said softly.

Morgon did not see Rood again, though he searched through the grounds and the cliff above the sea half the afternoon for him. He took supper with the Masters, and found, wandering outside afterward into the dead wind of twilight, the High One's harpist coming up the road.

Deth, stopping, said, "You look troubled."

"I can't find Rood. He must have gone down to Caithnard." He ran a hand through his hair in a rare, preoccupied gesture, and set his shoulders against the broadside of an oak. Three stars gleamed below his hairline, muted in the evening. "We had an argument; I'm not even sure now what it was about. I want him with me at Anuin, but it's getting late, and I don't know now if he'll come."

"We should board."

"I know. If we miss the tide, they'll sail without us. He's probably drunk in some tavern, wearing nothing but his boots. Maybe he would rather see me take a long journey to the High One than marry Raederle. Maybe he's right. She doesn't belong in Hed, and that's what upset him. Maybe I should go down and get drunk with him and go home. I don't know." He caught the harpist's patient, vaguely mystified expression and sighed. "I'll get my pack."

"I must speak to Master Ohm briefly before we leave. Surely Rood, of all people, would have told you the truth about how he feels toward the marriage."

Morgon shrugged himself away from the tree. "I suppose so," he said moodily. "But I don't see why he has to upset me at a time like this."

He retrieved his pack from the chaos of Rood's room and bade the Masters farewell. The sky darkend slowly as he and the harpist took the long road back to the city; on the rough horns of the bay the warning fires had been lit; tiny lights from homes and taverns made random stars against the well of darkness. The tide boomed and slapped against the cliffs, and an evening wind stirred, strengthened, blowing the scent of salt and night. The trade-ship stirred restlessly in the deep water as they boarded; a loosed sail cupped the wind, taut and ghostly under the moon. Morgon, standing at the stern, watched the lights of the harbor ripple across the water and vanish.

"We'll reach Anuin in the afternoon, the wind will—

ing," an affable, red-bearded trader with a weal down the side of his face said to him. "Sleep above or below as it pleases you. With the horses we carry, you may be happier up here in the air. There are plenty of skins from your own sheep to keep you warm."

"Thank you," Morgon said. Sitting on a great spool of cable, his arms resting on the rail, he watched the white wake furl to the turn of the silent helmsman's tiller. His thoughts slid to Rood; he traced the threads of their argument to its roots, puzzled over it, retraced it again. The wind carried voices of the handful of sailors manning the ship, a snatch of traders' discussion of the goods they carried. The masts groaned with the weight of wind; the ship, heavy with cargo, neatly balanced, cut with an easy roll from bow to stern through the waves. Morgon, the east wind numbing his cheek, lulled by the creak and dip of the vessel, put his head on his arms and closed his eyes. He was asleep when the ship shuddered as though the twelve winds had seized it at once, and, startling awake, he heard the furious, unchecked thump of the tiller.

He stood up, a call dying in his throat, for the deck behind him was empty. The ship, its sails full-blown to the harsh wind, reeled, throwing him back against the rail. He caught his balance desperately. The chart-house, where the traders had been lamp-lit as they pored over their papers, was dark. The wind, whimpering, drove hard into the sails, and the ship rolled, giving Morgon a sudden glimpse of white froth. He straightened slowly with it, his teeth set hard, feeling the prick of sweat on his back even in the cold spray.

He saw the hatch to the hold open reluctantly against the wind, recognized the web-colored hair in the moonlight. He made his way toward it in a lull of wind, clinging to whatever stay and spare corner he passed. He had to shout twice to make himself heard.

"What are they doing down there?"

"There's no one in the hold," Deth said. Morgon, staring at him, made no sense of the words.

"What?"

Deth, sitting in the open hatchway, put a hand on Morgon's arm. At the touch, and his quick, silent glance across the decks, Morgon felt his throat suddenly constrict.

"Deth—"

"Yes." The harpist shifted the harp slightly on his shoulder. His brows were drawn hard.

"Deth, where are the traders and sailors? They can't have just—just vanished like pieces of foam. They . . . Where are they? Did they fall overboard?"

"If they did, they put up enough sail before they left to take us with them."

"We can take it down."

"I think," Deth said, "we won't have time." The ship flung them both, as he spoke, backward in a strange, rigid movement. The animals screamed in terror; the deck itself seemed to strain beneath them, as though it were being pulled apart. A rope snapped above Morgon's head, slashing across the deck; wood groaned and buckled around them. He felt his voice tear out of him.

"We're not moving! In open sea, we're not moving!"

There was a rush of water beneath him, bubbling through the open hold; the ship sagged on its side. Deth caught Morgon as he slid helplessly across the deck; a wave breaking against the low side drenched them both, and he gagged on the cold, bitter water. He managed to stand, clinging with one hand to Deth's wrist, and flung his arms around the mast, tangling his fingers in the rigging. His face close to the harpist's, his feet sliding to the tilt of the deck, he shouted hoarsely,

"Who were they?"

If the harpist gave him an answer, he did not hear it. Deth's figure blurred in the sweep of a wave; the mast snapped with a jar Morgon felt to his bones, and the striped canvas weighted with rigging and yard slapped him loose from his hold and swept him into the sea.

3

E WOKE, FLUNG LIKE A RAG AMID A HARVEST OF dry kelp, his face in the sand, his mouth full of sand. He lifted his face; a bone-white beach strewn with seaweed and bleached driftwood blurred under one eye; his other eye was blind. He dropped his head, his eye closing again, and someone on his blind side touched him.

He started. Hands tugged at him, rolled him onto his back. He stared into a wild white cat's ice-blue eyes. Its ears were flattened. A voice said warningly, "Xel."

Morgon tried to speak, but made only the strange, harsh noise that a crow might make.

The voice said, "Who are you? What happened to you?"

He tried to answer. His voice would not shape the words. He realized, as he struggled with it, that there were no words in him anywhere to shape answers.

"Who are you?"

He closed his eyes. A silence spun like a vortex in his head, drawing him deeper and deeper into darkness.

He woke again tasting cool water. He reached for it blindly, drank until the crust of salt in his mouth dissolved, then lay back, the empty cup rolling from his hands. He opened his good eye again a moment later.

A young man with lank white hair and white eyes knelt beside him on the dirt floor of a small house. The threads of the voluminous, richly embroidered robe he wore were picked and frayed; the skin was stretched taut, hollow across his strange, proud face.

He said as Morgon blinked up at him, "Who are you? Can you speak now?"

Morgon opened his mouth. Like a small wave receding, something he had once known slipped quietly, silently away from him. The breath exploded out of him suddenly, violently; he dug the heels of his hands into his eyes.

"Be careful." The man pulled his hands from his face. "It looks as though you hit your head on something; blood and sand are caked over your eye." He washed it gently. "So you can't remember your name. Did you fall off a ship in that storm last night? Are you of Ymris? Of Anuin? Of Isig? Are you a trader? Are you of Hed? Of Lungold? Are you a fisher from Loor?" He shook his head in puzzlement at Morgon's silence. "You are mute and inexplicable as the hollow gold balls I dig up on Wind Plain. Can you see now?" Morgon nodded, and the man sat back on his haunches, frowning down at Morgon's face as though it held a name in it somewhere. His frown deepened suddenly; he reached out and brushed at the hair plastered dry with salt against Morgon's forehead. His voice caught. "Three stars."

Morgon lifted his hand to touch them. The man said softly, incredulously, "You don't remember even that. You came out of the sea with three stars on your face, with no name and no voice, like a portent out of the past. . . ." He stopped as Morgon's hand fell to his wrist, gripped it, and Morgon made the grunt of a question. "Oh. I am Astrin Ymris." Then he added formally, almost bitterly, "I am the brother and land-heir of Heureu, King of Ymris." He slid an arm under

Morgon's shoulders. "If you'll sit, I'll give you some dry clothes."

He pulled the torn, wet tunic off Morgon, washed the drying sand from his body, and helped him into a long, hooded robe of rich dark cloth. He fetched wood, stirred up the embers under a cauldron of soup; by the time it had heated, Morgon had fallen asleep.

He woke at dusk. The tiny house was empty; he sat up, looking around him. It had little furniture: a bench, a large table cluttered with odd objects, a high stool, the pallet Morgon had slept on. Tools leaned against the doorway: a pick, a hammer, a chisel, a brush; dirt clung to them. Morgon rose, went to the open door. Across the threshold a great, wind-blown plain swept westward as far as he could see. Not far from the house, dark, shapeless stoneworks rose, blurred in the fading light. To the south lay, like a boundary line between lands, the dark line of a vast forest. The wind, running in from the sea, spoke a hollow, restless language. It smelled of salt and night, and for a moment, listening to it, some memory reeled into his mind of darkness, water, cold, wild wind, and he gripped the door posts to keep from falling. But it passed, and he found no word for it.

He turned. Strange things lay on Astrin's broad table. He touched them curiously. There were pieces of broken, beautifully dyed glass, of gold, shards of finely painted pottery, a few links of heavy copper chain, a broken flute of wood and gold. A color caught his eye; he reached for it. It was a cut jewel the size of his palm, and through it flowed, as he turned it, all the colors of the sea.

He heard a step and looked up. Astrin, Xel at his side, came in, dropped a heavy, stained bag by the hearth.

He said, stirring the fire. "It's beautiful, isn't it. I found that at the foot of Wind Tower. No trader I showed it to could give me the name for that stone, so I took it to Isig, to Danan Isig himself. He said that

41

never in his mountain had he seen such a jewel, nor did he know anyone beside himself and his son, who could have cut it so flawlessly. He gave me Xel out of friendship. I had nothing to give him, but he said I had given him a mystery, which is sometimes a precious thing." He checked the pot above the flames, then reached for the bag and a knife hanging by the fire. "Xel caught two hare; I'll cook them for supper . . ." He looked up as Morgon touched his arm. He let Morgon take the knife from him. "Can you skin them?" Morgon nodded. "You know you can do that. Can you remember anything else about yourself? Think. Try to——" He stopped at the helpless, tormented expression on Morgon's face, gripped Morgon's arm briefly. "Never mind. It will come back to you."

They ate supper by firelight, the door closed against a sudden drenching rain. Astrin ate quietly, the white huntress Xel curled at his feet; he seemed to have settled back into a habit of silence, his thoughts indrawn, until he finished. Then he opened the door a moment to the driving rain, closed it, and the cat lifted its head with a yowl. Astrin's movements became restless as he touched books and did not open them, set shards of glass together that did not fit and dropped them, his face expressionless as though he were listening to something beyond the rain. Morgon, seated at the hearth, his head aching and the cut over his eye pressed against cool stones, watched him. Astrin's prowling brought him finally in front of Morgon; he gazed down at Morgon out of his white, secret eyes until Morgon looked away.

Astrin sat down with a sigh beside him. He said abruptly, "You are as secret as Wind Tower. I've been here five years in exile from Caerweddin. I speak to Xel, to an old man I buy fish from in Loor, to occasional traders, and to Rork, High Lord of Umber, who visits me every few months. By day I go digging out of curiosity in the great ruined city of the Earth-Masters on Wind Plain. By night, I dig in other directions, sometimes in books of wizardry I've learned to open, sometimes out there in the darkness above Loor, by the sea. I take Xel with me, and we watch something that is building on the shores of Ymris under night cover, something for which there is no name. . . . But I can't go tonight; the tide will be rough in this wind, and Xel hates the rain." He paused a moment. "Your eyes look at me as though you understand everything I'm saying. I wish I knew your name. I wish . . ." His voice trailed away; his eyes stayed, speculative, on Morgon's face.

He rose as suddenly as he had sat down, and took from his shelves a heavy book with a name on it stamped in gold: Aloil. It was locked with two apparently seamless bindings of iron. He touched them, murmuring a word, and they opened. Morgon went to his side; he looked up. "Do you know who Aloil was?" Morgon shook his head. Then his eyes widened a little as he remembered, but Astrin continued, "Most people have forgotten. He was the wizard in service to the Kings of Ymris for nine hundred years before he went to Lungold, then vanished along with the entire school of wizards seven hundred years ago. I bought the book from a trader; it took me two years to learn the word to open it. Part of the poetry Aloil wrote was to the wizard Nun, in service to Hel. I tried her name to open the book, but that didn't work. Then I remembered the name of her favorite pig out of all the pig herds of Hel: the speaking pig, Hegdis-Noon—and that name opened the book." He set the heavy book on the table, pored through it.

"Somewhere in here is the spell that made the stone talk on King's Mouth Plain. Do you know that tale? Aloil was furious with Galil Ymris because the king refused to follow Aloil's advice during a seige of Caerweddin, and as a result Aloil's tower was burned. So Aloil made a stone in the plain above Caerweddin speak for eight days and nights in such a loud voice that men as far as Umber and Meremont heard it, and the stone recited all Galil's secret, very bad attempts at writing poetry. From that the plain got its name." He glanced up to see Morgon's smile. He straightened. "I haven't talked so much in a month. Xel can't laugh. You make me remember I'm human. I forget that sometimes, except when Rork Umber is here, and then I remember, all too well, who I am." He looked down, turned a page. "Here it is. Now if I can read his handwriting. . . ." He was silent a few moments, while Morgon read over his shoulder and the candle-light spattered over the page. Astrin turned to him finally. He held Morgon gently by the arms and said slowly, "I think if this spell can make a stone speak, it may make you speak. I haven't done much mind-work; I've gone into Xel's mind, and once into Rork's, with his permission. If you are afraid, I won't do this. But perhaps if I go deep enough, I can find your name. Do you want me to try?"

Morgon's hands touched his mouth. He nodded, his eyes holding Astrin's, and Astrin drew a breath. "All right. Sit down. Sit quietly. The first step is to become as the stone. . . ."

Morgon sat down on the stool. Astrin, standing across from him, grew still, a dark shape in the flickering light. Morgon felt an odd shifting in the room, as if another vision of the same room had superimposed itself over his own, and refocussed slightly. Odd pieces of thought rose in his mind: the plain he had looked at, Xel's face, the skins he had hung to dry. Then there was nothing but a long darkness and a withdrawal.

Astrin moved, the fire reflected strangely in his eyes. He whispered, "There was nothing. It is as though you have no name. I couldn't reach the place where you have your name and your past hidden from yourself. It's deep, deep. . . ." He stopped as Morgon rose. His hands closed tight on Astrin's arms; he shook Astrin a little, imperatively, and Astrin said, "I'll try. But I've never met a man so hidden from himself. There must be other spells; I'll look. But I don't know why you care so much. It must be the essence of peace, having no name, no memory. . . . All right. I'll keep looking. Be patient."

Morgon heard him stirring at sunrise the next day and got up. The rain had stopped; the clouds hung broken above Wind Plain. They ate a breakfast of cold hare, wine and bread, then, carrying Astrin's tools, Xel following, they walked across the plain to the ancient, ruined city.

It was a maze of broken columns, fallen walls, rooms without roofs, steps leading nowhere, arches shaken to the ground, all built of smooth, massive squares of brilliant stone all shades of red, green, gold, blue, grey, black, streaked and glittering with other colors melting through them. A wide street of gold-white stone, grass thrusting up between its sections, began at the eastern edge of the city, parted it, and stopped at the foot of the one whole building in the city: a tower whose levels spiraled upward from a sprawling black base to a small, round, deep-blue chamber high at the top. Morgon, walking down the center street at Astrin's side, stopped abruptly to stare at it.

Astrin said, "Wind Tower. No man has ever been to the top of it—no wizard either. Aloil tried; he walked up its stairs for seven days and seven nights and never reached the end of them. I've tried, many times. I think at the top of that tower there must lie the answer to questions so old we've forgotten to ask them. Who were the Earth-Masters? What terrible thing happened to them that destroyed them and their cities? I play like a child among the bones of it, finding a fine stone here, a broken plate there, hoping that one day I'll find a key to the mystery of it, the beginning of an answer. . . . I took a chip off these great stones also to Danan Isig; he said he knew of no place in the High One's realm where they quarried such stone." He touched Morgon briefly, to get his eyes. "I'll be there, in that chamber without a roof. Join me when you wish."

Morgon, left to his own in the hollow, singing city, wandered through the roofless halls and wall-less chambers, between piles of broken stones rooted deep to the earth by long grass. The winds sped past like wild horses, pouring through empty rooms, thundering down the street to spiral the tower and moan through its secret chamber. Morgon, following them, drawn to the huge, bright structure, put one hand flat on its blue-black wall, one foot on its first step. The gold steps curved away from him; the winds pushed at him like children, tumbled past him. He turned away after a moment, went to find Astrin.

He worked all day at Astrin's side, digging quietly in a little room whose floor was sunk beneath the earth, crumbling the earth in his hands, searching it for bits of metal, glass, pottery. Once, his hands full of the moist black earth, he caught the strong, good smell of it, and something leaped in him, longing, responding. He made a sound without knowing it. Astrin looked up.

"What is it? Did you find something?"

He dropped the earth and shook his head, feeling tears behind his throat and not knowing why.

Walking home at dusk, their finds carefully wrapped in old cloth, Astrin said to him, "You are so patient here. Perhaps you belong here, working among these forgotten things, in silence. And you accept my strange ways so unquestioningly, as though you can't remember how men do live with one another. . . ." He paused a moment, then went on slowly, as if remembering himself, "I haven't always been alone. I grew up in Caerweddin, with Heureu, and the sons of our father's High Lords, in the beautiful, noisey house Galil Ymris made out of the Earth-Master's stones. Heureu and I were close then, like shadows of each other. That was before we quarrelled." He shrugged the words away as Morgon looked at him. "It makes no difference here. I'll never go back to Caerweddin, and Heu-

46

reu will never come here. I had just forgotten that once I wasn't alone. You forget easily."

He left Morgon that night after supper. Morgon, brushing dirt off pieces of pottery they had found, waited patiently. The wind rose hours after sunset; he grew uneasy, feeling them pull at the joints of the small house, heave at it as if to uproot it. He opened the door aimlessly once to look for Astrin; the wind tore it from his grip, sent it crashing back and fought with him, face-to-face, as he edged it closed.

When the wind died finally, a silence dropped like thin fingers of moonlight across Wind Plain. The tower rose out of broken stone, whole and solitary, yielding nothing to the moon's eye. Morgon added wood to the fire, made a torch of an oak branch, and went outside. He heard heavy breathing suddenly from the side of the house, an odd, dragging step. He turned and saw Astrin hunched against the wall of the house.

He said, as Morgon put out his torch underfoot and went to help him, "I'm all right." His face was mistcolored in the light from the window; he flung an arm around Morgon heavily, and together they stumbled across the threshold, Astrin sat down on the pallet. His hands were scratched raw; his hair was tangled with sea spray. He held his right hand against his side and would not move it, until Morgon, watching the dark stain bloom under his fingers, made a harsh noise of protest. Astrin's head dropped back on the pallet; his hand slid down. He whispered as Morgon ripped a seam open, "Don't. I'm short of clothes. He saw me first, but I killed him. Then he fell in the sea, and I had to dive for him among the rocks and tide, or they would have found him. I buried him in the sand. They won't find him there. He was made . . . He was shaped out of seaweed and foam and wet pearl, and the sword was of darkness and silver water. It bit me and flew away like a bird. If Xel hadn't warned me, I would be dead. If I hadn't turned . . ." He flinched as Morgon touched his side with a wet cloth. Then he was silent, his teeth locked, his eyes closed, while Morgon washed the shallow wound gently, closed it and bound it with strips from his dry robe. He heated wine; Astrin drank it and his shivering stopped. He lay back again. "Thank you. Xel—thank you. If Xel comes back, let her in."

He slept motionlessly, exhausted, waking only once near dawn, when Xel came whining to the door, and Morgon sleepless by the fire, rose to open it for the wet, bedraggled huntress.

Astrin said little of the incident the next day. He moved stiffly, with a tight, sour expression that eased only when his eyes fell on Morgon's mute, worried face. They spent the day indoors, Astrin prowling through wizards' books like an animal scenting, and Morgon trying to wash and mend Astrin's robe while questions he could not ask struggled like trapped birds in the back of his throat.

Astrin came out of his grim thoughts, finally, near sunset. He closed a book with a sigh, its iron bonds locking automatically, and said, staring out at the plain, "I should tell Heureu." Then his hand snapped down flat on the book and closed. He whispered, "No. Let him see with his own eyes. The land is his business. Let him put his own name to this. He drove me out of Caerweddin five years ago for speaking the truth; why should I go back?"

Morgon, watching from the hearth as he struggled with needle and seam, made a questioning sound. Astrin, a hand to his side, turned to add wood to the fire for their evening meal. He paused a moment, to drop one hand on Morgon's shoulder. "I am glad you were here last night. If there is anything I can possibly do for you, I will do it."

He did not go out again at night for a while. Morgon worked at his side during the days, digging in the city; in the long, quiet evenings he would try to piece together shards of pottery, of glass, while Astrin searched through his books. Sometimes they hunted with Xel in the wild oak forest just south of them, which stretched from the sea far west beyond the limits of Ymris.

Once Astrin said, as they walked through the gentle, constant fall of dead oak leaves, "I should take you to Caithnard. It's just a day's journey south of these woods. Perhaps someone knows you there." But Morgon only looked at him blankly, as if Caithnard lay in some strange land at the bottom of the sea, and Astrin did not mention it again.

Morgon found a few days later a cache of lovely red and purple glass in a corner of the chamber they were working in. He took the fragments to Astrin's house, brushed off the dirt and puzzled over them. It rained heavily the next day; they could not go out. The small house smelled damp, and the fire smoked. Xel prowled restlessly, wailing complaints every now and then to Astrin, who sat murmuring over a spell-book he could not open. Morgon, some rough paste Astrin had made in front of him, began to fit together, piece by piece, the shards of glass.

He looked up as Astrin said irritably, "Xel, be quiet. I've run out of words. Yrth was the most powerful of the wizards after the Founder, and he locked his books too well."

Morgon opened his mouth, made a small sound, a puzzled look on his face. He turned abruptly, found a half-burned twig in the fire and blew it out. He wrote on the tabletop in ash, "You need his harp."

Astrin, watching, slid rather abruptly off the stool. He stood looking over Morgon's shoulder. "I need his what? Your handwriting is as difficult as Aloil's. Oh. Harp." His hand closed on Morgon's shoulder. "Yes. Perhaps you're right. Perhaps he did lock the book with a series of notes from the harp he made—or with the one low string that is said to shatter weapons. But where would I find it? Do you know where it is?"

Morgon shook his head. Then he dropped the twig, staring down at it as if it had been writing of its own volition. He turned his head after a moment, met Astrin's eyes. Astrin opened one of Aloil's spell-books abruptly, pushed a quill into Morgon's hand. "Who paid for his shape with the scars on his hands and to whom?"

Morgon began to write slowly down the margins of one of Aloil's spells. When he had finished the answer to the ancient Osterland riddle and begun the stricture, Astrin's voice broke from him in a little hiss.

"You studied at Caithnard. No man without a voice studies at that college—I know; I spent a year there myself. Can you remember it? Can you remember anything of it?"

Morgon stared back at him. He rose as if to go at once, the bench overturning behind him; Astrin caught him as he reached the door.

"Wait. It's nearly dusk. I'll go with you to Caithnard tomorrow, if you'll wait. There are some questions I want to ask the Masters myself."

They rose before dawn the next morning, to the soft drizzle of rain batting against the roof. It cleared before sunrise; they left Xel sleeping beside the fire and headed south across the wet, grassy plain toward the border of Ymris. The sun rose behind rain clouds drifting like ships above the grey sea. The wind shivered through the trees, plucked the last few wet leaves as they entered the woods, heading for the great traders' road that ran the length of Ymris and beyond, connecting the ancient city of Lungold to Caithnard.

"We should reach the road by noon," Astrin said. Morgon, the hem of his long robe drenched with dew, his eyes on the numberless trees as though he could see through them to a city he did not know, made an absent, answering noise. Crows flicked black through the distant branches; their harsh voices echoed back at him, mocking. He heard voices; a couple of traders, laughing, startled a tree full of birds as they rode through the early morning, their packs bulging. They came abreast of Morgon and Astrin; one of them stopped, bowing his head courteously.

"Lord Astrin. You're a ways from home." He turned, slipping his pack-strings loose. "I have a message from Mathom of An to Heureu Ymris concerning —I believe—the man who won Peven's crown. As a matter of fact, I have messages for half the landrulers of the realm. I was going to stop by your house and put it into your care."

Astrin's white brows closed. "You know I haven't seen Heureu for five years," he said rather coldly. The trader, a big, red-haired man with a scar down the side of his face, lifted a brow.

"Oh? You see, the difficulty is I'm taking ship from Meremont, so I will not be going to Caerweddin." He reached into his pack. "I would ask you to take him this message."

The silver of a blade soared in an arc out of the pack, flashed with a whistle down at Astrin. The trader's horse startled, and the sword blade, skimming past Astrin's face, shirred the sleeve of Morgon's outflung arm. He leaped forward after the first stunned, incredulous moment, caught the trader's wrist before it could lift again; the second trader, whirling his mount behind Morgon, brought the edge of his own blade down, high under Morgon's uplifted arm.

The blade tangled a little in the dark, heavy cloth. Morgon, the breath and sound knocked out of him by the blow, heard Astrin groan, then, for a moment, heard nothing. An odd quietness rose in his mind, a sense of something green, familiar, that smelled not unlike the wet, crushed grass; it faded away before he could name it, but not before he knew it held his name. Then he found himself swaying on his knees, breathing heavily, his lips caught between his teeth, blinking away something he thought was blood but was only the rain beginning again.

A horse, bare backed, galloped away into the trees; Astrin, a bloodstained sword in one hand, was unbuckling the saddle from the other. He wrenched it off, led the horse by the bit over to Morgon. There was a smear of blood across his face; the traders lay sprawling beside their packs and saddles.

He said, his own breath fast, "Can you stand? Where are you hurt?" He saw the black stain spreading down under Morgon's arm and winced. "Let me see."

Morgon shook his head, holding the arm clamped to his side with his hand. He struggled to his feet, swallowing sound after sound that would have set the crows mocking; Astrin got a firm grip on his good arm. His face, always colorless, seemed grey in the rain.

"Can you make it back to the house?"

He nodded and managed to make it as far as the edge of the plain.

He woke again as Astrin, dismounting behind him, pulled him gently down from the horse and into the house. He kicked the door shut with his foot as Xel, scenting them at the door, streaked out. Morgon collapsed on the pallet; Astrin, taking a skinning knife to the robe, managed despite Morgon's mute argument, to find the wound that began in the soft skin of the armpit and slanted down to lay three ribs bare.

Astrin made a sound in his throat. There was a knock on the door then; he whirled, reaching in a single, skilled movement for the sword by the pallet, and rising. He flung the door open; the point of the bloody sword came to rest on the breastbone of a trader who said, "Lord . . ." and then became uncharacteristically inarticulate.

"What?"

The trader, a broad man in a flowing Herun coat, black-bearded, kindly-faced, backed a step. "I have a message from . . ." He stopped again as the sword, shivering in Astrin's grip, rose from his breast to his throat. He finished in a whisper, "Rork Umber. Lord, you know me—"

"I know." Morgon, lifting his head with an effort, saw the skin stretched waxen across Astrin's face.

"That's why if you turn now, and go very quickly, I might let you leave this place alive."

"But, Lord . . ." His eyes broke from Astrin's face in helpless curiosity, met Morgon's, and Morgon saw the flash of his own name in the dark, astonished eyes. He made an eager, questioning noise; the trader drew a breath. "That's what happened to him? He can't talk—"

"Go!" The harsh, desperate edge in Astrin's voice startled even Morgon. The trader, his face white under his beard, held his ground stubbornly.

"But the High One's harpist is in Caerweddin, looking—"

"I have just killed two traders, and by the High One's name, I swear I will kill a third if you don't get off my doorstep!"

The trader disappeared from the doorway; Astrin watched until the sound of hooves died. Then, his hands shaking, he leaned the sword against the doorpost and knelt beside Morgon again.

"All right," he whispered. "Lie still. I'll do what I can."

He was forced to leave Morgon at the end of two days, to get help from an old fisherman's wife at Loor, who picked the herbs for him he needed and watched Morgon while he slept and hunted. After five days, the old woman went back home with chips of the Earth-Masters' gold in her hand; and Morgon, too weak to walk, could at least sit up and drink hot soup.

Astrin, worn himself with short nights and worry, said, after half a day of silence, as though he had resolved something in his own mind, "All right. You can't stay here; I don't dare take you to Caithnard or Caerweddin. I'll take you to Umber, and Rork can send for Deth. I need help."

He did not leave Morgon alone after that. As Morgon became stronger, they spent hours painstakingly piecing together the fragments of red and purple glass that Morgon had found; it began to take the shape of a fragile bowl, beautifully dyed, the red streaks becoming figures moving around the sides in the pattern of some ancient tale. Excited by it, Morgon, his pen scratching across Aloil's spells, talked Astrin into searching for the remaining pieces. They spent a day in the ruined city, found three more pieces and returned to meet the fisherman's wife on Astrin's doorstep. She had brought them a basket of fresh fish; she harried Morgon back into bed, scolded Astrin, and cooked supper for them.

The next morning they finished the bowl. Astrin placed the final pieces carefully, Morgon hovering at his shoulder, scarcely breathing. The red figures became whole, moving through the misty purple in some strange action. Astrin, trying to decipher it without touching the bowl as the paste dried, gave an impatient murmur as someone knocked on the door. Then his face tightened. He reached for the sword, held it loosely as he opened the door. He said, "Rork!" and then nothing more.

Three men came past Astrin into the house. They wore silver-white mail under long, heavy, beautifully embroidered coats; swords were slung on jewelled belts at their hips.

The black-bearded trader whom Astrin had driven from his door said, looking at Morgon, "There he is. The Prince of Hed. Look at him. He's hurt, he can't speak. He doesn't even know me, and I bought grain and sheep from him five weeks ago; I knew his father."

Morgon stood up slowly. Other men entered: a tall, richly dressed, red-haired man with a harried expression on his face; another guard; a pale-haired harpist. Morgon looked for Astrin's face in the confusion of faces, found in it the same incredulous horror he saw in the strangers' eyes.

Astrin breathed, "Rork, it's not possible. I found him tossed up by the sea—he couldn't speak, he couldn't . . ."

The eyes of the High Lord of Umber met the harpist's, received affirmation; he said wearily, "He's the Prince of Hed." He ran a hand through his bright hair, sighing. "You had him. Deth has been looking for him for five weeks, and this trader finally brought some tale to the King at Caerweddin that you had gone mad and killed two traders, wounded the Prince of Hed, kept him imprisoned, somehow—through a spell, I suppose—stole his voice. Can you imagine what Heureu thinks? There's a strange rebellion building in Meremont and Tor, among the coastal lords, that not even the High Lords can account for. We're bidden to arms for the second time in a year, and on top of that the land-heir of Ymris is accused of murder and imprisoning a land-ruler. The King sent armed men to take you if you resist; the High One sent his harpist to place you under the doom if you try to escape, and I came ... I came to listen to you."

Astrin put a hand over his eyes. Morgon, his eyes moving bewilderedly from one face to another, hearing a name that belonged to him yet had no meaning, made another sound. The trader sucked a breath.

"Listen to him. Five weeks ago he could talk. When I saw him, he was lying there making noises, with the blood pouring out of his side, and Lord Astrin standing at the door with blood on his sword, threatening to kill me. It's all right," he added soothingly to Morgon. "You're safe now."

Morgon drew a breath. The sound he wanted to make was cut short before it came; instead he lifted the bowl they had put together so patiently and smashed it against the table. He had their attention then, but as they stared at him, startled, he could not speak. He sat down again, his hands sliding over his mouth.

Astrin took a step toward him, stopped. He said to Rork, "He can't ride all that way to Caerweddin; his wound is barely healed. Rork surely you don't believe —I found him washed up on the beach, nameless, voiceless—You can't believe I would harm him."

"I don't," Rork said. "But how did he get hurt?"

"I was taking him to Caithnard, to see if the Masters recognized him. We met two traders who tried to kill us both. So I killed them. And then this one came, knocking on my door when I had just brought the Prince of Hed in, hardly knowing if he were dead or alive. Can you blame me for being something less than hospitable?"

The trader took off his cap and passed a hand through his hair. "No," he admitted. "But Lord, you might have listened to me. Who were these traders? There hasn't been a renegade trader in fifty years. We see to that. It's bad for business."

"I have no idea who they were. I left the bodies in the woods, not far from the edge, as you would go straight south from here to reach the trade-road."

Rork nodded briefly to the guards. "Find them. Take the trader with you." He added, as they left, "You'd better pack. I brought two mounts and a packhorse from Umber."

"Rork." The white eyes were pleading. "Is it necessary? I've told you what happened; the Prince of Hed can't speak, but he can write, and he'll bear witness for me before you and the High One's harpist. I have no wish to see Heureu; I have nothing to answer for."

Rork sighed. "I will have, if I don't bring you back with me. Half the High Lords of Ymris gathered at Caerweddin heard this tale, and they want an answer to it. You have white hair and white eyes, you meddle with ancient stones and books of wizardry; no one has seen you at Caerweddin in five years, and for all anyone knows it's entirely possible that you have gone mad and done exactly what the trader said you did."

"They'll believe you."

"Not necessarily."

"They'll believe the High One's harpist."

Rork sat down on the stool, rubbed his eyes with his fingers. "Astrin. Please. Go back to Caerweddin."

"For what?"

Rork's shoulders slumped. The High One's harpist

said then, his voice quiet, even, "It's not that simple. You are under the doom of the High One, and if you choose not to answer to Heureu Ymris, you will answer to the High One."

Astrin's hands went down flat on the table among the glass shards. "For what?" He held the harpist's eyes. "The High One must have known the Prince of Hed was here. What can he possibly hold me accountable for?"

"I cannot answer for the High One. I can only give you that warning, as I have been instructed. The doom for disobedience is death."

Astrin looked down at the splinters of glass between his hands. He sat down slowly. Then he reached out, touched Morgon. "Your name is Morgon. No one told you." He added wearily to Rork, "I'll have to pack my books; will you help me?"

The guards and the trader returned an hour later. The trader, an odd expression on his face, replied only vaguely to Rork's questions.

"Did you recognize them?"

"One of them, yes. I think. But . . ."

"Do you know his name? Can you attest to his character?"

"Well. Yes. I think. But . . ." He shook his head, his face strained. He had not dismounted, as though he wanted to stay no longer than necessary in the lonely, wild corner of Ymris. Rork turned, seized with the same impatience.

"Let's go. We have to reach Umber by nightfall. And——" He glanced up as a stray tear of rain caught his eyes, "It's going to be a weary ride to Caerweddin."

Xel, too wild to live at Caerweddin, sat on the doorstep as they left, watching them curiously. They rode eastward across the plain, while the clouds darkened behind the ancient, ruined city, and wind passed like some lost, invisible army across the grass. The rain held miraculously until early evening, when they crossed a river at the northern edge of the plain and caught a road that led through the rough hills and green woods of Umber to Rork's house.

They spent the night there, in the great house built of red and brown stones from the hills, in whose vast hall all the lesser lords of Umber seemed to be gathered at once. Morgon, knowing only the silence of Astrin's house, was uneasy among the men whose voices rumbled like the sea with talk of war, the women who treated him with a fine, bewildering courtesy and spoke to him of a land he did not know. Only Astrin's face, closed and aloof to the strangeness, reassured him; and the harpist, playing at the supper's end, wove a sound within the dark, fire-washed stones that was like the wind-haunted peace Morgon remembered. At night, alone in a chamber big as Astrin's house, he lay awake listening to the hollow wind, groping blindly for his name.

They left Umber at dawn, rode through a morning mist that coiled and pearled on black, bare orchards. The mist resolved into a rain that stayed with them all the way up the long road from Umber to Caerweddin. Morgon, riding hunched against it, felt the damp collect in his bones, like a mildew. He bore it absently, vaguely aware of Astrin's concern, something drawing his thoughts forward, an odd pull out of the darkness of his ignorance. Finally, racked by a nagging cough as he rode, he felt the half-healed wound in his side scored as with fire, and he reined sharply. The High One's harpist put a hand on his shoulder. Looking at the still, austere face, Morgon drew a sudden breath, but the moment's strange recognition wavered and passed. Astrin, riding back to them, his face taut, unapproachable, said briefly, "We're almost there."

The ancient house of the Ymris Kings stood near the sea on the mouth of the Thul River, which ran eastward across Ymris from one of the seven Lungold Lakes. Trade ships were anchored in its deep waters; a fleet of ships with the scarlet and gold sails of Ymris were docked at the mouth of the river like colorful birds. As they rode across the bridge, a messenger, sighting them, turned hurriedly into the open gates of a sprawling stone wall. Beyond it, on a hill, stood the house that Galil Ymris had built, its proud face and wings and towers alive with beautiful patterns of color formed by the brilliant stones of the Earth-Masters.

They rode through the gates, up the gentle incline of a cobbled road. Thick oak doors in the mouth of a second wall were opened for them: they entered a courtyard where serving men took their horses as they dismounted and flung heavy fur cloaks over their shoulders. They went in silence across the wide yard, the rain gusting against their faces.

The King's hall, built of smooth, dark, glittering stones, held a fire that ran half the length of the inner wall. They were drawn to the fire like moths, shuddering and dripping, unaware of the men falling silent, motionless around them. A quick step on the stones made them turn.

Heureu Ymris, lean, big boned, his dark hair speckled with rain, bent his head courteously to Morgon and said, "You are welcome to my house. I met your father not too long ago. Rork, Deth, I am in your debt. Astrin—" He stopped then, as though the word he had spoken was strange or bitter to his mouth. Astrin's face was closed as surely as one of Yrth's books; his white eyes were expressionless. He looked placeless in the rich hall, with his colorless face and worn robe. Morgon, suddenly possessed of a father he did not know, wished futilely, desperately, that he and Astrin were back where they belonged, in the small house by the sea fitting pieces of glass shard together. He glanced around at the silent, watching strangers in the hall. Something snagged his eye then, down the long hall, something that flamed across the distance, turning his face toward it like a touch.

A sound came out of him. In the shifting torchlight, a great harp stood on a table. It was of beautiful, ancient design, with gold twisted into pale, polished wood inlaid with moons and quarter moons of ivory or bone. Down the face of it, among full moons, inset in gold, were three flawless blood-red stars.

Morgon went toward them, feeling as though his voice and name and thoughts had been stripped from him a second time. There was nothing in the room but those flaming stars and his movement toward them. He reached them, touched them. His fingers moved from them to trace the fine network of gold buried deep in the wood. He ran his hand across the strings, and at the rich, sweet sounds that followed, a love of that harp filled him, overpowering all care, all memory of the past, dark weeks. He turned, looked back at the silent group behind him. The harpist's quiet face rippled a little in the firelight. Morgon took a step toward him.

"Deth."

4

NO ONE MOVED. MORGON, FEELING A WORLD SLIP easily, familiarly into place as though he were waking from a dream, gave a second look at the massive, ancient walls of the house, at the strangers watching him, jewelled, double-linked chains of rank flashing on their breasts. His eyes went back to the harpist. "Eliard . . ."

"I went to Hed to tell him—somehow—that you might have drowned; he said you must be still alive since the land-rule had not passed to him. So I searched for you from Caithnard to Caerweddin."

"How did you—?" He stopped, remembering the empty ship sagging on its side, the screaming horses. "How did we both survive?"

"Survive what?" Astrin said. Morgon gazed at him without seeing him.

"We were sailing to An at night. I was taking the crown of Peven of Aum to Anuin. The crew just vanished. We went down in a storm."

"The crew did what?" Rork demanded.

"They vanished. The sailors, the traders, in open sea . . . In the middle of a storm, the ship just stopped and sank, with all its grain and animals." He stopped again, feeling the whip of the wet, mad winds, remembering someone who was himself and yet not himself lying half-drowned on the sand, nameless, voiceless. He reached out to touch the harp. Then, staring down at the stars burning under his hand like the stars on his face, he said sharply, amazed, "Where in the world did this come from?"

"Some fisherman found it last spring," Heureu Ymris said, "not far from where you and Astrin were staying. It had washed up on the beach. He brought it here because he thought it was bewitched. No one could play it."

"No one?"

"No one. The strings were mute until you touched them."

Morgon moved his hand away from it. He saw the awed expression in Heureu's eyes repeating itself in Astrin's as they looked at him, and he felt again, for a moment, a stranger to himself. He turned away from the harp, walked back to the fire. He stopped in front of Astrin; their eyes met in a little, familiar silence. Morgon said softly, "Thank you."

Astrin smiled for the first time since Morgon had met him. Then he looked over Morgon's shoulder at Heureu. "Is that sufficient? Or do you still intend to bring me to judgment for trying to murder a land-ruler?"

Heureu drew a breath. "Yes." His face, set with the same stubbornness, was a dark reflection of Astrin's. "I will, if you try to walk out of this hall without giving me any explanations of why you killed two traders, and threatened to kill a third when he saw the Prince of Hed wounded in your house. There have been enough unfounded rumors spreading through Ymris about you; I will not have something like this added to them."

"Why should I explain? Will you believe me? Ask the Prince of Hed. What would you have done with me if he hadn't found his voice?"

Heureu's own voice rose in exasperation. "What do

you think I would have done? While you've been at the other end of Ymris digging up potshards, Meroc Tor has been arming half the coastal lands of Ymris. He attacked Meremont yesterday. You would be dead by now if I hadn't sent Rork and Deth to get you out of that hut you've been clinging to like a barnacle."

"You sent—?"

"What do you think I am? Do you think I believe every tale I hear about you—including the one that you go out in animal-shape every night and scare cattle?"

"I do what?"

"You are the land-heir of Ymris, and you are my brother whom I grew up with. I'm tired of sending messengers to Umber every three months to find out from Rork if you are alive or dead. I have a war on my hands that I don't understand and I need you. I need your skill and your mind. And I need to know this: who were those traders that tried to kill you and the Prince of Hed? Were they men of Ymris?"

Astrin shook his head. He looked dazed. "I have no idea. We were . . . I was taking him to Caithnard to see if the Masters knew him when we were attacked. He was wounded; I killed the traders. I don't believe they were traders."

"They weren't," the trader who had come with them said glumly; and Morgon said, suddenly, "Wait. I remember. The red-haired man—the one who spoke to us. He was on the ship."

Heureu looked at them bewilderedly. "I don't understand." Astrin turned to the trader.

"You knew him."

The trader nodded. His face was white, unhappy in the firelight. "I knew him. I've looked at that face I saw in the woods night and day, tried to tell myself that the death in it was playing tricks on me. But I can't. There was the same front tooth gone, the same scar he got when a loading cable snapped and hit him in the face—it was Jarl Aker; from Osterland."

"Why would he attack the Prince of Hed?" Heureu asked.

"He wouldn't. He didn't. He's been dead for two years."

Heureu said sharply, "That's not possible."

"It's possible," Astrin said grimly. He was silent, struggling a little with himself while Heureu watched. "Meroc Tor's rebels aren't the only men arming themselves in Ymris."

"What do you mean?"

Astrin glanced at the curious, expectant faces of the gathering in the hall. "I would rather tell you privately. That way if you don't—" He stopped abruptly. A woman had joined Heureu quietly; her dark, shy eyes, flicking over the group, lingered a little on Morgon's face, then moved to Astrin's.

She said, her brows crooked, her voice soft in the murmurings of the fire, "Astrin, I'm glad you've come back. Will you stay now?"

Astrin's hands closed at his sides, his eyes going to Heureu's face. There was a mute, brittle struggle between them; the Ymris King, without moving, seemed to shift closer to the woman.

He said to Morgon, "This is my wife, Eriel."

"You don't favor your father," she commented interestedly. Then the blood burned into her face. "I'm sorry—I wasn't thinking."

"It's all right," Morgon said gently. The firelight brushed like soft wings over her face, her dark hair. Her brows crooked again, troubled.

"You don't look well. Heureu—"

The Ymris King stirred. "I'm sorry. You could all do with some dry clothes and food; you've had a rough ride. Astrin, will you stay? The only thing I ask is that if you ever speak of that matter that came between us five years ago, you give me unshakable, absolute proof. You've been away from Caerweddin long enough; there's no one I need more now."

Astrin's head bowed. His hands in his frayed sleeves were still closed. He said softly, "Yes."

An hour later, Morgon, washed, shorn of five weeks' growth of hair, the edge taken off his hunger, surveyed the fur-covered bed in his chamber and lay down without undressing. There was a knock on his door in what seemed only a moment later; he sat up, blinking. The room, except for the low fire, was dark. The stone walls seemed to move and settle around him as he rose; he could not find the door. He considered the problem, murmured the stricture of an ancient riddle from An:

"See with your heart what your eyes cannot, and you will find the door that is not."

The door opened abruptly in front of him, light flaring in from the hall. "Morgon."

The harpist's face and silver hair were oddly blurred with torchlight. Morgon said with an odd sense of relief, "Deth. I couldn't find the door. For a moment I thought I was in Peven's tower. Or the tower Oen of An built to trap Madir. I just remembered that I promised Snog Nutt I would fix his roof before the rains start. He's so addled he won't think of telling Eliard; he'll sit there all winter with the rain dripping down his neck."

The harpist put a hand on his arm. His brows were drawn. "Are you ill?"

"I don't think so, no. Grim Oakland thinks I should get another pigherder, but Snog would die of uselessness if I took his pigs away from him. I'd better go home and fix his roof." He started as a shadow loomed across the threshold.

Astrin, unfamiliar in a short, close-fitting coat, his hair neatly trimmed, said brusquely to Deth, "I have to talk to you. Both of you. Please." He took a torch from the hall; the shadows flitted away in the room, sat hunched in corners, behind furniture.

Astrin closed the door behind them, turned to Morgon, "You have got to leave this house."

Morgon sat down on the clothes chest. "I know. I was just telling Deth." He found himself shivering suddenly, uncontrollably, and moved to the fire that Deth was rousing.

Astrin, prowling through the room like Xel, demanded of Deth, "Did Heureu tell you why we quarrelled five years ago?"

"No. Astrin—"

"Please. Listen to me. I know you can't act, you can't help me, but at least you can listen. I left Caerweddin the day Heureu married Eriel."

An image of the shy, fragile face, richly colored with firelight, rose in Morgon's mind. He said sympathetically, "Were you in love with her, too?"

"Eriel Meremont died five years ago on King's Mouth Plain."

Morgon closed his eyes. The harpist, kneeling with his hands full of wood, was so still not even the light trembled on the chain across his breast. He said, his voice changeless as ever, "Do you have proof?"

"Of course not. If I had proof, would that woman who calls herself Eriel Meremont still be married to Heureu?"

"Then who is married to Heureu?"

"I don't know." He sat down finally beside the fire. "The day before the wedding, I rode with Eriel to King's Mouth Plain. She was tired of the preparations and wanted a few moments of peace, and she asked me to go with her. We were close; we had known each other since we were children, but there was nothing more than deep friendship between us. We rode to the ruined city on the plain and separated. She went to sit on one of the broken walls to watch the sea, and I just walked through the city, wondering as always what force had scattered the stones like leaves on the grass. At one moment, as I walked, everything grew suddenly very quiet: the sea, the wind. I looked up. I saw a white bird flying above me against the blue sky. It was very beautiful, and I remember thinking that the

silence must be like the still eye of a maelstrom. Then
I heard a wave break, and the wind rise. I heard a
strange cry; I thought the bird had made it. Then I
saw Eriel ride past me without looking back or speaking. I called to her to wait, but she didn't look back. I
went to get my horse, and when I passed the rock she
had been sitting on, I saw a white bird lying dead on it.
It was still warm, still bleeding. I held it in my hands,
and felt sorrow and terror overwhelm me as I remembered the silence, and the cry of the bird and Eriel riding away from me without looking back. I buried the
bird there among the ancient stones above the sea.
That night I told Heureu what I had seen. We ended
up shouting at each other, and I swore as long as he
was married to that woman I would never return to
Caerweddin. I think Rork Umber is the only man to
whom Heureu told the truth about why I left. He
never told Eriel, but she must know. I only began to
realize what she must be as I watched the army being
gathered, ships built, arms unloaded at night from Isig
and Anuin. . . . I've seen, late at night, what Meroc
Tor has not: that part of this army he has formed is
not human. And that woman is of this nameless, powerful people." He paused, his eyes moved from Deth's
face to Morgon's. "I decided to stay at Caerweddin for
one reason only: to find proof of what she is. I don't
know what you are, Morgon. They gave you a name
in my house, but I've never heard of a Prince of Hed
winning a riddle-game with death, playing an ancient
harp made only for him by someone, sometime, who
put the touch of a destiny on that harp's face."

Morgon leaned back in his chair. He said wearily,
"I can't use a harp to fix Snog Nutt's roof."

"What?"

"I've never heard that a destiny is of any use at
all to a Prince of Hed. I'm sorry Heureu married
the wrong woman, but that's his business. She's beautiful, and he loves her, so I don't see why you're upset.
I was on my way to Anuin to get married myself when

I nearly got killed. Logically it would seem that some-one wants to kill me, but that's their business; I don't want to be bothered trying to figure out why. I'm not stupid; once I start asking questions—even one ques-tion: What are three stars—I'll begin a riddle-game I don't think I'll want to finish. I don't want to know. I want to go home, fix Snog Nutt's roof, and go to bed."

Astrin gazed at him a moment, then turned to Deth. "Who is Snog Nutt?"

"His pigherder."

Astrin reached out, touched Morgon's face. "You may as well have died in that woods for all the good four days' riding in the rain has done you. I'd row you back to Hed and patch your pigherder's roof myself if I thought you could even walk out of this room and stay alive. I'm afraid for your life in this house, especially now since you found that harp so conveniently here, under the eyes of Eriel Ymris. Deth, you nearly lost your own life because of those people; who does the High One say they are?"

"The High One, beyond saving my life and doubt-lessly Morgon's, for his own reasons, has said ab-solutely nothing to me. I had to find out for myself whether Morgon was alive, and where he was. It was unexpected, but the High One follows his own inclinations." He settled a log on the fire and stood up. Lines had formed, faint, taut, down the sides of his mouth. He added, "You know I can do nothing without his instructions. I cannot in any way offend the King of Ymris, since I act in the High One's name."

"I know. You'll notice I haven't asked you if you believe me or not. But do you have any suggestions?"

Deth glanced at Morgon. "I suggest you send for the King's physician."

"Deth—"

"There is nothing either one of us can do but wait. And watch. As ill as Morgon is, he should not be left alone."

Something eased in the lean, colorless face. He rose

abruptly. "I'll get Rork to help us watch. He may not believe me, but he knows me well enough to be uneasy about this."

The King's physician, the Lady Anoth, an elderly, comforting, dry-voiced woman took one look at Morgon, and, ignoring his arguments, gave him something that whirled him into a drugged sleep. He woke hours later, light-headed, restless. Astrin, who had stayed to keep watch over him, had fallen asleep by the fire, exhausted. Morgon eyed him a moment, wanting to talk, then decided to let him sleep. His thoughts strayed to the harp in the hall; he heard again the light, rich voice of it, felt the taut, perfectly tuned strings under his fingers. A thought occurred to him then, a question underlying the agelessness, the magic behind the harp. He rose a little unsteadily, wrapped himself in fur from the bed, and left the room soundlessly. The hallway was empty, quiet; the torchlight flared over the private faces of closed doors. With an odd certainty, he found his way down a stairway that led to the great hall.

The stars gleamed like eyes in the shadows. He touched the harp, picked it up, feeling the unexpected lightness of it in spite of its size. The fine, ancient scroll and web of gold burned under his fingers. He touched a string, and at the lovely, solitary sound, he smiled. Then a fit of coughing shook him, tearing painfully at his side; he dropped his face in the fur to still the sound.

A startled voice said behind him, "Morgon."

He straightened after a moment, white, exhausted. Eriel Ymris came down the stairs, followed by a girl with a torch. He watched her come to him quietly through the long hall, her unbound hair making her look very young. He said curiously, "Astrin told me you were dead."

She stopped. He could not read the expression in her eyes. Then she said composedly, "No. You are."

His hands shifted position slightly on the harp.

Somewhere, too distant to trouble him, something in him was crying out a warning. He shook his head. "Not yet. Who are you? Are you Madir? No, she's dead. And she didn't kill birds. Are you Nun?"

"Nun is dead, too." She was watching him without blinking, her eyes fire-flecked. "You don't go back far enough, Lord. Go back as far as your mind will take you, to the earliest riddle that was asked, and I am older than that."

He threw his mind back to his studies, touched riddle after riddle but found her nowhere. He said incredulously, "You don't exist in the books of the Masters—not even in the books of wizardry that have been opened. Who are you?"

"The wise man can give a name to his enemy."

"The wise man knows he has enemies," he said a little bitterly. "What is it? Is it the stars? Would it help to tell you that the last thing I want to do is fight you; I simply want to be left alone to rule Hed in peace."

"Then you shouldn't have left your land to begin weaving riddles at Caithnard. The wise man knows his own name. You don't know my name; you don't know your own. It's better for me if you die that way, in ignorance."

"But why?" he said bewilderedly, and she took a step toward him. At her side, the young girl turned suddenly into a big, red-haired trader with a weal across his face, who wielded instead of a torch a sword of lean, ash-colored metal. Morgon moved back, felt the wall behind him. He watched the sword rise in a dreamlike slowness. It burned the skin of his throat, and he started.

"Why?" The blade had drained the sound from his voice. "At least tell me why."

"Beware the unanswered riddle." She looked away from him, nodded at the trader.

Morgon closed his eyes. He said, "Never under-

70

estimate another riddler," and plucked the lowest string of the harp.

The sword shattered in midair, and he heard a cry like a faint bird cry. Then all around him came a terrible cacophony of sound as ancient shields lining the far wall burst with hollow, metallic ringing, and their split pieces drummed on the floor. Morgon felt himself drop from a great distance, fall like a shield to the floor, and he buried the noise of his falling in the fur. Voices followed the din and hum of metal, flurried, indistinct.

Someone tugged at him. "Morgon, get up. Can you get up?" He lifted his head; Rork Umber, dressed in little more than a cloak and a knife belt, helped him up.

Heureu, staring down at them from the stairs, with Eriel behind him, demanded amazedly, "What is going on? It sounds like a battlefield in here."

"I'm sorry," Morgon said. "I broke your shields."

"You did. How in Aloil's name did you do that?"

"Like this." He plucked the string again, and the knife in Rork's belt, and the pikes of the guards in the doorways snapped. Heureu drew a breath, stunned.

"Yrth's harp."

"Yes," Morgon said. "I thought it might be." His eyes moved to Eriel's face as she stood behind Heureu, her hands against her mouth. "I thought—I dreamed you were here with me."

Her head gave a little, startled shake. "No. I was with Heureu."

He nodded. "It was a dream, then."

"You're bleeding," Rork said suddenly. He turned Morgon toward the light. "How did you get that cut on your throat?"

Morgon touched it. He began to shake then, and he saw, above Eriel, Astrin's haggard, bloodless face.

Drugged again, he dreamed of ships tossing in a wild, black sea, decks empty, sails ripped to ribbons; of a beautiful, black-haired woman who tried to kill him by playing the lowest string on a starred harp, and who wept when he shouted at her; of a riddle-game weaving through his dreams that never ended, with a man whose face he never saw, who asked riddle after riddle, demanding answers, yet never answered any himself. Snog Nutt appeared from somewhere, waiting patiently with rainwater falling down his neck for the game to end, but it was interminable. Finally the strange riddler turned into Tristan, who told him to go home. He found himself in Hed, walking through the wet fields at dusk, smelling the earth. Just as he reached the open doors of his house, he woke.

The room with its beautiful patterned walls of blue and black stone was filled with a grey afternoon light. Someone sitting by the fire bent over to settle a falling log. Morgon recognized the lean, outstretched hand, the loose, silver hair.

He said, "Deth."

The harpist rose. His face was hollowed, faintly lined with weariness; his voice, calm as always, held no trace of it. "How do you feel?"

"Alive." He stirred and said reluctantly, "Deth, I have a problem. I may have been dreaming, but I think Heureu's wife tried to kill me."

Deth was silent. In a rich, dark, full-sleeved robe he looked a little like a Caithnard Master, his face honed from years of study. Then he touched his eyes briefly with his fingers and sat down on the edge of the bed.

"Tell me."

Morgon told him. The rain he had heard now and again in his dreaming began to tap softly against the wide windows; he listened to it a moment when he had finished, then added, "I can't figure out who she might be. She has no place in the tales and riddles of the kingdoms . . . just as the stars have no place. I can't accuse her; I have no proof, and she would just look at me out of her shy eyes and not know what on earth I was talking about. So I think I should leave this place quickly."

"Morgon, you have been lying ill for two days since you were found in that hall. Assuming you have the strength to leave this room, what would you do?"

Morgon's mouth crooked. "I'm going to go home. The wise man does not shake a hornet's nest to see what's buzzing in it. I've left Hed without a land-ruler for six weeks; I want to see Eliard and Tristan again. I'm accountable to the High One for the name I was born with in Hed, not for some strange identity I seem to have beyond Hed." He paused; the rain changed, began battering hard at the glass. His eyes strayed to it. "I am curious," he admitted. "But this is one riddle-game I have sense enough to stay out of. The High One can play it."

"The High One is not the one being challenged."

"It's his realm; I'm not responsible for the power games in Ymris."

"You may be if the stars on your face set them in motion."

Morgon looked at him. His mouth drew taut; he turned restlessly, wincing a little, the shadows of pain and exhaustion in his face deepening. Deth dropped a hand on his arm. "Rest," he said gently. "If you choose, when you're well enough to leave, to go back to Hed, unless the High One gives me other instructions, I'll travel with you. If you disappear again between Hed and Ymris, I would only have to search for you."

"Thank you. I don't understand, though, why the High One left you ignorant of where I was. Did you ask him?"

"I'm a harpist, not a wizard to throw my mind from here to Erlenstar Mountain. He comes into my mind at will; I cannot go into his."

"Well, he must have known you were searching for me. Why didn't he tell you?"

"I can only guess. The High One's mind is the

73

great web of the minds of those in his realm. He weaves to his own ends, threading back and forth between action and action to make a pattern, which is why his reactions to events are often unexpected. Five years ago, Heureu Ymris married, and Astrin Ymris left Caerweddin carrying a fact like a stone in him. Perhaps the High One used you to bring Astrin and his fact back to Caerweddin to face Heureu."

"If that's true, then he knows what she is." He stopped. "No. He could have acted when Heureu married, that would have been simpler. Her children will be the land-heirs of Ymris; if she were that powerful, that lawless, surely the High One would have acted then. Astrin must be wrong. I must have been dreaming, that night. And yet . . ." He shook his head, his hand sliding over his eyes. "I don't know. I'm glad all this is none of my business."

The King's physician checked him, forbade him to set one foot on the floor, and gave him a hot, heady mixture of wine and herbs at evening that slid him into a dreamless sleep. He woke only once, sometime in the middle of the night, to find Rork Umber reading by the fire. The High Lord's bright hair blurred against the flames as Morgon's eyes closed and he slept again.

Heureu and Eriel came to see him the next afternoon. Astrin, who had relieved Rork, stood at the broad windows overlooking the city; Morgon saw the eyes of the king and his land-heir meet a moment, expressionlessly. Then Heureu pulled chairs to the bedside and sat down.

He said tiredly, "Morgon, Anoth ordered me not to disturb you, but I must. Meroc Tor has laid seige to the High Lord of Meremont; I am leaving in two days with a force from Ruhn, Caerweddin and Umber to break it. I have had word that there is a fleet of warships on the coasts of Meremont ready to set sail for Caerweddin if Meremont falls. If those ships succeed in reaching Caerweddin, you're liable to be trapped here indefinitely. For your own safety, I think

you should be moved north, to the house of the High
Lord of Marcher."

Morgon did not answer for a moment. He said
slowly, "Heureu, I am grateful for the care you've
given me, and for your kindness. But I would rather
not go any farther from Hed than I am now. Can
you spare a ship to send me home?"

The dark, troubled face eased a little. "I can. But
I thought you might object to going home by sea.
I can send you in one of my own trade-ships, under
guard. I know my own traders well; I've sailed with
them."

"You have?"

"To Anuin, Caithnard, even Kraal . . ." He smiled
reminiscently. "That was when I was younger, and
my father was still alive. Astrin went to Caithnard
to study, but I chose to learn about the world beyond Ymris in a different way. I loved it, but since
I took the land-rule, I have rarely left Ymris."

"Is that when you met my father? On one of your
journeys?"

Heureu shook his head. "I met your parents last
spring, when Eriel and I visited Caithnard."

"Last spring." He drew a breath. "You saw
them then. I had no idea."

"You couldn't have," Eriel said softly, and Astrin,
at the window, turned. Her soft brows were crooked
a little anxiously, but she continued, "We met when
—when Heureu bumped into your mother, Spring, on
a crowded street and broke a glass bowl she was
carrying. She started crying. I think she was frightened
of all the people and the noise. And your father
tried to get her to stop—we all tried—but she wouldn't
come out from behind her hands. So we just talked
for a while. We told each other our names, and
your father began to tell us about you, how you went
to college there. He was very proud of you. And, of
course, your mother came out then, because we were
talking about her child." She smiled quickly at the

memory; then her brows drew together again, and her eyes dropped from his gaze. "We had supper together and talked into the night. Your mother . . . I had—I had a child that died a few months before that, and I was never able to speak about it to anyone until that night, to her. So when we returned to Caerweddin and heard what happened to them, I felt . . . I was deeply grieved."

Morgon's lips parted as he watched her. His eyes flicked once to Astrin, but the white eyes were unreadable. Heureu's hand touched hers, closed over it. He said gently, "Morgon, your father said something that I remembered suddenly last night. He told me he had bought a harp for you, a very beautiful, odd-looking harp he thought you'd like. He had paid almost nothing for it, to some wandering Lungold trader because it was cursed, it didn't play. He said no sensible man believed in curses. I asked him how you would be able to play it, then, and he just smiled and said he thought you could. He didn't show it to me because it was packed on the ship. I realized last night that your father must have known you could play that harp because it had your stars on its face."

Morgon tried to speak; his voice would not come. He rose suddenly, unsteadily, stood staring into the fire, oblivious to everything but one terrible thought. "Is that what happened? Someone saw those stars and made a death-ship for them, whose crew vanished, left them alone, helpless, with the ship tearing apart around them, not knowing, not understanding why? Is that how they died? Is that—" He turned abruptly, saw the wine in its glass flagon by the fire, the cups of glass and gold, and he swept them in a single, furious movement off the table to smash against the stones. The broken shards beaded with red wine on the floor brought him back to himself. He said, his face bloodless, drawn, "I'm sorry . . . I didn't . . . I keep breaking things."

Heureu had risen. He gripped Morgon firmly; his

voice sounded distant, then returned, full. "I should have thought a little—I should have thought. Lie down before you hurt yourself. I'll get Anoth."

Morgon, scarcely hearing them leave, pushed his face tightly against the crook of his arm, felt tears burn like seawater in his eyes.

He woke later, slowly, to the sound of low intense voices: Astrin's and Heureu's. The muted anger in the King's voice broke the web of his dark dreaming like a cold wind.

"Do you think I'm witless, Astrin? I don't have to ask where to find you or Rork Umber, or even the High One's harpist, even at midnight. What Deth does is the High One's business, but if you and Rork spent as much time concerning yourself with the problems at hand as you do exhausting yourselves guarding against an illusion in this room, I would feel easier about the fate of Caerweddin."

Astrin's voice came back at him, cold, edged. "There are more illusions in this land than the woman you married. Anyone could come in here wearing a face so familiar none of us would think to see beneath it—"

"What do you want me to do? Mistrust every man and woman in my house? Is that what moved you to the far corner of Ymris—such terrible mistrust? I've seen the way you look at her, talk to her. What is it? Is it her unborn children you are jealous of? Do you want the land-rule that badly? I've heard that rumour too, but I've never come close to believing it before."

Astrin stared at him, silent, motionless, his colorless face like a mask. Then something broke in it; he turned away. He whispered, "I can take anything from you but that. I'm going back to Wind Plain. That woman nearly killed the Prince of Hed in your hall three nights ago; I'm not staying to watch her succeed. You watch; you married her."

He left Heureu gazing at the open, empty doorway. Morgon saw the first, faint uncertainty in his eyes before he followed.

Morgon shifted restlessly. The irresolvable quarrel, the hopeless questioning, the black, heavy thought of his parents' deaths loomed like a growth in his mind. He tried to get up, yielded, and fell back into a half-sleep. He woke with a startled murmur as the door opened again. Astrin came to his side.

Morgon said huskily, "I keep dreaming of that bowl I broke: the figures are moving around it in some strange pattern, a riddle I am on the verge of answering when it shatters, and with it all the answers to all the riddles in the world shatter. Why did you come back? I wouldn't blame you if you had left."

Astrin did not answer. Instead, with brief, methodical movements, he pulled the furs off Morgon, bundled them in his arms, and pushed them with all his strength against Morgon's face.

The fur in Morgon's mouth stifled his startled cry. The heavy weight of it melted around him, forced into his dry mouth, his eyes. He gripped the hands that held it down, struggled to pull them apart to move from the bed while the blood snapped and sang in his ears, and the darkness seemed to eddy him in huge, ponderous circles.

Then he found air again, a clean edge of it, and knelt on the floor, his voice sobbing, rattling like pebbles as he breathed. Next to the fire, Heureu, his hands twisted in the shoulders of Astrin's robe, held the man against the wall, while Rork Umber's sword lay like a lick of flame against his breast.

Morgon pulled himself up. Heureu and Rork were gazing incredulously at the mute, white-eyed figure. Rork was whispering, as if he had no breath for speech, "I don't believe it. I don't believe—"

A movement in the doorway caught Morgon's eye. He tried to speak; his voice, bruised, trapped, made for one last time a harsh, desperate bird-cry that turned their uncomprehending faces towards him.

"Heureu."

The King whirled. Astrin stood in the doorway. For a moment neither he nor Heureu moved; then expression came into Heureu's eyes. He said, "Be careful. I haven't got your gift for seeing. If I get you confused, I'll never understand this."

Rork said sharply, "Heureu!"

The figure beneath his sword was fading. It drifted like smoke beyond their eyes into the air, until suddenly it was gone and a white bird shot through the air towards Astrin.

He flung up his arms as it struck his face. They cried out together, he and the bird; he stumbled and fell, his hands over his eyes. Morgon reached him first, held him, and saw the blood trickling between the taut fingers covering one eye. There was a crash behind them; wind moaned into the room through the colored, jagged spears of window glass the bird left in its passing.

Heureu went to Astrin. Murmuring gently, incoherently, he moved Astrin's fingers from his eye. He drew a sharp breath, and snapped to a white-faced page staring at them in the hall,

"Get Anoth."

Astrin, his head in the crook of Morgon's shoulder, his eyes closed, said raggedly, "I was going to leave, but I couldn't. I came back to Morgon's room to see if you were still there, and as I came down the hall, I saw . . . I saw myself go into the room ahead of me. So I did something I've never been able to do before. I threw a call to you through the stones, into your mind—the wizard's call. I wait—I waited. That was hard to do, but you wanted proof."

"I know. Lie still. You've done—" He stopped. For a moment nothing of him moved, his breath, his hands, his eyes, while the blood drained slowly from his face. He whispered, "So long ago. That white bird." He stopped, kneeling hunched over Astrin, and they were silent. He rose abruptly; Rork gripped his shoulder.

"Heureu."

The King pulled away from him, strode down the long, empty hallway. Morgon closed his eyes. The Lady Anoth came, grim and breathless, to bandage Astrin's eye. Rork helped him up. Relieved of his burden, Morgon stood alone for the moment. He went to the window, touched the broken glass. He saw then, beyond Caerweddin, the stones of the ruined city on King's Mouth Plain, scattered like the bones of some gigantic, nameless man.

He dressed, went downstairs to the great hall. Firelight coiled deep in the stars on the face of the harp. He picked it up, slung it by its jewelled strap over his shoulder. He heard a step behind him and turned. The High One's harpist, his hair web-colored in the hearthlight, reached out, touched the stars.

He said softly, "I was there when Yrth made this harp. I heard the first song it ever played . . ."

His hand moved, closed gently on Morgon's shoulder, and Morgon's trembling eased. He said, "I want to leave."

"I'll ask the king to put a ship and guards at your disposal. You should be well enough to travel to Hed, if you're careful."

"I'm not going to Hed. I am going to Erlenstar Mountain." The stars, as he looked down on them, seemed like a reflection of his own face. "I can ignore the threats to my own life. I can deny my curiosity. I can deny that there is in me, somewhere, a man whose name I do not know. But I can't deny that these stars on my face may be deadly to those I love. So I am going to Erlenstar Mountain to ask the High One why."

The harpist was silent; Morgon could not read the expression in his eyes. "Are you going by sea?"

"No. I want to get there alive."

"It's late in the year for travelling north. It will be a long, lonely, dangerous journey; you'll be away from Hed for months."

"Are you trying to dissuade me?" Morgon asked, surprised.

The hand at his shoulder tightened faintly. "I haven't been to Erlenstar Mountain for three years, and, barring instructions from the High One, I would like to go home. May I travel with you?"

Morgon bowed his head, touched the harp, and stray strings sounded gently, haltingly, as though he were feeling for the beginning of some great song. "Thank you. But will you mind travelling with a man tracked by death?"

"Not when that man is carrying the harp of the Harpist of Lungold."

They left at dawn the next morning, so quietly only Heureu and the half-blind Ymris land-heir knew they had gone. They rode northward through King's Mouth Plain, their long morning shadows splaying across the massive, patternless stones. A gull, wheeling in the cool air, gave one cry above them, like a challenge, then winged, bright in the clear morning, southward over the line of lean, blue-sailed warships taking the slow tide of the Thul toward the sea.

5

THEY JOURNEYED SLOWLY THROUGH YMRIS, AS Morgon fought the last stages of his illness, avoiding the great houses of the Ymris lords, taking shelter after an easy day's riding in small villages that blossomed at the crux of a patchwork of field, or in the curve of a river. Deth paid for their shelter with his harping. Morgon, nursing a cold in miserable silence, sipping hot broth the women made for him, watched weary farmers and unruly children settle quietly to the sound of Deth's beautiful, intricate harping, his fine, skilled voice. They were given without hesitation any song, ballad, dance they asked for; and occasionally someone would bring out his own harp, a harp that had been passed down for generations, and recite a curious history of it, or play a variation of a song that Deth could invariably repeat after listening once. Morgon, his eyes on the ageless face bent slightly above the polished oak harp, felt the familiar nudge of a question in the back of his mind.

In the rocky fields and low border hills of Marcher, where villages and farms were rare on the rough land, they found themselves camping for the first time in the open. They stopped beside a narrow stream under a stand of three oaks. The late sun in the clear, dark-blue sky glanced off the red faces of rocks pushing up in the soil, and turned the hill grass gold. Morgon, coaxing a young fire, paused a moment and looked around him. The rough, undulating land flowed toward old, worn hills that seemed in their bald, smooth lines like old men sleeping. He said wonderingly, "I've never seen such lonely land."

Deth, unpacking their store of bread, cheese, wine and the apples and nuts one villager had given them, smiled. "Wait until you reach Isig Pass. This is gentle country."

"It's immense. If I had travelled this long in a straight line across Hed, I would have been walking on the ocean bottom a week ago." He added a branch to the fire, watched the flames eat across the dry leaves. The dull ache and weariness of fever had dropped away from him finally, leaving him clear-headed and curious, enjoying the cool wind and the colors. Deth handed him the wineskin; he took a mouthful. The fire, rousing, shimmered in the clean air like some rich, strange cloth; Morgon, catching a reflection of it in his memories, said slowly, "I should write to Raederle."

He had not spoken her name since they had left Caithnard. The colors of the memory resolved into long, flighty, fiery hair, hands flashing with gold and amber, amber-colored eyes. He tossed another branch on the fire and felt the harpist's eyes on his face. He sat back against a tree, reached for the wine again.

"And Eliard. The traders will probably tell him enough to worry him grey-haired before any letter of mine reaches him. If I get killed on this journey, he'll never forgive me."

"If we skirt Herun, you may not be able to send letters until we reach Osterland."

"I should have thought of writing before." He passed the wineskin to the harpist and sliced a wedge of cheese; his eyes strayed again to the fire. "After our father died, we grew so close that sometimes we dream the same dreams. . . . I was that close to my father as his land-heir. I felt him die. I didn't know how or why or where; I simply knew, at that moment, that he was dying. And then that he was dead, and the land-rule had passed to me. For a moment I saw every leaf, every seed, every root in Hed . . . I was every leaf, every new-planted seed. . . ." He leaned forward, reached for the bread. "I don't know why I'm talking about that. You must have heard it a hundred times."

"The passage of the land-rule? No. From what little I have heard, though, the passing isn't so gentle in other lands. Mathom of An told me some of the various bindings that demand constant attention from the land-rulers of An: the binding of the spell-books of Madir, the binding of the ancient, rebellious lords of Hel in their graves, the binding of Peven in his tower."

"Rood told me that. I wonder if Mathom has set Peven free now that I have the crown. Or rather," he added ruefully, "now that Peven's crown is at the bottom of the sea."

"I doubt it. The kings' bindings are not broken lightly. Nor are their vows."

Morgon, tearing a chunk of bread from the loaf, felt a light flush burn his face. He looked at the harpist, said a little shyly, "I believe that. But I could never ask Raederle to marry me if she had no other reason than Mathom's vow to accept me. It's her choice, not Mathom's, and she may not choose to live in Hed. But if there's a chance, then I just want to write and tell her that I will come, eventually, in case—if she wants to wait." He took a bite of bread and cheese, asked rather abruptly, "How long will it take us to get to Erlenstar Mountain?"

"If we reach Isig Mountain before winter, it will take perhaps six weeks. If the snow gets to Isig before us, we may have to stay there until spring."

"Would it be faster to go around Herun to the west and up through the wilderness lands to Erlenstar without going through the Pass?"

"Through the back door of Erlenstar? You would

have to be part wolf to survive the backlands in this season. I've taken that way only a few times in my life, and never this late in the year."

Morgon tilted his head back against the tree. "It occurred to me a couple of days ago," he said "when I started to think again, that if you weren't with me, I would not have the slightest idea what direction to go next. You move through this land as though you've been across it a thousand times."

"I may have. I've lost count." He fed the fire, the eager flames flicking in his quiet eyes. The sun had gone down; the grey wind set the dry leaves chattering above them in some unknown tongue.

Morgon asked suddenly, "How long have you been in the High One's service?"

"When Tirunedeth died, I left Herun, and the High One called me to Erlenstar Mountain."

"Six hundred years. . . . What did you do before that?"

"Harped, travelled. . . ." He fell silent, his eyes on the fire; then he added almost reluctantly, "I studied awhile at Caithnard. But I didn't want to teach, so I left after taking the Black."

Morgon, raising the wineskin to his mouth, lowered it without drinking. "I had no idea you were a Master. What was your name, then?" As the question left his tongue, he felt the blood burn again in his face, and he said quickly, "Forgive me. I forget that some things I want to know are none of my business."

"Morgon—" He stopped. They ate in silence awhile, then Deth reached for his harp, uncased it. He ran a thumb softly across the strings. "Have you tried to play that harp of yours yet?"

Morgon smiled. "No. I'm afraid of it."

"Try."

Morgon took the harp out of the soft leather case Heureu had given him for it. The burning net of gold, the bone-white moons and polished wood held him wordless a moment with their beauty. Deth plucked the high string on his harp; Morgon echoed it softly, his own string perfectly pitched. Deth took him slowly down the gleaming run of strings, and he found note after note precisely tuned. Only twice the sounds jarred slightly, and each time Deth stopped to tune his own harp.

He said, as Morgon's fingers moved to the low note, "I don't have a string to tune that to."

Morgon moved his hand quickly. The sky was black above them; the wind had stilled. The firelight traced the groins and arches of the dark, twisted branches sheltering them. He said wonderingly, "How can it still be in tune after all these years, even after it was washed up from the sea?"

"Yrth bound the pitch into those strings with his voice. There is no harp more beautiful in the High One's realm."

"And neither you nor I can play it." His eyes moved to Deth's harp, its pale, carved pieces burnished in the firelight. It was adorned with neither metal nor jewels, but the oak pieces were finely scrolled on all sides with delicate carving. "Did you make your harp?"

Deth smiled, surprised. "Yes." He traced a line of carving, and something in his face opened unexpectedly. "I made it when I was young, by my standards, after years of playing on various harps. I shaped its pieces out of Ymris oak beside night fires in far, lonely places where I heard no man's voice but my own. I carved on each piece the shapes of leaves, flowers, birds I saw in my wanderings. In An, I searched three months for strings for it. I found them finally, sold my horse for them. They were strung to the broken harp of Ustin of Aum, who died of sorrow over the conquering of Aum. Its strings were tuned to his sorrow, and its wood was split like his heart. I strung my harp with them, matching note for note in the restringing. And then I retuned them to my joy."

Morgon drew a breath. His head bowed suddenly, his face hidden from the harpist. He was silent for a long time, while Deth waited, stirring the fire now and then, the sparks shooting upward like stars. He lifted his head finally.

"Why did Yrth put the stars on this harp?"

"He made it for you."

Morgon's head gave a swift, single shake. "No one could have known of me. No one."

"Perhaps," Deth said quietly. "But when I saw you in Hed, I thought of that harp; and the stars on it and the stars on your face fit together like a riddle and its answer."

"Then who . . ." He stopped again, his voice unsteady. He leaned back, his face blurring in the shadows. "I can't ignore all this and I can't understand it, though I've been trying very hard to do both. I'm a riddle-master. Why am I so terribly ignorant? Why did Yrth never mention the stars in his works? Who is behind me, trailing me in the dark, and where does she come from? If these stars signalled such a reaction from such strange, powerful people, why were the wizards themselves ignorant of both the stars and the people? I spent one entire winter with Master Ohm at Caithnard, looking for a reference to the stars in the history, poetry, legends and songs of the realm. Yrth himself, writing about the making of that harp at Isig, never mentioned the stars. Yet my parents are dead, Astrin lost an eye, and I've been nearly killed three times because of them. There's so little sense to this, sometimes I think I'm trying to understand a dream, except that no dream could be so deadly. Deth, I am afraid even to begin to untangle this."

Deth put a branch on the fire, and a wave of light etched Morgon's face out of the shadows. "Who was Sol of Isig and why did he die?"

Morgon turned his face away. "Sol was the son of Danan Isig. He was pursued through the mines of Isig Mountain one day by traders who wanted to steal from him a priceless jewel. He came to the stone door at the bottom of Isig, beyond which lay dread and sorrow older even than Isig. He could not bring himself to open that door, which no man had ever opened, for fear of what might lie in the darkness beyond it. So his enemies found him in his indecision, and there he died."

"And the stricture?"

"Turn forward into the unknown, rather than backward toward death." He was silent again, his eyes hidden. He righted the harp; his fingers moved over the strings, picked out the melody of a gentle ballad of Hed.

Deth, listening, said, " 'The Love of Hover and Bird' . . . Can you sing it?"

"All eighteen verses. But I can't play it on this—"

"Watch." He positioned his own harp. "When you open your mind and hands and heart to the knowing of a thing, there is no room in you for fear."

He taught Morgon chords and key changes on the great harp; they played late into the night, sending harp-notes like flurries of birds into the darkness.

They spent one more night in Ymris, then crossed the worn hills and turned eastward, skirting the low mountains, beyond which lay the plains and tors of Herun. The autumn rains began again, monotonous, persistent, and they rode silently through the wilderness between the lands, hunched into voluminous, hooded cloaks, their harps trussed in leather, tucked beneath them. They slept in what dry places they could find in shallow caves of rock, beneath thick groves of trees, their fires wavering reluctantly in wind and rain. Deth, when the rains slackened, played songs Morgon had never heard before, from Isig, Herun, Osterland, from the court of the High One. He would try to follow Deth's playing on his own harp, his notes lagging, faltering, then suddenly meeting Deth's, matching them, and the voices of the two harps would meld for a moment, tuned and beautiful, until he lost himself again and stopped, frustrated, bringing a smile to Deth's face. And somehow the sound of their harping reached the ears of the Morgol at the court deep in Herun.

They rode long one day through wet, rocky land. They camped late in the evening, too tired to do more than build a small fire when the rain drizzled to a stop, eat, and stretch out in their damp bedrolls to sleep. Morgon, restless on the rough ground, woke every now and then to grope at a stone beneath him. He dreamed of mile upon mile of lonely land, the rain drumming on it unceasingly, and he heard beneath the drumming the slower beat of hooves. Shifting, he felt the hard nudge of a rock underneath him, and opened his eyes. In the faint, orange wash of embers, he saw a face looming over Deth, a spearhead stopped above his heart.

Morgon, his mouth dry, reached for a stone the size of his fist, raised himself abruptly and threw it. He heard a thump and a gasp, and the face vanished. Deth woke with a start. He sat up, looking at Morgon, but before he could speak a rock, shot with fine accuracy out of the darkness, smacked against the arm Morgon was leaning on, and he dropped.

A voice said irritably, "Do we have to throw rocks at each other like children?"

Deth said, "Lyra."

Morgon raised his head. A girl of fourteen or fifteen stepped to their fire, stirred the embers until they caught, and tossed a handful of twigs on it. Her heavy, loose coat was the color of flame; her dark hair was drawn back from her face, coiled in a thick braid on the crown of her head. Finished, she straightened, holding one arm as though it pained her. In the other hand she held a light spear of ash and silver. Morgon sat up. Her eyes flicked to his face and the spear shifted swiftly to him.

"Are you done?"

Morgon demanded, "Who are you?"

"I am Lyraluthuin, daughter of the Morgol of Herun. You are Morgon, Prince of Hed. We are instructed to bring you to the Morgol."

"In the middle of the night?" Then he said, "We?"

She lifted an arm suddenly, and like a ring of color out of the darkness other young women in long, bright, richly woven coats surrounded their camp, spearpoints forming a jagged, glittering circle. Morgon, rubbing his arm, eyed them darkly. His eyes flicked to Deth in a sudden, urgent question. Deth shook his head.

"No. If this were a trap set by Eriel, you would be dead by now."

"I don't know who Eriel is," Lyra said. Her voice had lost its annoyance; it was light, assured. "And this is not a trap. It's a request."

"You have a strange way of making a request," Morgon commented. "I would like the honor of meeting the Morgol of Herun, but I dare not take the time now. We must reach Isig Mountain before the snow starts."

"I see. Would you like to ride into Crown City as befits a ruler, or would you rather ride slung over your saddle like a sack of grain?"

Morgon stared at her. "What kind of a welcome is that? If the Morgol ever came to Hed, she would never be welcomed with—"

"Rocks? You attacked me first."

"You were standing over Deth with a spear in your hand! Should I have stopped to ask why?"

"You should have known I wouldn't touch the High One's harpist. Please rise and saddle your horse."

Morgon lay back, folding his arms. "I'm not going anywhere," he said firmly, "except back to sleep."

"It's not the middle of the night," Lyra said calmly. "It's nearly dawn." In a swift movement, she thrust her spear across him and picked up his harp by the strap. He caught at it rising; the spearhead swooped away from him with its burden. She tilted the spear, let the harp slide down it to her shoulder. "The Morgol warned me of that harp. You could have broken our spears if you had been thinking. Now that you've gotten up, please saddle your horse."

Morgon drew an outraged breath, then saw somewhere in the clear look she gave him, a suppressed smile that reminded him oddly of Tristan. The anger left his face, but he sat down again on the bare ground and said, "No. I haven't time to go to Herun."

"Then you will be—"

"And if you take me bound into the City of Circles, the traders will have the tale all over the realm by spring, and I will complain first to the Morgol, and then to the High One."

She was silent for a breath; then her chin went up. "I am of the chosen guard of the Morgol, and I have a duty to perform. You will come, one way or another."

"No."

"Lyra," Deth said. There was an overtone of amusement in his voice, and his words seemed almost perfunctory. "We must get to Isig before winter. We have no time for delay."

She bowed her head respectfully. "I do not seek to delay you. I didn't even want to wake you. But the Morgol requires the Prince of Hed."

"The Prince of Hed requires the High One."

"I have a duty—"

"Your duty does not preclude the respectful treatment of land-rulers."

"Respectful or not," Morgon said, "I'm not going. Why are you discussing the matter with her? Tell her. She'll listen to you. She's a child, and we can't be bothered with children's games."

Lyra surveyed him composedly. "No one who knows me calls me that. I said you would come one way or another. The Morgol has questions she would like to ask you about the stars on your face and that harp. She has seen it before. I would have told you sooner, but I lost my temper when you threw that rock."

Morgon looked up at her. "Where?" he said. "Where did she see it?"

"She'll tell you. There is also a riddle I am to give you when we have crossed the mountains and the marshes, and Crown City is in our sight. She says it holds your name."

In the wash of the single flame, the blood ran suddenly out of Morgon's face. He rose. "I'll come."

Riding from dawn to sunset, they followed Lyra through a little-travelled pass in the low, ancient mountains, and camped on the other side of them the next night. Morgon, wrapped in his cloak by the fire, sat watching the chill, misty breath of the marshes ease toward them up the mountain. Deth, his hands seemingly inured to the cold, played a lovely, wordless song that danced into Morgon's thoughts, drawing him out of them until he yielded and listened.

He said when it ended, "What was that? It was beautiful."

Deth smiled. "I never gave it a name." He sat a moment in silence, then reached for the harp case. Lyra, appearing without a sound in their circle of firelight, begged, "Don't stop. Everyone is listening. That was the song you composed for the Morgol."

Morgon looked at the harpist, amazed. Deth said, "Yes," his fingers moving lightly down the strings, sliding into a new weave. Lyra took Morgon's harp from her shoulder and set it down beside him.

"I meant to give you this earlier." She sat down, held out her hands to the fire. The light gave her young face rich, rounded shadings; Morgon's eyes were drawn to it. He said abruptly, "Do you always wait outside the borders of Herun to abduct land-rulers passing by?"

"I didn't abduct you," she said imperturbably. "You chose to come. And—" she went on as he drew breath to expostulate, "I usually lead traders through the marshes. Visitors from other lands are rare, and when they come, sometimes they don't know enough to wait for me, and they fall in the marshes or get lost. Also, I protect the Morgol when she travels beyond Herun, and carry out whatever other duties she gives me. I'm skilled with a knife, a bow, and a spear; and the last man who underestimated my skill is dead."

"You killed him?"

"He forced me to. He was going to rob traders under my protection, and when I warned him to stop he ignored me, which was not wise. He was going to kill one of the traders, so I killed him."

"Why does the Morgol let you travel unattended, if such things happen to you?"

"I am in her guard, and I am expected to take care of myself. And you: why are you travelling unarmed as a child through the High One's realm?"

"I have the harp," he reminded her stiffly, but she shook her head.

"It's no use to you in its case. There are other enemies besides me in the out-lands: wild men who prey on traders beyond the boundaries of king's laws, exiles —you should arm yourself."

"I'm a farmer, not a warrior."

"There's not a man in the High One's realm who would dare touch Deth. But you—"

"I can take care of myself. Thank you."

Her brows flicked up. She said kindly, "I'm only trying to give you the benefit of my experience. No doubt Deth can take care of you if there's trouble."

Deth's voice trailed into his harping. "The Prince of Hed is remarkably adept at surviving. . . . Hed is a land renowned for its peace, a concept often difficult to understand."

"The Prince of Hed," Lyra said, "is no longer in Hed."

Morgon looked at her distantly across the fire. "An animal doesn't change its skin or its instincts because it travels out of one land into another."

She disregarded his argument and said helpfully, "I could teach you to throw a spear. It's simple. It might be useful to you. You had good aim with that rock."

"That's a good enough weapon for me. I might kill someone with a spear."

"That's what it's for."

He sighed. "Think of it from a farmer's point of

view. You don't uproot cornstalks, do you, before the corn is ripe? Or cut down a tree full of young green pears? So why should you cut short a man's life in the mist of his actions, his mind's work—"

"Traders," Lyra said, "don't get killed by pear trees."

"That's not the point. If you take a man's life, he has nothing. You can strip him of his land, his rank, his thoughts, his name, but if you take his life, he has nothing. Not even hope."

She listened quietly, the light moving in her dark eyes. "And if there is a choice between your life and his, which one would you choose?"

"My life, of course." Then he thought about it and winced a little. "I think."

She loosed a breath. "It's unreasonable."

He smiled in spite of himself. "I suppose so. But if I ever killed anyone, how would I tell Eliard? Or Grim Oakland?"

"Who is Eliard? Who is Grim Oakland?"

"Grim is my overseer. Eliard is my brother, my land-heir."

"Oh, you have a brother? I always wanted one. But I have no one except cousins, and the guard, which is like a family of sisters. Do you have a sister?"

"Yes. Tristan."

"What is she like?"

"Oh, a little younger than you. Dark, like you. A little like you except that she doesn't annoy me as much."

To his surprise, she laughed. "I did, didn't I? I wondered when you would stop being angry with me." She got to her feet in a single, lithe movement. "I think the Morgol may not be very pleased with me either, but I'm not generally polite to people who surprise me, as you did."

"How will the Morgol know?"

"She knows." She bent her dark head to them. "Thank you for your playing, Deth. Good night. We will ride at dawn."

She stepped out of the firelight, faded into the night

so quietly they could not hear a single footstep. Morgon reached for his bedroll. The mist from the marshes had come upon them and the night was damp and chill as a knife's edge. He put another branch on the fire and lay close to it. A thought struck him as he watched the flames, and he gave a short, mirthless laugh.

"If I were skilled in arms, I might have thrown a spear at her this morning instead of a rock. And she wants to teach me."

The next morning, he saw Herun, a small land ringed with mountains, fill like a bowl with dawn. Morning mists fell as they reached the flat lands, and great peaks of rock rose through them like curious faces. Low plains of grass, wind-twisted trees, and ground that sucked at their horse's hooves appeared and disappeared in the whorls of mist. Now and then Lyra stopped until the shifting mists revealed some landmark that showed her the path.

Morgon, accustomed to land that was predictable underfoot, rode unconcerned until Lyra, stopping a moment for him to catch up to her, said, "These are the great Herun marshes. Crown City lies on the other side of them. The path through them is a gift from the Morgol, which few people know. So if you must enter or leave Herun quickly, go north across the mountains rather than this way. Many people in a hurry have vanished here without a trace."

Morgon looked with sudden interest at the ground his horse walked on. "I'm glad you told me."

The mists rolled away eventually, baring a blue sky without a cloud, vibrant against the wet green plains. Stone houses, small villages rose on the crests of the undulating plain, huddled at the feet of stone peaks that rose without preface from the ground. In the distance, a road stroked the plain white here and there in its twistings. A smudge detached itself from the horizon smoky with mountains, and began to take shape. A pattern of stonework gleamed against the earth: a vast circle of red, upright stones like flaming sentinels around a black oval house. As they neared, a river spilling from the northern mountains rose to their view, split blue through the plain and ran into the heart of the stonework.

"Crown City," Lyra said. "It is also known as the City of Circles." She stopped her horse; and the guard behind her stopped.

Morgon said, his eyes on the distant stones, "I've heard of that city. What are the seven circles of Herun and who built them? Rhu, the fourth Morgol, structured the city, planning a circle for each of eight riddles his curiosity set to him and he answered. His journey to answer the eighth riddle killed him. What that riddle was no one knows."

"The Morgol knows," Lyra said. Her voice drew Morgon's eyes from the city. He felt something jump deep within him. She went on, holding his eyes. "The riddle that killed Rhu is the one I am to give you now from the Morgol: Who is the Star-Bearer, and what will he loose that is bound?"

Morgon's breath stopped. He shook his head once, his mouth shaping a word without sound. Then he shouted it at her, startling her: "No!"

He wrenched his horse around, kicked it, and it leaped forward. The grassy plain blurred beneath him. He bent low in the saddle, heading toward the marshlands innocently smooth under the sun, and the low mountains beyond. He did not hear the hooves behind him until a flick of color drew his eyes sideways. His face set, rigid, he urged his horse forward, the earth pounding beneath him, but the black horse stayed with him like a shadow, neither slowing nor speeding while he raced toward the line where the earth locked with the sky. He felt his horse falter suddenly, its speed slacken, and then Deth reached across for his reins, brought him jolting to a stop.

He said, his breathing quick, "Morgon—"

Morgon jerked his reins free from Deth's hold and backed his horse a step. He said, his voice shaking,

"I'm going home. I don't have to go any farther with this. I have a choice."

Deth's hand went out toward him quickly, as though to soothe a frightened animal. "Yes. You have a choice. But you will never reach Hed riding blind through the Herun marshes. If you want to go back to Hed, I'll take you. But Morgon, think a little first. You are trained to think. I can lead you through the marshes, but then what will you do? Will you go back through Ymris? Or by the sea from Osterland?"

"I'll skirt Ymris and go to Lungold—I'll take the traderoad to Caithnard—I'll disguise myself as a trader—"

"And if you reach Hed by some thread of chance, then what? You will be bound nameless on that island for the rest of your life."

"You don't understand!" His eyes were startled, like an animal's at bay. "My life has been shaped before me—shaped for me by something—someone who has seen my actions before I even see a reason for them. How could Yrth have seen me hundreds of years ago to make this harp for me? Who saw me two thousand years ago to set the riddle to my life that killed the Morgol Rhu? I am being forced into some pattern of action I can't see, I can't control—given a name I do not want—I have the right of choice! I was born to rule Hed, and that is where I belong—that is my name and my place."

"Morgon, you may see yourself as the Prince of Hed, but there are others seeking answers to those same questions you ask, and they will give you this name: Star-Bearer, and there will be no peace for them until you are dead. They will never let you live peacefully in Hed. They will follow you there. Will you open the doors of Hed to Eriel? To those that killed Athol, and tried to kill you? What mercy will they have for your farmers, for your toothless pigherder? If you go back to Hed now, death will ride behind you, beside you, and you will find it waiting for you beyond the open doors of your house."

"Then I won't go to Hed." His face struggled against itself; he turned it away from Deth. "I'll go to Caithnard, to take the Black, and teach—"

"Teach what? The riddles that are no truth to you, nothing more than ancient tales spun at twilight—"

"That's not true!"

"What of Astrin? Heureu? They are bound also in the riddle of your life; they need your clear vision, your courage—"

"I have none! Not for this! Death at least I have seen; I can look at it and give it a name, but this—this path that is building before me—I can't even see! I don't know who I am, what I was born to do. In Hed, at least I have a name!"

Deth's voice quieted. He had crossed the distance Morgon held between them; his hand gripped Morgon's forearm gently. "There is a name for you beyond Hed. Morgon, what use are the riddles and strictures of Caithnard, if not for this? You are Sol of Isig, caught up by fear between death and a door that has been closed for thousands of years. If you have no faith in yourself, then have faith in the things you call truth. You know what must be done. You may not have courage or trust or understanding or the will to do it, but you know what must be done. You can't turn back. There is no answer behind you. You fear what you cannot name. So look at it and find a name for it. Turn your face forward and learn. Do what must be done."

The winds breathed down the long plain, broke against them, turning the grass silver. Behind them, like a cluster of bright flowers, the guard of the Morgol waited.

Morgon's fingers crushed his reins and looked at them. He lifted his head slowly, "It's not your business, as the High One's harpist, to give me such advice. Or do you speak to me as one who can wear by right the Black of Mastery? No riddle-master at Caithnard ever gave me that name, Star-Bearer; they never knew it existed. Yet you accept it as though you expected it. What hope that no one else but you has ever seen, what riddle, are you seeing in me?" The harpist, his eyes falling suddenly from Morgon's, did not answer. Morgon's voice rose, "I ask you this: Who was Ingris of Osterland and why did he die?"

Deth shifted his hand on Morgon's arm. There was an odd expression on his face. He said after a moment, "Ingris of Osterland angered Har, the King of Osterland one night when he appeared as an old man at Ingris's door, and Ingris refused to take him in. So the wolf-King put this curse on him: that if the next stranger who came to Ingris's house did not give his name, then Ingris would die. And the first stranger who came after Har left was—a certain harpist. That harpist gave Ingris everything he asked for: songs, tales, the loan of his harp, the history of his travellings—everything but the name Ingris wanted to hear, though Ingris demanded it in despair. But the harpist could give him only one word, each time Ingris asked for his name, and that word, as Ingris heard it, was Death. So in fear of Har, and in despair of the curse, he felt his heart stop and he died." He paused.

Morgon, his face growing quiet as he listened, said haltingly, "I never thought . . . You could have given Ingris your name. Your true name. The stricture is: Give what others require of you for their lives."

"Morgon, there were things I could not give Ingris, and things I cannot give you now. But I swear this: if you finish this harsh journey to Erlenstar Mountain, I will give you anything you ask of me. I will give you my life."

"Why?" he whispered.

"Because you bear three stars."

Morgon was silent. Then he shook his head a little. "I will never have the right to ask that."

"The choice will be mine. Have you thought that the

stricture also applies to you? You must give what others require of you."

"And if I can't?"

"Then, like Ingris, you will die."

Morgon's eyes dropped. He sat motionless but for the winds that thrummed like harp notes about him, plucked at his hair, his cloak. He turned his horse finally, rode slowly back to the guard, who, accepting his return in silence, proceeded to the City of Circles.

6

THE MORGOL OF HERUN WELCOMED THEM INTO her courtyard. She was a tall woman with blue-black hair drawn back from her face, falling without a ripple against her loose robe of leaf-green cloth. Her house was a vast oval of black stone. Water from the river flowing beneath it fanned over stone fountains in her yard, formed tiny streams and pools where fish slipped like red and green and gold flames beneath the tracery of shadows from the trees. The Morgol went to Deth's side as he dismounted, smiling at him. They were of a height, and her eyes were luminous gold.

"I didn't mean for Lyra to disturb you," she said. "I hope you are not inconvenienced."

An answering smile tugged at his mouth. There was a tone in his voice Morgon had never heard before. "El, you knew I would go where the Prince of Hed chose to go."

"Now, how could I have known that? Your path has always been your own. But I'm glad you chose to come. I dream of your harping."

She walked with him to Morgon, as silent women took their horses out of the yard, and others carried their gear into the house. Her strange eyes melted over him. She held out her hand to him. "I am Elrhiarhodan,

103

the Morgol of Herun. You may call me El. I am very glad you've come."

He bent his head to her, aware suddenly of his travel-stained clothes and unkempt hair. "You gave me no choice."

"No," she said gently, "I did not. You look very tired. For some reason I expected you to be older, or I would have waited to tell you that riddle myself, instead of frightening you with it like that." She turned her head to greet Lyra. "Thank you for bringing the Prince of Hed to me. But was it necessary to throw a rock at him?"

A smile touched Lyra's eyes at Morgon's amazement. She said gravely, "Mother, the Prince of Hed threw a rock at me first, and I lost my temper. Also, I said things which were—not entirely diplomatic. But I don't think he's angry with me any more. He doesn't seem to be any kind of a warrior."

"No, but he had good aim, and if he had been armed, you would be dead, which I would not like at all. The people of Hed do not, as a habit, take arms against others, a laudable restraint. It was perhaps not wise to enter their camp in the dark; you must learn to avoid misunderstandings. But you brought them here safely, and for that I thank you. Now get some food, my child, and some sleep." Lyra left them, and the Morgol tucked her fingers into the crook of Deth's arm. "She has grown since you saw her last. But then you have not come to Herun in some time. Come in."

She led them into her house, through its doors of silver and pale wood. Within, the arched corridors wandered, seemingly without plan, from one room to another; the rooms, with delicate cloth tapestries, strange plants, rich woods and finely wrought metals, followed one another like treasure boxes. The Morgol stopped finally in a room warm with hangings of orange and gold, and bade them rest on soft, enormous cushions covered with white wool. She left them.

Morgon, drowning muscle by weary muscle in sheepskin, closed his eyes and whispered, "I can't remember the last time I touched a bed. . . . Does she go into our minds?"

"The Morgol has the gift of sight. Herun is a small, very rich land; the morgols have developed their sight since the Years of Settlement, when an army from north Ymris attacked Herun with an eye to its mines. Herun is ringed with mountains; the Morgols learned to see through them. I thought you knew that."

"I didn't realize their sight was that good. She startled me." Then he fell asleep, not even waking when, moments later, servants entered with trays of food and wine and all their gear.

He woke hours later to find Deth gone. He washed and dressed himself in the light, loose robe of orange and gold cloth the Morgol had left for him. She had given him also a knife of milky metal sheathed in bone, which he let lie. A servant led him to a broad room white from floor to ceiling. The guards in their bright robes chattered at one end of it on cushions around a firebed, with trays of steaming dishes on low tables before them. Deth, Lyra and the Morgol sat at a table of polished white stone, the silver cups and plate in front of them sparkling with amethyst. The Morgol, in a robe of silver and white, her hair braided and bound, beckoned to Morgon, smiling. Lyra shifted to give him a place beside her. She served him from dishes of hot spiced meats, seasoned fruits and vegetables, cheeses and wines. Deth, to one side of the Morgol, sat harping softly. He drew a song to a close, then, very lightly, played a phrase from the song he had composed for her.

Her face turned toward him as though he had spoken her name; she smiled and said, "I have made you harp long enough. Sit beside me and eat."

Deth put his harp down and joined her. He was dressed in a coat silver-white as his hair; a chain of silver and tiny, fire-white stones hung on his breast.

Morgon, watching their close faces as the Morgol

served him, was drawn out of his preoccupation by Lyra, who said, "Your food is getting cold. He didn't tell you then?"

"What? No." He took a bite of seasoned mushrooms. "At least not in words. I guessed from that song. I don't know why I'm surprised. No wonder he allowed you to take us into Herun."

She nodded. "He wanted to come, but of course the choice was yours."

"Was it? How did the Morgol know the one thing that would have brought me into Herun?"

Lyra smiled. "You are a riddle-master. She said you would answer to a riddle like a hound to scent."

"How did she know that?"

"When Mathom of An was searching for the man who had taken Peven's crown, his messengers came even to Herun with the tale. So, being curious, she made it her business to find out who had it."

"But so few people knew—Deth, Rood of An, the Masters—"

"And the traders who took you from Hed to Caithnard. The Morgol has a talent for finding things out."

"Yes." He moved his cup an inch on the table, frowned down at it a moment. Then he turned to the Morgol, waiting while she spoke with Deth until she paused, and he said, "El." Her coin-colored eyes came to his face. He drew a breath. "How did you know that riddle you gave me? It is listed nowhere in the books of the Masters, and it should have been."

"Should it, Morgon? It seems to be such a dangerous riddle, that only one man should try to answer it. What would the Masters have done with it?"

"They would have searched for the answer. That's their business. Riddles are often dangerous, but an unanswered riddle may be deadly."

"True, as Dhairrhuwyth found—which seems the more reason for keeping it private."

"No," he said, "ignorance is deadly. Please. Where

did you find it? I have—I have had to come to Herun to find my name. Why?"

Her eyes dropped, hidden from him a moment. She said slowly, "I found the riddle years ago in an ancient book the Morgol Rhu left as the record of his travellings. The book had been word-locked by the wizard Iff of the Unpronounceable Name, who was in the service to Herun at the time. I had a little difficulty opening the book. Iff had bound it with his name."

"And you pronounced it?"

"Yes. A wise old scholar at my court suggested that perhaps Iff's name should be sung as well as pronounced, and he spent many long hours with me trying to find the notes that belonged with the syllables of Iff's name. Finally, by sheer accident, I sang the name on the right tones, pronouncing it correctly, and unlocked the book. The last entry the Morgol had made in it was the riddle that he left Herun to answer: the riddle of the Star-Bearer. He wrote that he was going to Erlenstar Mountain. Danan found his body and sent it home from Isig. The scholar who helped me is dead, and I—with little more reason than instinct—kept the riddle to myself."

"Why?"

"Oh . . . because it is dangerous; because I had heard from the traders of a child growing up with three stars on his face in Hed; and because I asked a Master at Caithnard what he knew of three stars and he said he had never heard anything about them, and that Master's name was Ohm."

"Master Ohm?" he said startled. "He taught me. Why did his name stop you?"

"It was a small thing, but it set my mind on a train of thought . . . I took his name to be a shortening of a Herun name. Ghisteslwchlohm."

Morgon stared at her. His face lost color. "Ghisteslwchlohm. Who was the Founder of Lungold, and what are the nine strictures of his teachings? But he died.

Seven hundred years ago when the wizards disappeared from Lungold."

"Perhaps," she said. "But I wonder . . ." She stirred herself out of her thoughts, touched his wrist. "I'm disturbing your supper with my idle conjectures. But you know, a strange thing happened that I have always wondered about. I have good vision; I can see through anything I choose, though I don't generally choose to see through the people I'm talking to: it tends to be distracting. But while I was with Ohm in the Masters' Library, at one point he had turned to look for a book on his shelves, and as he put his hand on it, I looked through him automatically to see the title. But I couldn't see through him. I could see through the walls of the college, through the cliff and into the sea—but my vision could not pass through Ohm."

Morgon swallowed a tasteless mouthful. "Are you saying—?" His voice caught. "What are you saying?"

"Well, it took me months to put pieces together, since, like you, I would rather have complete faith in the integrity of the Masters of Caithnard. But now, especially since you have come and I can put that riddle to a name and a face, I tend to think that perhaps the Master Ohm is Ghisteslwchlohm, the Founder of the School of Wizards at Lungold, and that he destroyed Lungold."

Morgon made an inarticulate sound in the back of his throat. Lyra protested weakly, "Mother, it's very hard to eat when you say things like that. Why would he have destroyed Lungold after going through all the trouble to found it?"

"Why did he found the College a thousand years ago?"

Lyra shrugged a little. "To teach the wizards. He was the most powerful wizard in the High One's realm, and the other wizards were half-wild, undisciplined; they were unable to use their powers to the full extent. So why would Ohm have tried to teach them to be more powerful if all he wanted to do was destroy their power?

"Did he gather them there to teach them?" the Morgol said, "or to control them?"

Morgon found his voice again. He said softly, his hands gripping the rough edge of the stone table, "What evidence? On what evidence do you base your conclusions?"

The Morgol drew a breath. The food was growing cold in front of them all. Deth sat quietly listening, his head bent; Morgon could not see his face. Laughter drifted toward them occasionally from the lower tables; the fire in the bed probed to the heart of a log with soft, silken rustlings. "On evidence of an ignorance I do not like," she said. She held his eyes. "Why could the Masters tell you nothing of the stars on your face?"

"Because in their studies no mention was made of them."

"Why?"

"Because—the tales of the kingdoms, their songs and poetry have never mentioned them. The wizards' books that the Masters took from Lungold, which form the basis of their knowledge, say nothing of them."

"Why?"

He was silent, groping for a plausible answer. Then his face changed. He whispered, "Iff, at least, knew what riddle Rhu was trying to answer. He must have known. He talks about Rhu and his searchings in the books the Masters have opened at Caithnard; he listed every riddle Rhu went to answer except that one—"

"Why?"

"I don't . . . I don't know why. Are you saying that Ohm—Ghisteslwchlohm—brought them together to control their knowledge, to teach them only what he wanted them to know? That matters concerning the stars are things he kept them ignorant of—or perhaps even took from their minds?"

"I think it is possible. I think from what I have

109

learned about you from Deth today, that it's quite probable."

"But why? For what possible purpose would he have done that?"

"I don't know. Yet." She continued softly, "Suppose you were a wizard restless with power, drawn to Lungold by the powers of Ohm and his promises of great skill and knowledge. You placed your name in his mind; with your trust in his skill, your absolute faith in his teachings, you did without question whatever he asked of you, and in return he channelled your own energies into powers you scarcely dreamed you had. And then suppose, one day, somehow, you realized that this wizard, whose mind could control yours so skillfully, was false to his teachings, false to you, false to every man, king, scholar, farmer, that he had ever served. What would you do if you found that he had dangerous plans and terrible purposes that you could not even guess at, and that the very foundations of his teachings were a lie? What would you do?"

Morgon was silent. He looked down, watched his hands close on the table into fists, as though they belonged to someone else. He whispered, "Ohm." Then his head gave a quick shake and he said, "I would run. I would run until no one, man or wizard, could find me. And then I would begin to think."

"I would kill him," Lyra said simply. Morgon's hands opened.

"Would you? With what? He would vanish like a mist before your spear touched him. You can't solve riddles by killing people."

"Then if this Master Ohm is Ghisteslwchlohm, what are you going to do about him? You'll have to do something."

"Why me? The High One can deal with him—and the fact that he hasn't is a good proof that Master Ohm is not the Founder of Lungold."

Deth raised his head. "I recall you used that same argument at Caerweddin."

Morgon sighed. He said reluctantly. "It fits, I suppose, but I can't believe it. I can't believe that either Ohm or Ghisteslwchlohm are evil, although that might explain the strange, sudden disappearance of the wizards and the tales of the violence of their leaving. But Ohm—I lived with him for three years. He never . . . he treated me with great kindness. It makes no sense."

The Morgol looked at him thoughtfully. "It doesn't, no. All this reminds me of a riddle from An, I believe. Re of Aum."

"Who was Re of Aum?" Lyra asked, and the Morgol, at Morgon's silence, answered imperturbably, "Re of Aum offended the Lord of Hel once and became so frightened that he had a great wall built around his house in fear of revenge. He hired a stranger to build it, who promised him a wall no man could destroy or climb, either by force or wizardry. The wall was built; the stranger took his pay; and Re at last felt secure. One day, when he decided that the Lord of Hel had realized the futility of revenge, he decided to venture out of his lands. And then he travelled around his wall three times but found no gate to let him out. And slowly he realized that the Lord of Hel himself had built that wall." She paused. "I've forgotten the stricture."

"Never let a stranger build walls around you," Lyra guessed. "Then Ghisteslwchlohm built his wall of ignorance in Caithnard as well as Lungold, which is why Morgon does not know who he is. It's very complicated. I prefer problems I can throw spears at."

"What about Eriel?" Morgon said abruptly. "Has Deth told you about her?"

"Yes," the Morgol said. "But that, I think, is a completely different problem. If Ohm wanted you dead, he could easily have killed you while you were a student. He didn't react to the stars on your face the way those —those nameless people do."

"That woman," Morgon said, "has a name."

"Do you know it?"

"No. I have never heard of anyone like her. And I'm more frightened of her hidden name than I am of a man whose name I know."

"Perhaps Ohm hid her name, too," Lyra said. She shifted uneasily. "Morgon, I think you should let me teach you to defend yourself. Deth, tell him."

"It's not my business to argue with the Prince of Hed," Deth said mildly.

"You argued with him this afternoon."

"I didn't argue. I simply pointed out the illogic of his arguments."

"Oh. Well, why doesn't the High One do something. It's his business. There is a strange people on his coasts, trying to kill the Prince of Hed—we could fight them. Ymris has an army; the people of An bear arms; from Kraal to Anuin, the High One could gather an army. I don't understand why he doesn't."

"Osterland could arm itself," Morgon said; "Ymris, Anuin, even Caithnard, but those people could wash over Hed like a seawave, and it would be barren in a day. There must be a better way to fight them."

"Arm Hed."

Morgon's cup came down with a little clink on the table. "Hed?"

"Why not? I think you should at least warn them."

"How? The fishermen of Tol go out every morning, and the only thing they have ever found in the sea is fish. I'm not even sure the farmers of Hed believe anything exists beyond Hed, and the High One. Of all the six kingdoms, Hed is the only one the wizards never sought service in—there wasn't anything for them to do. The wizard Talies visited it once and said it was uninhabitable: it was without history, without poetry, and utterly without interest. The peace of Hed is passed like the land-rule, from ruler to ruler; it is bound into the earth of Hed, and it is the High One's business, not mine, to break that peace."

"But—" Lyra said stubbornly.

"If I ever carried a weapon into Hed and told the

people of Hed to arm themselves, they would look at me as though I were a stranger—and that is what I would be: a stranger in my own land, the weapon like a disease that would wither all the living roots of Hed. And if I did it without the High One's sanction, he could take the land-rule from me."

Lyra's dark brows crooked above her eyes. "I don't understand," she said again. "Ymris is always fighting within itself; An and Aum and Hel have had terrible wars in the past. The old lords of Herun have battled each other; why is Hed so different? Why should the High One care if it's armed or not?"

"It just evolved that way. It made its own laws in the Years of Settlement, and the laws grew to bind the Princes of Hed. It had nothing anyone would have fought for: no wealth, no great stretches of land, no seat of power or mystery, just good farm land and good weather, in a land so small not even the Kings of An in their years of conquering, were tempted by it. Men found the rulers they wanted to keep the peace, and their instinct for peace drove deep into the land like a seed. It's in my blood. To change that in me, I would have to change my name . . ."

Lyra was silent, her dark eyes on Morgon's face as he drank. He felt, as he put his cup down again, the light touch of her hand on his shoulder. "Well, then, since you won't protect yourself, I'll come with you and guard you," she said. "There's no one in the Morgol's guard who could do that better than I could —no one in all Herun." She looked across him to El. "May I have your permission?"

"No," Morgon said.

"Do you doubt my skill?" She picked up her knife, poised the blade between finger and thumb. "Do you see that rope at the far end of the room holding the torch?"

"Lyra, please do not set the room on fire," the Morgol murmured.

"Mother, I'm trying to show him—"

"I believe you," Morgon said. He turned to take the hand holding the knife in his hands. Her fingers were lean and warm, stirring a little, like a bird in his hold, and something he had half-forgotten in the long, rough weeks touched him unexpectedly. He kept his voice steady, gentle with an effort. "Thank you. But if you were hurt or killed trying to defend me, I would never forgive myself as long as I lived. My only hope is travelling as quickly and quietly as possible; doing that, I will be safe."

He saw the doubt in her eyes, but she said only, putting the knife down, "Well, in this house I will guard you. And even you can't argue with that."

Deth played for the Morgol after they finished supper—sweet, wordless songs from the ancient court of An, ballads from Ymris and Osterland. The room was hushed when he finished, empty but for the four of them; the candles were burned low in their holders. The Morgol rose reluctantly.

"It's late," she said. "I'll replenish your supplies so that you won't have to stop in Osterland, if you'll tell me what you need in the morning."

"Thank you," Deth said, slipping the harp strap over his shoulder. He looked at her a moment in silence, and she smiled. He added softly, "I want to stay. I will come back."

"I know."

She led them back through the wandering maze of corridors to their room. Water and wine, soft blankets had been left for them; the fire burned steadily, sending out a clean, elusive scent.

Morgon said before El turned to go, "May I leave some letters with you for the traders? My brother has no idea where I am."

"Of course. I'll have paper and ink brought to you. And may I ask something of you? May I see your harp?"

He took it out of the case for her. She turned it in her hands, touching the stars and the fine tracery of gold, the white moons. "Yes," she said softly. "I thought I recognized it. Deth told me some time ago about Yrth's harp, and when a trader brought this harp into my house last year, I was sure Yrth must have made it—it was a spell-bound harp, with its mute strings. I wanted so badly to buy it, but it was not for sale. The trader said it was promised to a man in Caithnard."

"What man?"

"He didn't say. Why? Morgon, what did I say to trouble you?"

He drew a breath. "Well, you see, my father—I think my father bought it in Caithnard for me last spring, before he died. So if you could remember what the trader looked like, or find out his name—"

"I see." Her hand closed gently on his arm. "I see. Yes, I will get his name for you. Good night."

Lyra, in a short, dark tunic, took her place at the doorway as the Morgol left, her straight back to them, her spear motionless, upright in her hand. A servant brought paper, pens, ink and wax; Morgon sat down in front of the fire. He stared into it, the ink drying on his pen, for a long time; he murmured once, "What am I going to say to her?" And slowly he began to write.

Finished finally with Raederle's letter, he wrote a brief note to Eliard, sealed it, and lay back against the cushions, watching the flames meld and separate, half-aware of Deth's quiet movements as he sorted and checked their gear. He lifted his head finally, looked at the harpist.

"Deth . . . did you know Ghisteslwchlohm?"

Deth's hands stilled. They moved again after a moment, loosening a knot in a bedroll. He said without looking up, "I spoke to him only twice, very briefly. He was a distant, awesome figure in Lungold, then, in the years before the wizards' disappearance."

"Did it ever occur to you that Master Ohm might be the Founder of Lungold?"

"There was no evidence of it that would have made such a thought occur to me."

Morgon reached out to add wood to the fire; shadows falling in webs and tapestries from the ceiling, shifted and settled. He murmured, "I wonder why the Morgol couldn't see through Ohm. I don't know what land he's from; it may be that he was born, like Rood, with some witchery in his blood. . . . I never thought to ask where he was born. He was simply Master Ohm, and it seemed he had been at Caithnard forever. If El told him she thought he was Ghisteslwchlohm, he would probably laugh . . . except I've never seen him laugh. It happened so long ago, the destruction of Lungold; the wizards have been silent as death since then. None of them could possibly be alive." His voice trailed away. He turned on his side, his eyes closing. A little while later he heard Deth begin to harp gently, dreamily, and he drifted asleep to the sound.

He woke to the song of a different harpist. The harping wove through him like a net, the slow, deep beat measured to the sluggish, jarring beat of his blood, the swift, wild high notes ripping at the fabric of his thoughts like tiny, panicked birds. He tried to move but something weighed on his hands, his chest. He opened his mouth to call for Deth; the sound that came out of him was again the squawk of the black crow.

He opened his eyes and found he had dreamed them open. He opened them again and saw nothing but the dark behind his eyelids. A terror rose in his throat, sending the birds in his mind into a frenzy. He reached out of himself as though he were swimming through deep, heavy swells of darkness and sleep, straining himself toward awareness. And finally he heard the harpist's voice and saw between his lashes the faint, fiery eyes of embers.

The voice was husky, rich, and word by word it bound him with a nightmare.

> *Withering your voice, as the*
> *roots of your land are withering.*
> *Slow your hearts'-blood*
> *slow as the dragging waters,*
> *the rivers of Hed.*
> *Tangling are your thoughts*
> *as the yellow vines are tangling,*
> *drying, snapping underfoot.*
> *Withering the life of you*
> *as the late corn is withering . . .*

Morgon opened his eyes. The darkness and the red, panting embers whirled around him until the darkness rose about his face like a tide, and the fire seemed tiny, far away. In the well of night he saw Hed drifting like a broken ship in the sea; he heard the vine leaves whispering drily, felt in his veins the rivers slowing, thickening, draining dry, their beds cracking to the harpist's weave. He made a harsh, incredulous noise, and saw the harpist finally, beyond the fire, his harp made of strange bones and polished shell, his face lost in shadows. The face seemed to lift a little at Morgon's voice; he caught a flick of fire-scorched gold.

> *Dry, dust dry, the earth*
> *the earth of you, land-ruler*
> *lord of the dying. Parching the fields*
> *of your body, moaning the wind*
> *of your last word*
> *across the waste of them,*
> *the wasteland of Hed.*

A tide seemed to be draining back from the dark, broken land, drawing the last of the river waters with it, drawing the stream-waters out of Hed, leaving the coasts bare, leaving a wasteland of shell and sand around Hed as it drained back to the black edges of the world. Morgon, feeling the dry, cold earth, the life of Hed draining away with the sea, fading away from him, drew a breath. He shouted with his last strength a protest that was no word but a bird cry against the impossibility of the harp song. The squawk brought him back to himself, as though his body, fraying into darkness, had pulled itself together again. He got to his feet, shaking, so weak he tripped over the hem of his long robe and fell near the fire. He picked up, before he rose again, handfuls of hot ash, chips of dead wood and flung them at the harpist. The harpist, his face jerking away from them, rose. His eyes in the dim light were pale, flecked with gold. He laughed, and the heel of his hand slammed upward against Morgon's chin. Morgon's head snapped back; he fell to his knees, dizzy, choking, at the harpist's feet. His fingers slid through harp strings sending a faint cacophony of sound into the darkness. The harpist's own harp, whistling down, brushed past Morgon's head as he moved and broke into pieces against his collarbone.

He cried out at the sharp, sickening snap of bone. Through the sweat and haze in his eyes, he saw Lyra standing motionless in the doorway, her back to him as if he were silent as a dream behind her. The hurt, unreasoning anger in him cleared his head a little. Still kneeling, he threw himself against the harpist, lunging with his good shoulder, knocking him off-balance against the heavy cushions. Then, his fingers tangled in the harp strap, he flung the harp in his hand out, arching toward the harpist. It crashed with a spattering of notes, and Morgon heard a faint, involuntary gasp.

He flung himself onto the shadowed figure. The harpist struggled beneath him; in the faint light from the hall Morgon saw blood streaking down his face. A knife seemingly made from air blurred towards Morgon; he caught desperately at the harpist's wrist; the harpist's other hand closed with a hawk's grip on Morgon's broken shoulder.

He groaned, the blood drained out of his face, the harpist darkening in his sight. And then he felt the shifting shape of the man he held, the fraying of form beneath him. His teeth clenched, he held onto the figure with his good hand as though he were holding onto his name.

He lost count of the brief, desperately struggling shapes he gripped. He smelled wood, the musk of animal fur, felt feathers beat against his hand, a marsh-slime ooze ponderously through his hold. He held the great, shaggy hoof of a horse whose effort to rear pulled him to his knees; a salmon slick and panicked, who nearly flipped out of his hold; a mountain cat who whirled in fury to slash at him. He held animals so old they had no names; he recognized them with wonder from their descriptions in ancient books. He held a great stone from one of the Earth-Masters' cities that almost crushed his hand; he held a butterfly so beautiful he nearly let it free rather than harm its wings. He held a harp string whose sound pierced his ears until he became the sound itself. And the sound he held turned into a sword.

He held the blade of it, silver-white, half as long as himself; strange whorls of design wound down the blade, delicately etched, snagging the light from the scattered embers. The hilt was of copper and gold. Set in gold, fire sparkling in their cores, were three stars.

His grip loosened. The dry, whistling breath in his throat stopped until there was no sound in the room. Then, with a sudden, furious cry, he flung the sword away from him, across the floor, where it spun on the stones of the doorway, startling Lyra.

She picked it up and whirled, but it came alive in her grasp and she dropped it again, backing away from it into the hall. She gave a shout; there was a flurry of voices down the hall. The sword vanished; in its place stood the master of the shapes.

He moved swiftly, turning toward Morgon; Lyra's spear, thrown a fraction of a second late, skimmed past him and ripped through one of the cushions beside Morgon. Morgon, still on his knees, watched the figure breaking through the web of shadows, the hair weaving into darkness, the face sparse, shell-colored, the eyes heavy-lidded, blue-green, gleaming with their own light. The body was fluid, blurred, the colors of foam, the colors of the sea; he moved without noise, his strange garments shifting lights the colors of wet seaweed, of set shell. As he came, inexorable as tide, Morgon sensed an enormous, undefined power, restless and unfathomed like the sea, impersonal as the light behind the eyes fixed on his face.

Lyra's cry jarred him as if out of a dream. "The spear! Morgon! The spear by your hand. Throw it!"

He reached for it.

There was a movement in the sea-colored eyes like a distant, faint flick of a smile. Morgon rose, backed slowly, holding the spear with both hands between them. He heard Lyra's desperate cry, "Morgon!" His hands began to shake; the smile deepened in the strange eyes. With the sob of a rare Ymris curse that tore out of him, Morgon drew back his arm and threw.

7

I'M GOING HOME," MORGON SAID.

"I don't understand you," said Lyra. She was sitting beside him at the fire, a light, crimson coat over her guard's tunic, her face smudged with sleeplessness. Her spear lay loosely under one hand at her side. Two other guards stood at the doorway facing opposite directions, their spearheads, in the fragile morning sunlight, forming a gleaming apex of light. "He would have killed you if you hadn't killed him. It's that simple. There is no law in Hed that forbids you to kill in self-defense, is there?"

"No."

"Then why?" She sighed, her eyes on his face as he stared into the flames. His shoulder was set and bound; his face was set, as accessible as a word-locked book. "Are you angry because you were not well-guarded in the Morgol's house? Morgon, I asked the Morgol this morning to be relieved of my place in the guard because of that, but she refused."

She had his attention, then. "There was no reason for you to do that."

Her chin rose slightly. "There was reason. Not only did I stand there doing nothing while you were fighting

121

for your life, when I finally did try to kill the shape-changer, I missed. I never miss."

"He created an illusion of silence; it wasn't your fault that you heard nothing."

"I failed to guard you. That's simple, too."

"Nothing is simple."

He leaned back against the cushions, wincing a little; his brows pinched together again. He was silent; she waited, asked tentatively, "Well, then are you angry with Deth because he was with the Morgol when you were attacked?"

"Deth?" He looked at her blankly. "Of course not."

"Then what are you angry about?"

He looked down at the silver cup and the wine she had poured for him, touched it. Finally, the words dredged slowly, painfully from him as out of some shameful place, "You saw the sword."

She nodded. "Yes." The perplexed line between her brows deepened. "Morgon, I'm trying to understand."

"It's hardly difficult. Somewhere in this realm there is a starred sword waiting for the Star-Bearer to claim it. And I refuse to claim it. I'm going home where I belong."

"But Morgon, its's only a sword. You don't even have to use it if you don't want to. Besides, you might need it."

"I will need it." His fingers were rigid on the circle of silver. "That would be inevitable. The shape-changer knew. He knew. He was laughing at me when I killed him. He knew exactly what I was thinking when no one except the High One himself could have known."

"What were you thinking?"

"That one man could accept the name the stars on that sword gave him and still keep the land-rule of Hed."

Lyra was silent. The uneasy sunlight faded, leaving the room grey with shadows; leaves, wind-tossed, tapped like fingers against the window. She said finally, her hands clasped tightly around her knees, "You can't just turn your back on this and go home."

"I can."

"But you—you're a riddle-master, too—you can't just stop answering riddles."

He looked at her. "I can. I can do anything I must to keep the name I was born with."

"If you go back to Hed, they'll kill you there. You don't even have guards in Hed."

"At least I will die in my own land, be buried in my own fields."

"How can it matter so much? How can you face death in Hed that you can't face in Herun?"

"Because it's not death I'm afraid of—it's losing everything I love for a name and a sword and a destiny I did not choose and will not accept. I would rather die than lose the land-rule."

She said wistfully, "What about us? What about Eliard?"

"Eliard?"

"If they kill you in Hed, they'll still be there and so will Eliard. And we'll be alive, asking questions without you to answer them."

"The High One will protect you," he said grimly. "That's his business. I can't do it. I'm not going to follow the path of some fate dreamed up for me thousands of years ago, like a sheep going to be fleeced." He took a sip of the wine finally, saw her uncertain, anxious face. He said more gently, "You are the landheir of Herun. Some day you will rule it, and your eyes will turn as gold as the Morgol's. This is your home; you would die to defend it; your place is here. At what price would you give up Herun, turn your face from it forever?"

She was silent; one shoulder gave a little shrug. "Where else could I go? I don't belong anywhere else. But it's different for you," she added, as he opened his mouth. "You do have another name, another place. You are the Star-Bearer."

"I would rather be a pigherder in Hel," he said tartly. He dropped his head back wearily, one hand massaging his shoulder. Rain began then, thin, tentative; the plants in the Morgol's garden bowed under it. He closed his eyes, smelled, unexpectedly, the autumn rains falling over three-quarters of Hed. There was a sound of fresh wood falling on the fire, and the eager snap of flame. The voices of the flames tangled together, turned familiar after a while; he heard Tristan and Eliard arguing comfortably, pointlessly, beside the hearth at Akren, with Snog Nutt, a handful of bones and cobweb, snoring like rain in the background. He half-listened to the argument woven into the soft whispers of the fire, until the voices began to fade and he had to strain to hear them; they finally died away, and he opened his eyes to the cold, grey rain of Herun.

Deth was sitting opposite him, speaking softly to the Morgol, uncoiling broken strings from his harp. Their faces turned as Morgon straightened. El, her long hair unbound, brushing her tired face, said, "I sent Lyra to bed. I have set guards at every crack and crevice of this house, but it's difficult to suspect the ground-mist, or the spider wandering in from the rain. How do you feel?"

"All right." Then, his eyes on Deth's harp, he whispered, "I remember. I heard strings break, when I struck the shape-changer. That was your harp."

"Only five strings," Deth said. "A small price to pay Corrig for your life. El gave me strings from Tirunedeth's harp to match them." He put the harp down.

"Corrig." Morgon drew breath; the Morgol was gazing at Deth wonderingly. "Deth, how of all things do you know that shape-changer's name."

"I harped with him once, years ago. I met him even before I entered the High One's service."

"Where?" the Morgol asked.

"I was riding alone down the northern coast from Isig, in the far reaches belonging neither to Isig nor Osterland. I camped one night on the beach, sat late in the night beside my fire, harping . . . and out of the darkness came an answering harping, beautiful, wild, flawless. . . . He came into the circle of my firelight, glistening with tide, his harp of shell and bone and mother of pearl, and demanded songs of me. I played as well for him as for the kings I had played to; I dared not do less. He gave me songs in return; he stayed with me until dawn, until the sun rose, and his song as the red northern sun flamed across the sea burned in my heart for days after I heard it. He melted like mist into the morning sea-mist, but first he gave me his name. He asked for mine. I told him, and he laughed."

"He laughed at me last night," Morgon whispered.

"He played for you, too, from what you told us, then."

"He played my death. The death of Hed." His eyes lifted from the core of the fire. "What kind of power could do that? Was it truth? Or illusion?"

"Did it matter?"

He shook his head. "No. He was a very great harpist. . . . Does the High One know what he was."

"The High One said nothing to me, beyond instructing me to leave Herun with you as quickly as possible."

Morgon was silent. He got to his feet awkwardly, went to the window. Through the glistening air, as though he had the Morgol's vision, he could see the wide, wet plains of Caithnard where trade-ships were setting sail for An, Isig, Hed. He said softly, "Deth, tomorrow, if I can ride, I am going east to the trade-port Hlurle, to take a ship home. I should be safe; no one will expect that. But even if they find me again at sea, I would rather die a land-ruler returning home than a nameless, placeless man being forced into a life I can't understand or control."

There was no answer but the rain pounding with impersonal fury against the glass. Then, as the sound tapered away, he heard the harpist rise, felt a hand on his shoulder, turning him. He met the dark, dispassionate gaze silently; the harpist said softly, "It's more than the killing of Corrig. Will you tell me what is troubling you?"

"No."

"Do you want me to accompany you to Hed?"

"No. There's no reason for you to risk your life again."

"How will you reconcile turning back with what you held true at Caithnard?"

"I have made a choice," Morgon said steadily, and the hand fell from his shoulder. He felt the tooth of an odd sorrow bite into him, the sorrow of an ending, and he added, "I'll miss you."

Something came into the harpist's face, breaking through the calm agelessness of it until Morgon sensed for the first time the concern, the uncertainty, the endless experience that ran through his mind like water beneath ice. Deth did not answer; his head bent slightly as to a king or an inevitability.

MORGAN LEFT THE CITY OF CIRCLES BEFORE DAWN two days later. He wore against the thin, icy mists a heavy, richly lined coat the Morgol had given him. A hunting bow that Lyra had made for him hung with his saddlebags. He had left the packhorse with Deth, since Hlurle lay scarcely three days away, a small port the traders used to unload goods bound for Herun. Deth had given Morgon what money he had had left in case he had to wait, for in late autumn, in the heavy seas, ships grew scarce on the northern coast.

Morgon's harp lay at his back, encased against the damp air; his horse's hooves made soft rhythmic whispers through the long grass of the pastures. The sky was clear before dawn; the stars, huge, cold, gave him light. In the distance tiny lights from farmhouses winked alive, golden eyes in the darkness. The fields of the city gave way to a plain where huge stones rose originless as wizards around him. He felt their shadows as he rode beneath them. Mists fell then, rolling down from the hills; following Lyra's advice he stopped, found shelter under a rare tree, and waited.

He spent the first night at the foot of the eastern hills. That night, among the silent trees, alone for the first time in many weeks, he watched the smoke-colored dusk fade gently into night, and, in the light of his small, solitary fire, he took out the starred harp and began to play. The sound was rich and true under his fingers, made for a delicate, expert skill. After an hour his playing slowed. He sat examining the harp as he had never done before, tracing every curve of gold, marvelling at the white moons untarnished by age, sea, use. He touched the stars softly, as though he were touching flame.

The next day he spent picking a path through the low, empty hills. He found a stream lancing between them and followed it, winding through groves of pale ash and oak trees with their beautiful, endless weavings of dark, bare branches. The stream, quickening, bouncing over tree roots and green rocks, led him out of the trees to the bald, whistling eastern slopes where he could see unexpectedly, the flat no-man's-land of the eastern coast running between Ymris and Osterland, the faint white heads of mountains rising in the farthest point of the High One's realm, and the broad, endless eastern sea.

The stream joined a wide river that had curled around north Herun; struggling with a mental map, he realized it was the Cwill that took its roaring white waters from White Lady Lake, the enormous lake deep in the wastelands that fed also the seven Lungold Lakes. Hlurle, he remembered, lay just north of its mouth. He camped that night on the joint of land between the stream and the river, his thoughts lulled by their two voices: one deep, secret, swift; the other light, high, hospitable. He lay quietly by the fire, his head resting on his saddle, reaching out now and then to add a branch or a pinecone to the flames. Gently as small birds landing in his mind came questions he no longer had to answer; he looked at each one curiously, as though it had never occurred to him before, dispassionately, as though the answers had nothing to do with him, or with the white-haired, half-blind Ymris landheir, or with the King of Ymris struggling with a strange war growing on his coasts, or with the Morgol, the peace of her house shattered by a hint of power that had no origins, no definition. He saw in his mind's eye the stars on his face, the stars on the harp, the stars on the sword. He looked at himself as though he were a figure in some ancient tale: a Prince of Hed reared to harvest bare-backed in the sun, to puzzle over the varied diseases of trees and animals, to read the weather from the color of a cloud, or a tension in a breathless afternoon, to the simple, hard-headed, uncurious life of Hed. He saw that same figure in the voluminous robe of a Caithnard student pouring late at night over ancient books, his lips shaping, soundlessly, riddle, answer, stricture, riddle, answer, stricture; walking, from pure choice, one morning into a cold tower in Aum, finding himself, in the face of death, with no name, no way of life, no birthright to save him but his mind. He saw a Prince of Hed with three stars on his face leave his land, find a starred harp in Ymris, a sword, a name, and a hint of doom in Herun. And those two figures out of the ancient tale: the Prince of Hed and the Star-Bearer, stood apart from each other; he could find nothing that reconciled them.

He broke a branch, fed it to the fire; his thoughts turned to the High One whose home lay in the heart of one of the distant mountains to the north. The High One, from the beginning, had left men free to find their own destinies. His sole law was land-law, the law that passed like a breath of life from land-heir to land-heir; if the High One died, or withdrew his immense and intricate power, he could turn his realm into a wasteland. The evidences of his powers were subtle and unexpected; he was thought of, when at all, with both awe and trust; his dealings with rulers, generally through his harpist, were invariably courteous. His one concern was the land; his one law, the law instilled deeper than thought, deeper than dreaming, in his land-rulers. Morgon thought of the terrible tale of Awn of An, who, trying to discourage an army from Hel, had set fire to An, sending flames billowing over half the land, burning harvests, orchards, shearing the hillsides and riverbanks. Safe at last, he had awakened out of a sleep of exhaustion to realize he had lost the wordless, gentle awareness of things beyond eyesight that had been with him, like a hidden eye, since the death of his father. His land-heir, running grief-stricken into the room, had stopped, astonished, to find him still alive. . . .

The fire sank low, like a beast curling to sleep. Morgon tossed a handful of twigs and dry acorns on it, and it started awake. Awn had killed himself. The wizard Talies, methodical and sharp-tongued, who had hated Awn's warring, recorded the incident with relish, mentioned it to a passing trader, and within three months, precarious as trading was in those years of turmoil, all battling had ceased abruptly in the High One's realm. Peace did not last long; the battles over boundary and kingship had not ended yet, but they grew less frequent, and less devastating. Then the ports and the great cities had begun to grow: Anuin, Caithnard, Caerweddin, Kraal, Kyrth. . . .

And now, some strange, dark power, unsuspected by most lands, unchecked by the High One, was building along the coasts. Not since the wizards lived had there been people of such power; the wizards, themselves skilled, restless and arbitrary, would never had dreamed of trying to kill a land-ruler. There had been scarcely a hint of their existence in the tales and histories of the land until breaking a silence of centuries, they had roused to meet the Star-Bearer at Caithnard. A face floated into the fire before Morgon's eyes: foam-white, blurred, eyes luminous like wet kelp, wet shell

. . . they held a smile, knowing what he was thinking, knowing. . . .

He touched the heart of the questioning; his lips moved, whispering it, "Why?"

A little cold breeze moved across the river; his fire shivered under it. He realized then how tiny that fire was against the enormous darkness. A fear prickled over him; he froze, straining to hear above the water the soft breaking of a twig, the stirring of leaves around him. But the chattering stream distorted sounds, and the wind rose, tuneless in the bare branches. He lay back. His fire sank into itself; the stars clinging to the black oak limbs seemed to shake and sway in the winds. A few drops of rain fell, hard as acorns, to the earth. As though the wind carried an echo of the vast emptiness about him, his fear died away. He turned on his side, slept without dreaming.

The next day, following the Cwill, he reached the sea. Hlurle, little more than a dock, a scattering of warehouses, inns, and small, worn houses, lay hunched under a mist of rain beating in from the sea. There were two ships moored among the fishing boats, their furled sails were blue. There seemed to be no one around. He rode, drenched and shivering, down the wharf, hearing beneath the rain, the rattle of chain, the musing creak of timber, the occasional nudge of a boat against the dock. Ahead of him, light from a small tavern spilled into the wet air. He stopped there, dismounted under its broad eaves.

Inside, the rough tables and benches, lit by smokey torches and an enormous fire, were full of sailors, traders with jewels on their hands, in their caps, disgruntled fishermen who had come in with the rain. Morgon, enduring a brief, casual scrutiny as he walked dripping to the fire, unbuttoned his coat with numb fingers and hung it to dry. He sat down on the bench in front of the fire; the tavern keeper paused at his elbow.

"Lord?" he said questioningly, and then, with a glance at the coat, "You are far from home."

Morgon nodded tiredly. "Beer," he said. "And what is that I smell?"

"A fine, thick stew, with tender lamb, mushrooms, and wine—I'll bring you a bowl."

He ate and drank in weary silence, the smoke and heat and tangle of voices lulling as the river's voice. He sat sipping his beer, which he realized probably came from Hed, when the smell of wet wool and a chill of rain and wind disturbed him. A trader, the fur trim on his cloak beaded with water, sat down beside him. Morgon felt eyes on his face.

The man rose after a moment, divested himself of his cloak with a sprinkle of rain, and said apologetically, "Your pardon, Lord. You're wet enough without my help."

He was richly dressed in black leather and velvet, his hair and his eyes in a rough, kindly face dark as blackbird's wings. Morgon, drowsy in the warmth, stirred himself and put his mind to practical matters. There was no way of knowing whether he spoke to a man or the illusion of a man; he accepted the risk and said, "Do you know where those ships are going?"

"Yes. They are bound back to Kraal, to go into dry dock for the winter." He paused, his shrewd eyes on Morgon's face. "You don't want to go north? What do you need?"

"Passage to Caithnard. I'm supposed to be at the college."

The man shook his head, his brow wrinkling. "It's late in the season. . . . Let me think. We just came from Anuin, stopping at Caithnard, Tol, and Caerweddin."

"Tol," Morgon said involuntarily. "For what?"

"To take Rood of An from Caithnard to Hed." He caught the tavern maid's attention and got wine. Morgon settled back against the bench, his brows drawn, hoping Rood had contented himself with going only as far as Hed in search of him. The trader took a long swallow of wine, sat back himself. He said moodily, "It was a depressing journey. There was a storm around Hed that blew us down the coast, and we were in living fear of losing both the ship and Rood of An. . . . He's got a sharp tongue when he's seasick," he added thoughtfully, and Morgon almost laughed. "At Tol, there was Eliard of Hed, and the young one— Tristan—pleading for news of their brother. All I could tell them was that he'd been seen in Caerweddin, but I couldn't tell them what he was doing there. We lost sail in that storm, but we found we couldn't land in Meremont; there were king's warships in the harbor there, so we limped to Caerweddin. I heard then, for the first time, that his young wife had vanished, and his brother was home again, half-blind. No one knows what to make of it." He sipped wine. Morgon, his eyes on the fire, felt his mind fill with faces: Astrin's, white-eyed, twisted with pain; the Lady Eriel's, shy, beautiful, merciless; Heureu's face, realizing slowly what kind of woman he had married. . . . He shivered. The trader glanced at him.

"You're wet through. That was a long ride from Herun. I wonder if I know your father."

Morgon smiled at the hint. "Probably. But he's got a name so long even I can't pronounce it for you."

"Ah." There was an answering smile in the dark eyes. "Your pardon. I wouldn't pry for the world. But I need some idle chatter to warm my bones. I've got a wife waiting for me in Kraal, if we make it there, and two little sons I haven't seen for two months. Passage to Caithnard. . . . The only ships would be coming down from Kraal, and I can't remember who's up there. Wait." He turned, shouted into the din behind them. "Joss! Who's left in Kraal?"

"Three of Rustin Kor's ships, waiting for a cargo of timber from Isig," a voice boomed back in answer. "We didn't pass them; they must be still up there. Why?"

"The Herun lordling needs to get back to the College. Will they stop here, do you think?"

"Rustin Kor has half a warehouse full of Herun wine here; he'll pay winter storage fees if he doesn't stop."

"He'll stop," the trader said, turning back to Morgon. "I remember. It's Mathom of An who wants the wine. Do you like riddling, then? Do you know who's a great riddler? The wolf of Osterland. I was in his court last summer at Yrye, trying to interest him in a pair of amber cups, when a man came in from Lungold to challenge him to a game. Har has a standing wager that any man who wins a game with him can have the first thing he asks for when the game is done. It's a tricky prize: there's a tale of one man, long ago, who won the game after a day and a night, and he was so dry the first thing he asked for was a cup of water. I don't know if that's true. Anyway, this man—he was a little, wizened, arrogant one, looked as if he'd been sucked dry by riddles—kept Har at it two days, and the old wolf loved it. Everyone got drunk listening, and I sold more cloth and jewels there than I had all year. It was wonderful. Finally the wolf-king asked a riddle the little man couldn't answer—he'd never heard of it. He got angry and challenged the riddle. Har told him to go take the riddle to the Masters at Caithnard, and then he asked ten riddles in a row the man couldn't answer, one right after another—I thought the little one was going to burst with choler. But Har soothed him and said he hadn't played such a great game in years."

"What was the first riddle the man couldn't answer?" Morgon asked curiously.

"Oh—let me think. What will one star call out of dark. . . . No. What will one star call out of silence, one star out of darkness, and one star out of death?"

Morgon's breath caught sharply. He straightened, his face rigid, white, his eyes narrowed, searching the trader's. For a moment the dark face wavered before him in the flames, elusive, expressionless as a mask;

and then he realized that the trader was staring at him in utter astonishment.

"Lord, what did I say?" Then his face changed, and his hand went out abruptly toward Morgon. "Oh," he whispered, "I think you are no Herun lordling."

"Who are you?"

"Lord, my name is Ash Strag from Kraal; I have a wife and two children, and I would sooner cut off my hand than hurt you. But do you realize how they've been looking for you?"

Morgon's hand eased open. He said after a moment, his eyes unwavering on the anxious face, "I know."

"You're going home, now? From Anuin to Caerweddin, I heard always the same question: Have you news of the Prince of Hed? What is it? Are you in trouble? Can I help you?" He paused. "You don't trust me."

"I'm sorry—"

"No. I heard. I heard a tale from Tobec Rye, the trader who found you with Lord Astrin in Ymris. He gave me some mad story that you and the High One's harpist had been nearly drowned on a trade-ship whose crew vanished, and that one of the traders on it had been Jarl Acker. I saw Jarl Acker die, two years ago during a run from Caerweddin to Caithnard. He caught a fever, and he asked to be buried in the sea. So we —so we did that." His voice dropped again, hushed. "Someone stole his shape back out of the sea?"

Morgon dropped against the bench back. His blood was still jumping sickly. "You didn't—you didn't tell that to my brother."

"Of course not." He was silent again, studying Morgon, his dark brows winging together. "It was true, about the vanishing traders? Someone wants to kill you? That's why you're afraid of me. But you weren't afraid until I mentioned the stars. Those stars. Lord, is someone trying to kill you because of the stars on your face?"

"Yes."

"But why? Who in the world could benefit, killing a Prince of Hed? It's irrational."

Morgon drew a breath. The familiar din was unchanged behind him; there was no one near enough to hear them, or who even looked curious. All knew that if anything of interest were gleaned from Morgon's presence, it would be promptly shared in his absence. He rubbed his face with his hands. "Yes. Did Har answer the riddle about the stars?"

"No."

"How are Eliard and Tristan?"

"Worried sick. They asked if you were on your way home from Caerweddin, and I said as tactfully as possible that perhaps you were pursuing a circuitous route because no one knew where you were. I never expected to see you as far north as Hlurle."

"I've been in Herun."

Ash Strag shook his head. "It's unheard of." He sipped wine, brooding. "I don't like it. People of strange power impersonating traders—are they wizards?"

"No. I suspect they're even more powerful."

"And they're pursuing you? Lord, I'd go straight to the High One."

"They've tried to kill me four times," Morgon said wearily, "and I'm only as far as Herun."

"Four times, once at sea—"

"Twice at Ymris, and once again in Herun."

"Caerweddin." The sharp eyes flicked to him. "You went to Caerweddin, and now the King's wife is vanished, and Astrin Ymris, who came with you, is blind in one eye. What happened while you were there? Where is Eriel Ymris?"

"Ask Heureu."

The drawn breath hissed away into the sound of rain. "I don't like it," the trader whispered. "I've heard tales I wouldn't repeat to my own brother, met men who had hearts made of the leavings of animals, but

I've never heard anything like this. I've never heard of anything that could strike at the land-rulers before, so quietly, so powerfully. And it's all because of your stars?"

Morgon winced. "I'm going home," he said, almost to himself. The trader, holding their cups up in the air to get the tavern maid's attention, got them filled, pushed Morgon's back to him. He said carefully, "Lord, is it wise to go by sea?"

"I can't go back through Ymris. I've got to risk it."

"Why? You're halfway to Isig—more than halfway. Lord, come with us to Kraal—" He sensed Morgon's faint withdrawal, and said gently, "I know. I know. I don't blame your mistrust. But I know myself, and there's not a man in this room I mistrust. It would be better for you to risk going north with us than to take a strange ship to Hed. If you wait here too long, your enemies may find you."

"I'm going home."

"But, Lord, they'll kill you in Hed!" His voice had risen; he checked, glancing around him. "How do you expect your farmers to protect you? Go to the High One. How can you find answers to anything in Hed?"

Morgon, staring at him, began to laugh suddenly. He covered his eyes with his fingers; felt the trader's hand on his shoulder. He whispered, "I'm sorry, but I've never had a trader hand me the heart of a maze of riddles so aptly before."

"Lord . . ."

He dropped his hands, his face quieting. "I will not go with you. Let the High One answer a few riddles; I'm doing no good. The realm is his business; Hed is mine."

The hand at his shoulder shook him lightly, as if to wake him. "Hed is doing well as it is, Lord," the trader said softly. "It's the rest of us, the world outside of Hed you've troubled in your passing, that I'm worried about."

THE SHIPS SAILED WITH THE EVENING TIDE. MORGON watched them leave in an eerie, beautiful band of lavender-white twilight stretching across the sea beneath the rain clouds. He had stabled his horse, taken a room in the tavern to wait for Rustin Kor's ships; the rain-streaked window gave him a view of the quiet docks, the wild sea, and the two ships, taking the sullen waves with the grace of sea birds. He watched them until the light faded and their sails darkened. Then he lay on the bed, something nagging at the back of his mind, something he could not touch, though he wove strand after strand of thought trying to trace it. Raederle's face slipped unexpectedly into his mind, and he was startled at the joylessness he felt in himself at the thought of her.

He had raced her up the hill to the College once, years ago, she in a long, green dress she had hiked to her knees to run in. He had let her win, and, at the top, happy, panting, she had mocked his courtesy. Rood came behind with a handful of jewelled pins that had fallen out of her hair; he tossed them to her; they caught light like a swarm of strange, glittering insects, scarlet, green, amber, purple. Too tired to catch them, she had let them fall around her, laughing, her red hair massed like a mane in the wind. And Morgon had watched her, forgetting to laugh, forgetting even to move, until he saw Rood's black eyes on his face, quizzical, for once almost gentle. And, remembering back, he heard Rood's voice, harsh, stripped of pity on the last day they had met: *If you offer the peace of Hed to Raederle, that will be a lie.*

He sat up on the bed, knowing now what bothered him. Rood had known from the beginning. He could not go to Anuin taking honor for winning a game of riddles in a tower in Aum when all round him riddles were forming, deadly and imperative, for a game he refused to play. He could turn his back on other kingdoms, close the doors of the peace of Hed about himself, but to reach out to her would be to reach out to the strangeness, the uncertainty of his other name, for he could offer her nothing less than himself.

He rose, sat on the window ledge a long time, watching the wet world grow dark before him. An impossible web of riddles was being woven about his name; he had wrenched himself from it once; he had only to lift his hand to touch it, become ensnared in it again. He had a choice, for the moment: to return to Hed, live quietly without Raederle, asking no questions, waiting for the day when the storm brewing, growing on the coasts and the mainland would unleash its full fury at Hed—that day, he knew, would come soon. Or to set his mind to a riddle-game he had no hope of winning, and whose prize, if he did win, was a name that might cut every tie that bound him to Hed.

He moved after a while, realized the room was black. He got up, felt for a candle in the dark, lit it. The flame etched his face in the window, startling him. The flame itself was a star in his hand.

He dropped the candle to the floor, ground the flame underfoot, and lay back down on the bed. Late that night, after the rain had stopped and the wind's voice had dropped to a murmur, he fell asleep. He woke again at dawn, went downstairs to buy food and a skin of wine from the tavern keeper. Then he saddled his horse, left Hlurle without looking back, heading north to Yrye, to ask the King of Osterland a riddle.

8

TWO WEEKS AFTER HE LEFT HLURLE, THE WINTER
snow began to fall. He had felt its coming, tasted it
in the air, heard it coming in the voices of wild,
restless winds. He had gone up the coast to the mouth
of the Osc, the great river whose roots lay in the heart
of Erlenstar Mountain. The river ran through Isig Pass,
past the doorstep of Isig Mountain, to form the south-
ern boundary of Osterland on its way to the sea. Morgon followed it upriver patiently, through unclaimed
land, forgotten forests that only traders sailing down
from Isig ever saw, rough, rocky country where herds
of deer, elk, mountain sheep ranged, their coats thick
against the winter. Once he thought he saw moving
through a far stretch of forest a herd of vesta, their
legendary horns thin slivers of gold among the trees.
But against the white, empty sky, they could have been
a drift of mist, and he was uncertain.

He moved as quickly as possible through the wild
country, feeling the snow at his heels, hunting sporad-
ically, wondering in the back of his mind if the wilderness would ever end, or if there were any men left in
the High One's realm, or if the river he followed were
perhaps not the Ose but some unmapped water that
wound westward into the vast, uninhabited backlands

of the realm. That thought woke him more than once at night, to wonder what he was doing in the middle of nowhere, where a broken bone, a frightened animal, a sudden storm could kill him as easily as his enemies. The constant fears ran like a current in his mind. Yet there was an odd peace he sometimes felt when at night there were no colors but the fire and the black sky, and no sounds in the world but his harp. At those moments he belonged to the night; he felt nameless, bodiless, as though he could take root and become a tree, drift apart and become the night.

Finally, he began to see farms in the distance, herds of sheep, cattle grazing by the river, and knew somewhere he had crossed into Osterland. Partly from caution, partly out of a habit of silence that had grown with him the past weeks, he avoided the farms and small towns along the river. He stopped only once to buy bread, cheese and wine, and to get directions to Yrye. The curious glances made him uneasy; he realized how strange he must seem, neither trader nor trapper, coming out of the backlands of Osterland with a bright, worn, Herun coat and hair like an ancient hermit's.

Yrye, the wolf-king's home, lay north, in the arms of Grim Mountain, the central peak in a range of low, border mountains; there was a road leading to it out of one of the villages. Morgon, riding out of the town, camped for the night in a woods nearby. The winds whined like wolves through the pine; he woke near dawn chilled to the bone, made a fire that fluttered like a helpless bird. The winds moved about him as he rode that day, speaking to one another in some rough, deep language. At evening they quieted; the sky was a smooth fleece of cloud beyond which the sun wandered and set unnoticed. In the night the snow began to fall; he woke beneath a coat of white.

The fall was gentle, the cold winds were still; he rode through the day in a dreamlike silence of white broken only by the flick of a blackbird's wing, a brown hare's scuttle to shelter. He fashioned a tent, when he stopped at evening, out of the tanned skin he had been sleeping on, and found a snarled patch of dry bramble for kindling. His thoughts turned, as he ate, to the strange, ancient king who in his riddle-gatherings had chanced upon another the Masters at Caithnard had never learned. Har, the wolf-king, had been born even before most of the wizards; he had ruled Osterland since the years of Settlement. Tales of him were numerous and awesome. He could change shape. He had been tutored by the wizard Suth, during Suth's wildest years. He bore scars on his hands the shape of vesta horns, and he riddled like a Master. Morgon leaned back against a boulder, sipped hot wine slowly, wondering where the king had got his knowledge. He felt again the faint stirrings of curiosity that had been dulled for weeks, of a longing to return to the world of men. He finished his wine, reached out to pack the cup. And then he saw, beyond the circle of his fire, eyes watching him.

He froze. His bow lay on the other side of the fire; his knife was stuck upright on the wedge of cheese. He began to reach for it slowly. The eyes blinked. There was a gathering, a soft stirring; then a vesta walked into his firelight.

Something jumped in the back of Morgon's throat. It was huge, broad as a farmhorse, with a deer's delicate, triangular face. Its pelt was blazing white; its hooves and crescents of horn were the color of beaten gold. It eyed him fathomlessly out of eyes of liquid purple, then reached up above his head to nibble at a pine bough. Morgon, his breath still as though he were reaching toward a forbidden thing, lifted one hand to the white, glowing fur. The vesta did not seem to notice the gentle touch. After a moment Morgon reached for his bread, tore a piece. The vesta's head lowered curiously at the scent, nuzzled at the bread. Morgon touched the narrow bone of its face; it jerked beneath his hand, and the purple eyes rose again, huge and dimensionless, to his face. Then the vesta lowered its head, continued eating, while he gently scratched the space between its horns. It finished the piece, sniffed his hand for more. He fed it the rest, piece by piece, until there was no more. It searched his empty hands, his coat a moment, then turned, faded with scarcely a sound back into the night.

Morgon drew a full breath. The vesta, he had heard, were shy as children. It was a rare pelt seen in trade-shops, for they were wary of men, and the weight of Har's wrath lay on any man, trader or trapper, caught killing vesta. They followed snow, wandering farther and farther into the mountains during the summer. Morgon, with a sudden touch of unease, wondered what it had smelled in the air that night that had brought it so far from the mountains.

Before morning he found out. A wind, wailing like a bee swarm, wrenched the tent loose over his head and spun it into the river. Huddled beside his horse, his eyes stinging with snow, he waited for a dawn that it seemed would never come. When it did come finally, it only turned the blankness of night into a milky chaos through which Morgon could not even see the river running ten steps away from him.

A helpless, terrible despair rose in him. Chilled even beneath the thick hooded coat, the winds snarling like wolves around him, he lost sense of the river's position, felt the whole world a blind, patternless turmoil. He forced himself to remember. He rose stiffly, feeling his horse trembling with cold under the blanket he had thrown over it. He murmured something to it out of numb lips; heard it thrashing nervously to stand as he turned. Head bent against the snow, he walked almost blindly to where he thought the river was. It loomed out of the blizzard at him unexpectedly, swift, eddied with snow; he nearly stepped headlong into it. He turned back to get his horse, bent to retrace his footsteps. When he reached the end of them, he found his horse gone.

He stood still and called to it; the wind pushed the words back into his mouth. He took a step toward a shadow in the snow, and it melted away before his eyes into whiteness. When he turned again, he could not see in the drift of snow, either his pack or his harp.

He went forward blindly, dug in the snow with his hands, beneath boulders and trees that melted out of the blizzard. He tried to see; the wind spat flakes huge as coins into his eyes. He searched desperately, furiously, losing what fragile sense of direction he had gained, moving patternlessly, dazed by the incessant, whining winds.

He found the harp finally, already half-buried; as he held it in his hands, he began to think again. It lay where he had left it, beneath the boulder he had slept beside; the river, he knew, was to his left. His pack, and saddle were somewhere in the mist in front of him; he did not dare lose sense of the river again to look for them. He hung his harp over his shoulder and slowly, carefully, found his way back to the river.

His trek upriver was painfully slow. He stayed dangerously close to the water in order to see the faint, slate-grey glints of it; sometimes when everything melted before his eyes into one monotonous white blur, he would stop short, wondering if he had been threading his way along an illusion. His face and hands grew numb; the hair outside of his hood was icy. He lost all sense of time, not knowing if moments or hours had passed since he had started walking, not knowing whether it was noon or evening. He dreaded the coming of night.

He walked headlong into a tree once, instead of moving around it; he stood where he had stopped, his face resting against the cold, rough bark. He wondered absently how long he could continue, what would happen when he could not move another step, when night fell and he could no longer follow the river. The tree, swaying rhythmically in the wind, was soothing. He knew he should move, but his arms refused to loose the trunk. Unexpectedly, for his thoughts were formless as the blizzard, he saw Eliard's face in his mind, angry, troubled, and he heard his own voice out of some long-lost past. *I swear this: I will come back.*

His grip on the tree loosened reluctantly. He remembered the belief in Eliard's eyes. If Eliard had not believed him, he could root himself like a tree in the middle of the Osterland blizzard; but Eliard, stubborn, literal, would expect him to keep his vow. He opened his eyes again; the colorless world was still there, just beyond his eyelids, and he wanted to weep with the weariness of it.

Imperceptibly, the world began to darken. He did not notice at first, intent on the water, and then he realized that the river itself was melting into the wind. He stumbled frequently over roots, icy rocks, found it more and more tiring to fling an arm out to catch his balance. Once a rock slid into the water under his foot; only a wild grab at a branch saved him from following it. He found his footing again, gripped the tree, shivering uncontrollably like a dog. Looking up to keep himself awake, he was appalled at the color of the wind.

He set his face hard against the bark, tried to think. Night he could not outwit. He could find shelter—a cave, a hollow tree—try to build a fire; the chances of doing either were minute. He could not follow the river in the dark, yet if he left it, he would probably wander aimlessly for a short time, then simply stop and disappear into the snow and wind, become, in his vanishing, another curiosity of Hed, like Kern, for the Masters to put on their lists. He considered the problem stubbornly, staring at the whorls of bark to keep his eyes open. Shelter, a fire, impossible as they seemed, were his only hope. He straightened stiffly, realized that the tree, not his body, had been supporting him. An odd, moist warmth, frightening him more than anything else that day, touched his face; he startled, turning. The head of a vesta loomed over him out of the snow.

He did not know how long he stared into the purple eyes. The vesta was motionless, the wind rippling through its fur. His hands began to move of their own accord, brushing over the face, the neck; he murmured things almost to soothe himself more than it. He inched away from the tree, his hands following the arch of its neck, its back, until he stood at its side, his numb hands curled into the thick hair on its back. It moved finally, reaching for a pinecone on the tree. Poised, his lips tight between his teeth, he leaped for its back.

He was unprepared for the sudden, incredible explosion of speed that shot him like an arrow into the heart of the storm. He gripped the horns, his teeth clenched, his eyes closed, the harp crushed against his ribs; he was almost unable to breathe from the winds slamming against his face. A sound came out of him; as if in answer to it, the wild sprint of panic melted slowly into a slower, steadier pace that was effortless and faster than any horse he had ever ridden. He clung close to the creature's warmth, not wondering where it was going, nor how long it would permit him to stay on its back, simply concentrating on the single thought of staying with it until it could run no more.

He fell into a light sleep, feeling beneath his sleep the effortless, rhythmic movement. His hands, cramped around the horns, loosened; he lost his balance and fell, hitting the earth hard. The sky was black, blazing overhead; silence lay above the light snow like an element. He got to his feet, gazing at star after star blurring together into light, curving down to meet the white horizon. He saw the vesta looking back at him, motionless, white against the snow. He went towards it. For a moment it simply watched him as though he were a curious animal. Then, its steps delicate, barely breaking the snow, it walked to meet him. He lifted

himself onto its back, his arms shaking with the effort.
It began to run again toward the stars.

He woke to the curious touch of snow on his face.
The vesta walked sedately through the empty, snow-
covered streets of a city. Beautiful, brightly painted
wood houses and shops lined the streets, their doors
and shutters closed in the early dawn. Morgon straightened with an effort, breaking a crust of snow on his
coat. The vesta turned a corner; ahead of him Morgon
saw a great unwalled house, its weathered walls pat-
terened with wood gathered from distant corners of
the realm; oak, pale birch, red-toned cedar, dark, rich
timber; the eaves, window frames and double doors
were traced with endless whorls of pure gold.

The vesta walked fearlessly into the yard and
stopped. The dark house sat dreaming in the snow.
Morgon stared at it senselessly a moment; the vesta
made a little restless movement beneath him, as though
it had finished a task and were anxious to leave. Morgon slid off its back. His muscles refused to hold him;
he fell sharply to his knees, the harp jerked down beside him. Under the deep, curious gaze of the vesta, he
tried to get up, fell back helplessly, trembling with
exhaustion. The vesta nudged at him, its warm breath
in his ear. He slid his arm around its neck, his face
dropping against its face. It was still for a moment in
his hold. Then it broke free with a sudden movement,
its head jerking back; and as the circle of gold horn
lifted like the rim of the sun against the white sky, the
vesta faded, and a man stood in its place.

He was tall, lithe, white-haired, half-naked in the
snow. His eyes in his lean, lined face were ice-blue;
his hands, reaching down to Morgon, were scarred
with the white imprint of vesta-horns.

Morgon whispered, "Har." A little smile flared
like a flame behind the light eyes. The wolf-king slid
a powerful arm under Morgon's arm, lifted him to
his feet.

"Welcome." He helped Morgon patiently up the

steps, flung open the wide doors to a hall the size of the barn at Akren, with a firebed running almost the length of it. Har's voice rose, shearing the silence; a couple of crows squawked, startled, on the ledge of a long window. "Is this house hibernating for the winter? I want food, wine, dry clothes, and I will not wait for them until my bones snap like ice with old age and my teeth drop out. Aia!"

Servants scurried blearily into the hall; dogs, springing up, swarmed eagerly about their legs. Half a tree trunk was thrown on the drowsing fire; sparks shot up toward the roof. A mantle of white wool was put over Har's shoulders; Morgon's clothes were stripped from him with unexpected thoroughness on the threshold. A long woolen tunic was pulled over his head, and a mantle of many colored furs thrown over his shoulders. Trays of food were brought in, placed by the fire; Morgon caught the smell of hot bread and hot, spiced meat. He sagged in Har's grip; wine, cold, dry, was forced into his mouth. He swallowed it and choked, felt the blood begin to move again in him, sluggishly, painfully.

A woman came into the hall as they sat down at last and began to eat. She had a strong, lovely old face, hair the color of old ivory braided to her knees. She came to the fire, tightening a belt as she walked, her eyes moving from Har's face to Morgon's.

She dropped a gentle kiss on Har's cheek and said placidly, "Welcome home. Whom did you bring this time?"

"The Prince of Hed."

Morgon's head turned sharply. His eyes caught Har's, held them in an unspoken question. The little perpetual smile deepened in the wolf-king's eyes. He said, "I have a gift for naming. I'll teach it to you. This is my wife, Aia. I found him wondering on foot in a blizzard beside the Ose," he added to her. "I have been shot at, in vesta form; a trapper threw a weighted net over me once in the hills behind Grim

Mountain before he realized who I was; but I have never been fed a loaf of bread by a man half the traders in the realm have been trying to find." He turned again to Morgon, who had stopped eating. He said, his voice gentle in the snapping fire, "You and I are riddle-masters; I will play no games with you. I know a little about you, but not enough. I don't know what is driving you to Erlenstar Mountain, or who you are hiding from. I want to know. I will give you whatever you ask of me in knowledge or skills in return for one thing. If you had not come into my land I would have gone to yours eventually, in one form or another: an old crow, an old trader at your door selling buttons in exchange for knowledge. I would have come."

Morgon put his plate down. Strength was coming back into his body and a strength, a sense of purpose was waking, at Har's words, in his mind. He said haltingly, "If you hadn't found me by the river, I would have died. I will give you whatever help you need."

"That's a dangerous thing to promise blindly in my house," Har commented.

"I know. I've heard a little of you, too. I will give you what help you need."

Har smiled. His hand came to rest a moment, lightly, on Morgon's shoulder. "You made your way inch by inch up the Ose, against the wind in a raging blizzard, clinging to that harp like your life. I tend to believe you. The farmers of Hed are known for their stubbornness."

"Perhaps." He leaned back, his eyes closing in the hot drift of the fire. "But I left Deth in Herun to go back to Hed. I came here instead."

"Why did you change your mind?"

"You sent a riddle out of Osterland to find me. . . ." His voice trailed silent. He heard Har say something from the heart of the fire, he saw the blizzard again, formless, whirling, darkening, darkening. . . .

He woke in a small rich room, dark with evening. He lay without thought, his arm over his eyes, until a scrape of metal by the hearth made him turn his head. Someone was probing the fire; at the sudden lift of a white head, Morgon said, startled, "Deth!"

The head turned. "No. It's me. Har said I am to serve you." A boy rose from the fireside, lit the torch beside Morgon's bed. He was a few years younger than Morgon, big-boned, his hair milky-white. His face was impassive, but Morgon sensed a shyness, a wildness beneath it. His eyes in the torchlight were a lustrous familiar purple. Under Morgon's puzzled gaze, his voice went on, breaking a little now and then as though it were not frequently used. "He said . . . Har said I am to give you my name. I am Hugin. Suth's son."

Morgon's blood shocked through him. "Suth is dead."

"No."

"All the wizards are dead."

"No. Har knows Suth. Har found . . . he found me three years ago, running among the vesta. He looked into my mind and saw Suth."

Morgon stared up at him wordlessly. He gathered the tangled, aching knot of his muscles and bones, and rolled upright. "Where are my clothes? I have got to talk to Har."

"He knows," Hugin said. "He is waiting for you."

Washed, dressed, Morgon followed the boy to Har's great hall. It was filled with people, rich men and women from the city, traders, trappers, musicians, a handful of simply dressed farmers, drinking hot wine by the fire, talking, playing chess, reading. The informality reminded Morgon of Akren. Har, Aia beside him scratching the dog at her knee, sat in his chair by the fire, listening to a harpist. As Morgon made his way through the crowd, the king's eyes lifted, met his, smiling.

Morgon sat down on a bench beside them. The dog

left Aia to scent him curiously, and he realized then with a slight shock, that it was a wolf. Other animals lay curled by the fire: a red fox, a squat badger, a grey squirrel, a pair of weasels white as snow in the rushes.

Aia said tranquilly as he scratched the wolf's ears gingerly, "They come in from the winter, Har's friends. Sometimes they spend a season here, sometimes they come bringing news of both men and animals in Osterland. Sometimes our children send them when they can't come to visit us—that white falcon sleeping high on the rafters, our daughter sent."

"Can you speak to them," Morgon asked. She shook her head, smiling.

"I can only go into Har's mind, and then when he is in his own shape. It's better that way; otherwise I would have worried much more about him when I was younger and he wandered away, prowling his kingdom."

The harp song came to an end; the harpist, a lean, dark man with a dour smile, rose to get wine. The wolf moved to Har as the king reached for his own cup. The king poured Morgon wine, sent a servant for food. Then he said, his voice soft in the weave of sounds about them, "You offered me your help. If you were any other man, I would not hold you to that, but you are a Prince of Hed, that most unimaginative of lands. What I ask will be very difficult, but it will be valuable. I want you to find Suth."

"Suth? Har, how can he be alive? How, after seven hundred years?"

"Morgon, I knew Suth." The voice was still soft, but there was an edge to it as to a chill wind. "We were young together, so long ago. We hungered for knowledge, not caring how it was got, how we used ourselves, one another. We played riddle-games even before Caithnard existed, games that lasted years as we were forced to search for answers. He lost an eye during those wild years; he himself scarred my hands with the vesta-horns, teaching me how to change shape. When he vanished with the school of wizards, I thought he must be dead. Yet three years ago, when a young vesta changed shape to a boy in front of my eyes, and when I looked into the thoughts and memories of his mind, I saw the man he knew as his father, and I knew that face as I know my heart. Suth. He is alive. He has been running, hiding for seven hundred years. Hiding. When I asked him once how he lost his eye, he laughed and said only that there was nothing that may not be looked upon. Yet he has seen something, turned his back to it and run, vanished like a snowfall in a land of snow. He did well to hide. He knows me. I have been at his heels like a wolf for three years, and I will find him."

Patterns were shattering, shifting in Morgon's mind, leaving him groping, blind. "The Morgol of Herun suggested that Ghisteslwchlohm, the Founder of Lungold, is also alive. But that was pure conjecture, there is no evidence. What is he running from?"

"What is driving you to Erlenstar Mountain?"

Morgon put his cup down. He slid his fingers through his hair, drawing it back from his face so that the stars shone blood-red against his pallor. "That."

Har's hands shifted slightly, his rings flashing. Aia sat motionless, listening, her eyes hooded with thought. "So," the king said, "the movement of this great game of power revolves upon Hed. When did you first realize that?"

He thought back. "In Ymris. I found a harp with three stars matching the stars on my face, which no one else could play. I met the woman married to Heureu Ymris, who tried to kill me, for no other reason than those stars, who said she was older than the first riddle ever asked—"

"How did you come to be in Ymris?"

"I was taking the crown of Aum to Anuin."

"Ymris," Har pointed out, "is in the opposite direction."

"Har, you must know what happened. Even if all the traders in the realm had gone to the bottom of the sea with the crown of Aum, you would still probably know, somehow."

"I know what happened," Har said imperturbably. "But I do not know you. Be patient with me, an old man, and begin at the beginning."

Morgon began. By the time he finished the tale of his travellings, the hall was empty but for the king, Aia, the harpist playing softly, listening, and Hugin, who had come in to sit at Har's feet with his head against the king's knees. The torches burned low; the animals were sighing, dreaming in their sleep. His voice ran dry finally. Har got up, stood looking into the fire. He was silent a long time; Morgon saw his hands close at his sides.

"Suth . . ."

Hugin's face flashed toward him at the name. Morgon said tiredly, "Why would he know anything? The Morgol thinks that knowledge of the stars must have been stripped from the wizards' minds."

Har's hands eased open. He turned to look at Morgon, weighing a thought. He said, as though he had not heard Morgon's question, "You dislike killing. There are other methods of defense. I could teach you to look into a man's mind, to see beyond illusion, to close the doors of your own mind against entrance. You are vulnerable as an animal without its winter pelt. I could teach you to outwit winter itself . . ."

Morgon gazed back at him. Something moved in his mind, the glint of a half-surfaced thought. He said, "I don't understand," though he had begun to.

"I told you," Har said "you should never promise a thing blindly in my house. I believe Suth is running with the vesta behind Grim Mountain. I will teach you to take the vesta-shape; you will move among them freely through the winter as a vesta, yet not a vesta. Your body and instincts will be the vesta's, but your mind will be your own; Suth may hide from the

High One himself, but he will reveal himself to you."

Morgon's body shifted a little. "Har, I have no gift for shape-changing."

"How do you know?"

"I'm not . . . No man of Hed was ever born with gifts like that." He shifted again, feeling himself with four powerful legs honed to speed, a head heavy with gold horn, no hands for touching, no voice for speaking.

Hugin said hesitantly, unexpectedly, "It's a thing to love—being the vesta. Har knows."

Morgon saw Grim Oakland's face, Eliard's face, staring at him uncomprehendingly, baffled: You can do what? Why would you want to do that? He felt Har watching him, and he said softly, reluctantly, "I will try, because I promised you. But I doubt if it will work; all my instincts go against it."

"Your instincts." The king's eyes reflected fire suddenly like an animal's, startling Morgon. "You are stubborn. With your face toward Erlenstar Mountain, a thousand miles farther than any Prince of Hed has ever gone beyond his land, a harp and a name in your possession, you still cling to your past like a nestling. What do you know about your instincts? What do you know about yourself? Will you doom us all with your own refusal to look at yourself and give a name to what you see?"

Morgon's hands closed on the edge of the bench. He said evenly, struggling to keep his voice from shaking, "I am a land-ruler, a riddle-master and a star-bearer, in that order—"

"No. You are the Star-Bearer. You have no other name but that, no other future. You have gifts no land-ruler of Hed was ever born with; you have eyes that see, a mind that weaves. Your instincts took you out of Hed before you even realized why; out of Hed to Caithnard, to Aum, to Herun, to Osterland, whose king had no pity for those who run from truth."

"I was born—"

"You were born the Star-Bearer. The wise man knows his own name. You are no fool; you can sense as well as I can what chaos is stirring beneath the surface of our existence. Loose your grip on your past; it is meaningless. You can live without the land-rule if you must; it's not essential——"

Morgon found himself on his feet before he even realized he had moved. "No——"

"You have a very capable land-heir, who stays home and farms instead of answering obscure riddles. Your land can exist without you; but if you run from your own destiny, you are liable to destroy us all."

He stopped. A sound had come out of Morgon, involuntarily, a harsh, indrawn sob without tears. Aia's face, Hugin's face, seemed etched of white stone in the light; only the king's face moved in the shifting fire, alien, neither man's nor animal's. Morgon put his hands over his mouth to still the sound and whispered, "What price do you put on landlaw? What incentive will you offer me to forsake it? What price will you pay me for all the things I have ever loved?"

The light, glittering eyes were unmoved, unwavering on his face. "Five riddles," Har said. "Coin for the man who has nothing. Who is the Star-Bearer and what will he loose that is bound? What will one star call out of silence, one star out of darkness, and one star out of death? Who will come in the time's ending and what will he bring? Who will sound the earth's harp, silent since the Beginning? Who will bear stars of fire and ice to the Ending of the Age?"

Morgon's hands slid slowly away from his mouth. The hall was soundless. He felt tears run like sweat down his face. "What ending?" The wolf-king did not answer. "What ending?"

"Answering riddles is your business. Suth gave me those riddles one day, like a man giving his heart to a friend for safekeeping. I have carried them unanswered since his disappearance."

"Where did he learn them?"

"He knows."

"Then I will ask him." His face was bloodless,
streaked with fire; his eyes, the color of charred wood,
held Har's, seemed to draw from them, in that moment, something of their pitilessness. "I will answer
those riddles for you. And I think, when I have done
that, you will wish to the last breath of your life that
I had never set foot beyond Hed."

HE SAT THE NEXT MORNING IN A ROUND STONE SHED
behind Har's house, waiting for the fire Hugin had
built to bring some relief of warmth to the icy floor.
He wore a light, short linen tunic; his feet were bare.
There were pitchers of watered wine in a corner, cups,
but nothing else, neither food nor bedding. The door
was closed; there were no windows, only the hole
in the roof through which the smoke billowed out, flurries of snow burning, melting, in it. Har sat opposite
him, his face shaping and reshaping in the flames.
Hugin, cross-legged behind him, was motionless as
though he did not breathe.

"I am going into your mind," the face beyond the
fire said. "I will see things you keep there privately.
Do not try to fight my prying. If you wish to elude me,
simply let the thoughts drain out of you like water,
become formless, invisible as wind."

Morgon felt a light touch sorting his thoughts. Isolated moments, past events, rose unbidden in his mind:
Rood, studying with him late at night, a candle hunched
between them; the Lady Eriel speaking softly to him
in a dark hall as his fingers slid toward the last, low
string of a harp; Tristan, her feet muddy, watering
her rose bushes; Lyra, picking up a sword that came
alive in her hands, changing shape. He let the strange
knowledge of another mind, the sense of other un-
trapped thoughts stay in his mind without struggling
until unexpectedly out of the darkness of his thoughts
he saw a man's body whirl away from him, the spear
in his chest holding the fluid, shifting, sea-colored

155

lines of him still until his face became clear for one moment before he fell. Morgon started, murmuring. Har's eyes gazed at him from the flames, unblinking.

"There is nothing that may not be faced, nothing that may not be looked upon. Again."

The memories of his life ran behind his eyes in a current of slowly changing scenes, some of which Har seemed to linger over in his curiosity. As the hours passed, unmeasured except by the ashes of dying wood, Morgon accepted the probing patiently, learned to yield without flinching to memories buried deep in him. Then, wearied, he began to ease away from the incessant searching, let his thoughts slip away from him, become shapeless, like a mist through which the groping mind moved without finding a resting place. Finally, abruptly, he found himself on his feet, pacing back and forth in the tiny room, thinking of nothing but the hunger worrying at him like an animal, the cold that burned his feet as he walked, the cry of his body, like the incessant, unbearable cry of a child for sleep. He prowled the small hut, not hearing Har when he spoke, not seeing Hugin staring up at him, not noticing the door open to deep night when Hugin left to get more wood. Then he felt something forming in his mind that Har had not touched yet, the most private moment of his life: an uneasiness, a growing terror, the beginning of a grief so terrible that any moment he might drown in it. He tried to elude the probing, pitiless mind, felt the grief welling, blooming, struggled furiously against it, against Har without success, until he saw again in the firelight the unmoved, curious eyes, and he took the only escape left to him, slipping out of his own thoughts beyond the surface of another mind.

It was as though he had stepped into another world. He saw the shed from Har's eyes, saw himself standing, surprised in the shadows. He tapped hesitantly the continuous spring of memory deep in Har's mind. He saw a young woman with sun-colored hair he knew was Aia, watching the soaking and bending of the wood that would pattern the walls of her new home. He saw a wizard with wild white hair and grey-gold eyes standing barefoot in snow, laughing before he melted into a lank wolf's form. He saw the private world of Osterland: a fox's den in the warm earth under the snow swarming with red pups, a white owl's nest in the hollow of a high tree, a herd of starving deer in the sparse, cold backlands, a farmer's simple house, the plain walls gleaming with tools, his children rolling like puppies in front of the fire. He followed Har's path through his kingdom, sometimes in animal form, sometimes as a slightly wealthy, slightly foolish old man, his sharp mind gleaning knowledge beneath his sleepy eyes. He realized as he began to recognize places Har had travelled, that he had not confined his wanderings to Osterland. A familiar house rose in Har's mind: with a shock of surprise that threw Morgon back into himself, he recognized the threshold of his own home.

He said, "When? . . ." His voice grated as though he had wakened from sleep.

"I went to Hed to meet Kern. I was curious about a tale I heard of him and a Thing without a name. I had forgotten about that. You did well."

Morgon sat down again on the stones. The demands of his body seemed vague, impersonal, as though they came from his shadow. The fire in the hearth died, flared again, dwindled, flared. The stones grew warm. Morgon went into Hugin's mind, discovered his word-less language, shared with him a complaint of hunger that surprised a smile into the vesta eyes. Then Har held Morgon's mind, probing constantly, teaching him to thrust past the barriers of a locked mind, to defend his own barriers, attacking and parrying again and again until Morgon, ready to explode with a rage of weariness, cleared his mind beyond possibility to try again. Har loosed him; he felt the sweat dripping down his face, his back, felt himself trembling even in the heat.

"How long . . . how long have we? . . ." His throat was parched.

"What is that to either of us? Hugin, get wine."

Hugin knelt next to Morgon with a cup. The boy's face was drawn, the skin beneath his eyes was dark with weariness. But his still face gave back to Morgon something of a smile. The small shed was dim with smoke. Morgon could not tell whether it was day or night beyond the smoke hole in the roof. Hugin opened the doors a moment; winds, blade-sharp, leaped in, scattering snow. The world was black beyond. The sweat froze on Morgon's arms. He began to shiver, and Hugin closed the door.

"Again," Har said softly, and slipped into Morgon's mind like a cat, while Morgon groped, surprised, for the memory of his teachings. The long hours began again, Morgon struggling either to keep his mind free from Har's probing, or to find a path through Har's closed mind. Hugin sat shadow-still beside him. Sometimes Morgon saw him sleeping, stretched on the stones. Sometimes when he pulled away from Har, exhausted, the purple eyes turned to him, and he saw through them an image of the vesta. Then he began to see a vesta where Hugin sat, and was unsure afterward if Hugin had put the thought into his mind, or if the boy's shape were shifting back and forth. Once he looked across the fire and saw not Har but a lean grey wolf with yellow, smiling eyes.

He rubbed his eyes with the heels of his hands, and Har returned saying, "Again."

"No," he whispered, feeling his mind and body slip away from him. "No."

"Then leave."

"No."

The smoke engulfed him like a wind. He seemed to look down at himself from a distance, as though the man half-blind, too weak to move had nothing to do with him. Hugin and Har seemed formed of smoke, now king and wizard's boy, now wolf and vesta, watching, waiting. The wolf began to move closer to him, closer, circling him, fire in its eyes, until it stood next to him. Morgon felt his hands opened, a pattern traced with ash on his palms.

Then the wolf said, "Now."

The pain brought him abruptly back to himself. He opened his eyes, blinking at the salt tears of sweat that ran into them, and the purple eyes of the vesta gazed deep into his. A blade flashed in the corner of his eye; a sound split through his dry throat. Turning, fleeing away from the smoke, the agony of his weariness, the sear of the knife, he stumbled into the world beyond the vesta-eyes.

The stone walls melted away into the single flat line of winter horizon. He stood alone in a privacy of snow and sky, listening to the winds, untangling the scents in them. Somewhere within him, behind him, he sensed a struggling, a turmoil of thought; he avoided it, groping away from it, searching more deeply into the easy silence he had discovered. The winds snapped out of the sharp blue of the sky, carrying shades and tones of smell he could suddenly give names to: water, hare, wolf, pine, vesta. He heard the high, whirling voices of the winds, knew their strength, but felt them only vaguely. The chaotic, fearful voices he fled from weakened, mingled with the wind's meaningless wail. He drew a long, clean breath of the winter, felt the voice fade. The wind traced its passage through him, molded the sinews of his heart, flowed through his veins, honed his muscles to its unfaltering strength and speed. He felt it urge against him, challenging him; and the hard, restless muscles of his body locked suddenly for a race with the wind.

The stones rose out of the unknown. He moved bewilderedly, seeking escape, aware of strange, silent figures watching him. The fire snapped at him;

he backed away from it and turned. His horns scraped against the stones. Then, with a panic exploding through him, he realized that he had horns. He found himself in his own shape, trembling, staring at Har, his hands throbbing again, sticky with blood.

Hugin opened the door. A weak midday light stained the snow on the threshold. Har rose, his own hands trembling slightly. He said nothing, and Morgon, as familiar with the mind of the King as he was with his own, felt the panic die away, a stillness take its place. He went to the door, his steps halting, and leaned on the frame, breathing the wind, his limp hands staining his tunic. He felt an odd sorrow, as though he had turned away forever from something nameless in him. Har put a hand on his shoulder.

"Rest, now. Rest. Hugin—"

"I know. I will take him."

"Bind his hands. Stay with him. Both of you: rest."

9

AS MORGON'S HANDS HEALED, HAR CONTINUED THE training; Morgon learned to take the vesta-shape for long periods of time. Hugin guided him around Yrye; they ate pine in the forest fringing Yrye, climbed the steep crags and forests of Grim Mountain, rising behind Yrye. The vesta-instincts confused Morgon at first; he struggled against them as against deep water, and would find himself standing half-naked in deep winter, with Hugin nuzzling at him, his mind-voice running into Morgon's.

Morgon, let's run. You like vesta-running; you are not afraid of that. Morgon, come out of the cold.

And they would run for miles in the snow without tiring, their hooves barely skimming the snow, the great hearts and muscles of their bodies fine-tuned to the effortless movement. They would return to Yrye in the evenings, sometimes late at night, bringing back within them the silence of the still winter night. Har would be waiting for them in the hall, talking to Aia or listening to his harpist play softly beside the hearth. Morgon spoke little to Har during this time, as though something in his mind were healing along with his hands. Har waited, watched, silent himself. Finally one night Morgon and Hugin returned late, and the unexpected sound of their laughter, curtailed sharply as they entered, made Aia smile. Morgon went to Har unhesitantly, sat down beside him, while Hugin went to get food. He looked down at the palms of his hands, the bone-white imprint of vesta-horns on them.

Har said, "It's not such a terrible thing to be, a vesta, is it?"

He smiled. "No. I love it. I love the silence of it. But how will I explain to Eliard?"

"That," Har said a little drily, "is liable to be the least of your worries. Other men have come to me through the years begging me to teach them the mind-work, shape-changing; very, very few have ever left that room with the vesta-scars on their hands. You have great gifts. Hed was far too small a world for you."

"It's unprecedented. How will I explain that to the High One?"

"Why must you justify your abilities?"

Morgon looked at him. He said peacefully, "Har, you know, in spite of the arguments you used with me, that I am still answerable to the High One as the land-ruler of Hed, no matter how many deadly harpists out of the sea call me Star-Bearer. I would like to keep it that way, if possible."

The smile deepened in Har's eyes. "Then perhaps the High One will justify yourself to you. Are you ready to look for Suth?"

"Yes. I have some questions to ask him."

"Good. I believe he may be in the lake-lands north of Grim Mountain, on the fringe of the great northern wastes. There is a large herd of vesta on the other side of the mountain; I rarely join them. I've searched the rest of my kingdom and have found no sign of him. Hugin will take you there."

"Come with us."

"I can't. He would only run from me, as he has done for seven hundred years." He paused. Morgon saw his thoughts drift back into some memory, his eyes narrow.

He said, "I know. That's the blade that harrows the brain: Why? You knew Suth: what would he have run from?"

"I thought he would have died rather than run from anything. Are you sure you are ready? It may take months."

"I'm ready."

"Then leave at dawn, quietly, with Hugin. Look beyond Grim; if you cannot find Suth there, look along the Ose—but watch for trappers. Let the vesta know you. They will sense you are also a man, and Suth will hear of you if he is in contact with them. If there is even a hint of danger, return to Yrye at once."

"I will," Morgon said absently. He saw suddenly, in his mind's eye, long, quiet weeks beyond the snow-covered mountain, in the backlands of the world, where he would move to a rhythm of night and day, wind, snow and silence he had come to love. Har's eyes, insistent on his face, brought him out of his dreaming. There was a wry edge of warning in them.

"If you die in vesta-shape on my lands, I will have that imperturbable harpist on my doorstep asking why. So be careful."

They left at dawn, both in vesta-shape. Hugin led Morgon up the slopes of Grim Mountain, through high rocky passes where mountain goats stared at them curiously and hawks wheeled on the wind, searching for food. They slept that night among the rocks, then descended the next day into the lake-land beyond Grim, where no one but a few trappers lived, collecting skins for traders on the edge of the northern wastes. Herds of vesta passed like mist through the land, untouched, untroubled. Morgon and Hugin joined them quietly, unchallenged by the leaders of the herds who accepted them as they accepted Har, as strange but not threatening. They moved with the herds, ranging through the lake-lands, feeding on pine. They slept in the open at night, the winds scarcely penetrating their long fur. Wolves circled them occasionally, hungry yet wary; Morgon heard their distant howling in his dreams. He responded to them without fear, yet aware of their power if they came upon a young or aged vesta strayed from the herd. When he and Hugin had searched one herd for images of the one-eyed Suth, they moved to find another in the deep forests, or beside frozen, moon-colored lakes. Finally, Morgon found a pattern of images repeating itself in the minds of one herd: the image of a vesta with one eye purple, the other white as web.

He stayed with that herd, eating, sleeping with it, waiting in hope that the half-blind vesta would join it. Hugin, troubled by the same image, ranged away from the herd among the lakes and hills, searching. The moon grew round above them, dwindled and began to grow again, and Morgon grew restless himself. He began to roam in curiosity, searching the low hills of the northern boundaries. One day he went over them and looked across at the flat, empty wastes. The winds lifted snow, swept it like sand across the plains, honed into a single, unbroken line the bounds of the world. No life seemed hidden beneath the snow; the sky itself was empty, colorless. In the far west, he saw the great head of Erlenstar Mountain, and the flat, white lands behind it. He turned, oddly cold, and went back into Osterland.

Coming back down from the hills, he saw a vesta, grey-white with age, with its horns oddly trapped by something beneath the snow. Its head lowered, shoulders and haunches straining against the hold on its horns, it could not see the grey slink of wolves gathering behind it. Morgon caught a scent of them, thick, acrid in the wind. He found himself suddenly racing towards them, making a sound he had never heard from himself before.

The wolves scattered, whining, among the rocks. One of them, mad with hunger, snapped at Morgon's face then turned to leap at the trapped vesta. An odd rage surged through Morgon. He reared, striking. His sharp hooves caught the wolf's head, crushed it, spattering blood on the snow. The cloying smell welled over him; a sudden confusion of instinct thrust him out of the vesta-shape. He found himself barefoot in the snow, struggling with a wrench of nausea.

He moved upwind, knelt before the vesta. He groped in the snow beneath its horns, feeling the hidden branch that had trapped it. He reached up to soothe the vesta with one hand, and found himself looking into a blind eye.

He sat back on his heels. The wind searched the threads of his light tunic, racking his body, but he did not notice. He let his thoughts drift curiously beyond the blind eye, and the swift, skillful withdrawal of thought told him what he wanted to know.

"Suth?" The vesta eyed him, motionless. "I've been looking for you."

A darkness welled over his mind. He struggled with it desperately, not knowing how to avoid the single, insistent command that beat over and over in his mind like the single beat of water in a soundless cave. He felt his hands slip into the snow, wrench at the hidden branch. Then the impulse ceased abruptly. He felt his thoughts searched and did not move until the strange mind withdrew and he heard the command again: *Free me.*

He heaved the branch loose. The vesta straightened, flinging back its head. Then it vanished. A man stood before Morgon, lean, powerful, his white hair fraying in the wind, his single eye grey-gold.

His hand brushed across Morgon's face, seeking the stars; he lifted Morgon's hand, turned it palm-upward, traced the scar on it, and something like a smile flashed in his eye.

Then he put his hands on Morgon's shoulders, as though feeling the humanness of him, and said incredulously, "Hed?"

"Morgon of Hed."

"The hope I saw a thousand years ago and before is a Prince of Hed?" His voice was deep, like a wind's voice; long-disused. "You have met Har; he left his mark on you. Good. You'll need every bone of help you can get."

"I need your help."

The wizard's thin mouth twisted. "I can give you nothing. Har should have known better than to send you for me. He has two good eyes; he should have seen."

"I don't understand." He was beginning to feel the cold. "You gave Har riddles; I need answers to them. Why did you leave Lungold? Why have you hidden even from Har?"

"Why would anyone hide from the tooth of his own heart?" The lean hands shook him a little. "Can you not see? Not even you? I am trapped. I am dead, speaking to you."

Morgon was silent, staring at him. Behind the flame of laughter like Har's in his single eye, there was an emptiness vaster than the northern wastes. He said, "I don't understand. You have a son; Har cares for him."

The wizard's eyes closed. He drew a deep breath. "So. I hoped Har might find him. I am so tired, so tired of this. . . . Tell Har to teach you to guard against compulsion. What are you of all people doing with three stars on your face in this game of death?"

"I don't know," Morgon said tautly. "I can't escape them."

"I want to see the end of this; I want to see it —you are so impossible, you might win this game."

"What game? Suth, what has been happening for seven hundred years? What keeps you trapped here living like an animal? What can I do to help you?"

"Nothing. I am dead."

"Then do something for me! I need help! The third stricture of Ghisteslwchlohm is this: The wizard who hearing a cry for help turns away, the wizard who watching an evil does not speak, the wizard who searching for truth looks away from it: these are the wizards of false power. I understand running, but not when there is no place left to run to."

Something stirred deep in the emptiness of the gold eye. Suth smiled, again with the wry twist of mouth that reminded Morgon of Har.

He said with an odd gentleness, "I place my life in your hands, Star-Bearer. Ask."

"Why did you run from Lungold?"

"I ran from Lungold because—" His voice stopped. He reached suddenly to Morgon, his breath coming in sharp, white flashes. Morgon caught at him, felt himself pulled down in the grip and sag of the wizard.

"Suth!"

Suth's hands twisted the cloth at his throat, forced him closer to the open, straining mouth that gave him one final word formed with the husk of its breath.

"Ohm . . ."

HE CARRIED THE DEAD WIZARD ON HIS BACK TO YRYE. Hugin walked beside him, sometimes in vesta shape, sometimes, for a mile or so, in his own shape, a tall, silent boy with one hand holding Suth balanced on the vesta beside him. As they travelled over the mountain, Morgon felt in some deep place an impatience with the vesta-form, as though he had worn it too long. The land stretched before them, white to the white sky under the mold of winter. Yrye itself lay half-hidden in drifts of snow. When they reached it at last, Har was on the threshold to meet them.

He said nothing, took the body from Morgon's back and watched him turn at last into himself, with two months' growth of hair and the scars puckered on his hands. Morgon opened his mouth to say something; he could not speak. Har said softly, "He has been dead for seven hundred years. I'll take him. Go in."

"No," Hugin said. Har, bent over Suth's body, looked up at him.

"Then help me."

They carried him together around the back of the house. Morgon went inside. Someone threw fur over his shoulders as he passed; he drew it around him absently, scarcely feeling it, scarcely seeing the handful of curious faces turned toward him, watching. He sat down by the fire, poured himself wine. Aia sat down on the bench beside him. She put a hand on his arm, gripped it gently.

"I'm glad you're safe, you and Hugin, my children. Don't grieve for Suth."

He found his voice. "How did you know?"

"I know Har's mind. He'll bury his sorrow like a man burying silver in the night. Don't let him."

Morgon looked down into his cup. Then he put it on the table, pushed the heels of his hands against his eyes. "I should have known," he whispered. "I should have thought. One wizard, alive after seven centuries, and I forced him out of hiding so he could die in my arms . . ." He heard Har and Hugin come in, dropped his hands. Har sat down in his chair. Hugin sat at his feet, his white head resting against Har's knee. His eyes closed. Har's hand rested a moment in his hair. His eyes went to Morgon's face.

"Tell me."

"Take it from me," Morgon said wearily. "You knew him. You tell me." He sat passively while memories of the days and long white nights passed through his mind, culminated in the wolf killing, in the last few moments of the wizard's life. Finished, Har loosed him, sat quietly, his eyes impassive.

"Who is Ohm?"

Morgon stirred. "Ghisteslwchlohm, I think—the founder of the School of Wizards of Lungold."

"The Founder is still alive?"

"I don't know who else it could be." His voice caught.

"What troubles you? What have you not told me?"

"Ohm—Har, one of the . . . one of the Masters at Caithnard was named Ohm. He . . . I studied with him. I respected him greatly. The Morgol of Herun suggested that he might be the Founder." Har's hands closed suddenly on the arms of his chair. "There was no evidence—"

"The Morgol of Herun would not say something like that without evidence."

"It was scant—just his name, and the fact that she couldn't . . . she couldn't see through him—"

"The Founder of Lungold is at Caithnard? Still controlling whatever wizards may be alive?"

"It's conjecture. It's only that. Why would he have kept his own name for all the world to guess—"

"Who would guess, after seven centuries? And who would be powerful enough to control him?"

"The High One—"

"The High One." Har rose abruptly; Hugin started. The wolf-king moved to the fire. "His silence is almost more mysterious than Suth's. He has never been one to meddle greatly in our affairs, but this much restraint is incredible."

"He let Suth die."

"Suth waited to die," Har said impatiently, and Morgon's voice snapped away from him furiously.

"He was alive! Until I found him!"

"Stop blaming yourself. He was dead. The man you spoke to was not Suth but a husk that had no name."

"That's not true—"

"What do you call life? Would you call me living if I turned in fear away from you, refused to give you something that would save your life? Would you call me Har?"

"Yes." His voice softened. "Corn bears its name in the seed in the ground, in the green stalk, in the yellow dried stalk whose leaves whisper riddles to the wind. So Suth bore his name, giving me a riddle in the last breath of his life. So I blame myself because there is no longer anywhere in this world the man that bore his name. He took the vesta-form; he had a son among them; there were things that somewhere beneath his fear and helplessness, he remembered how to love."

Hugin's head dropped forward against his knees. Har's eyes closed. He stood at the fire without speaking, without moving, while lines of weariness and pain worked themselves through the mask of his face.

Morgon twisted on the bench, dropped his face in his arms on the table behind him. He whispered, "If Master Ohm is Ghisteslwchlohm, the High One will know. I'll ask him."

"And then?"

"And then . . . I don't know. There are so many pieces that don't fit. . . . It's like the shards I tried to fit together once in Ymris, not having all the pieces, not even knowing if the pieces belonged together at all."

"You can't travel alone to the High One."

"Yes, I can. You've taught me how. Har, nothing alive could stop me from finishing this journey now. If I had to, I'd drag my own bones out of a grave to the High One. I must have answers."

He felt Har's hands on his shoulders, unexpectedly gentle, and raised his head.

Har said softly, "Finish your journey; there's nothing any of us can do without answers. But go no farther than that alone. There are kings from Anuin to Isig who will help you, and a harpist at Erlenstar Mountain who is skilled at more things than harping. Will you give me this promise? That if Master Ohm is Ghisteslwchlohm, you will not rush blindly back to Caithnard to tell him you know?"

Morgon shrugged a little, wearily. "I don't believe he is. I can't. But I promise."

"And come back to Yrye, rather than going straight to Hed. You will be far more dangerous when you are less ignorant, and I think the forces gathering against you will move swiftly then."

Morgon was silent; a pain touched his heart and

withdrew. He whispered, "I won't go home. . . . Ohm, the shape-changers, even the High One—they seem to be balanced in a false peace, waiting for some kind of signal to act. . . . When they finally do, I don't want to give them any reason to be near Hed." He stirred, his face turning to Har's. Their eyes met a moment in an unspoken knowledge of one another. Morgon's head bowed. "Tomorrow, I will go to Isig."

"I'll take you as far as Kyrth. Hugin can ride with us, carry your harp. In vesta-shape, it should take only two days."

Morgon nodded. "All right. Thank you." He paused, looking again at Har; his hands moved a little, helplessly, as though groping for a word.

"Thank you."

They left Yrye at dawn. Morgon and the wolf-king were in vesta-form; Hugin rode Har, carrying the harp and some clothes Aia had packed for Morgon. They ran westward through the quiet day, across farmland buried in a crust of unbroken snow, skirting towns whose chimney smoke wove into an ash-white sky. They ran far into the night, through moonlit forests, up the low rocky foothills until they reached the Ose, winding down northward from Isig. They fed there, slept awhile, then rose before dawn to continue up the Ose, across the foothills into the shadow of Isig Mountain. The white head of the mountain, blind with snow, loomed over them as they ran, its depths secret, inexhaustible with minerals, metals, bright, precious jewels. The trade-city Kyrth sprawled at its roots; the Ose wandered through it on its long journey toward the sea. West of Kyrth, rocky peaks and hills jutted like a rough sea, parting between waves to form the winding pass that led to Erlenstar Mountain.

They stopped just before they reached the city. Morgon took his own shape, put the heavy, furred cloak Hugin had carried for him over his shoulders, slid the harp and pack straps around his neck. He stood, waiting for the great vesta beside him to take Har's shape once again, but it only watched him out of eyes that seemed to glint in the fading afternoon, with a familiar, elusive smile. So he slid an arm around its neck, pushed his face a moment against the white, cold fur. He turned to Hugin, embraced him; the boy said softly, "Find what killed Suth. And then come back. Come back."

"I will."

He left them without looking back. He followed the river into Kyrth, found the main road through the city crowded even in mid-winter with traders, trappers, craftsmen, miners. The road wound up the mountain above the city, the snow on it broken and scarred by cartwheels. It grew quiet in the twilight; the trees began to blur together. In the distance, obscured sometimes by the jut of mountain, Morgon saw the dark walls of Danan Isig's house, the jagged lines of its walls shaped as though the wind and weather and restless earth had formed them. After a while, out of the corner of his eye, he saw a man who walked beside him quietly as a shadow.

Morgon stopped abruptly. The man was big, thewed like a tree, with hair and beard grey-gold against the white fur of his hood. His eyes were the color of pine. He said quickly,

"I mean no harm. I am curious. Are you a harpist?"

Morgon hesitated. The green eyes were gentle, mild on his face; he said finally, his voice still a little rough from the long months away from men, "No. I'm travelling. I wanted to ask Danan Isig for shelter for the night, but I don't know—does he keep his house open to strangers?"

"In midwinter, any traveller is welcome. Did you come from Osterland?"

"Yes. From Yryr."

"The wolf-king's lair . . . I'm going to Harte now myself. May I walk with you?"

Morgon nodded. They walked a little in silence, the hard, broken snow crunching underfoot. The man drew a deep breath of pine-scented air, let it mist away. He said placidly, "I met Har once. He came to Isig disguised as a trader selling furs and amber. He told me privately he was trying to find a trapper who had been selling vesta-pelts to the traders, which was true, but I think he also came out of curiosity, to see Isig Mountain."

"Did he find the trapper?"

"I believe so. He also walked the veins and roots of Isig before he left. Is he well?"

"Yes."

"I'm glad to hear it. He must be an aged wolf now, as I am an ancient tree." He stopped. "Listen. You can hear where we stand the waters running deep below us through Isig."

Morgon listened. The murmur and hiss of water endlessly falling wound deep below the wind's voice. Cliffs bare of snow reared above them, melting into grey-white mists. Kyrth looked small below them, sheltered in a single curve of mountain.

"I would like to see the inside of Isig," he said suddenly.

"Would you? I'll show it to you. I know that mountain better than I know my own mind."

Morgon looked at him. The aged, broad face crinkled a little under his gaze. He said softly, "Who are you? Are you Danan Isig? Is that why I didn't hear you? Because you had just come out of your own shape-changing?"

"Was I a tree? Sometimes I stand so long in the snow watching the trees wrapped in their private thoughts that I forget myself, become one of them. They are as old as I am, old as Isig . . ." He paused, his eyes running over Morgon's untrimmed hair, his harp, and added, "I heard something from the traders about a Prince of Hed travelling to Erlenstar Mountain, but that may only have been rumor; you know how they gossip . . ."

Morgon smiled. The pine-colored eyes smiled back

at him. They started walking again; snow began to drift down, catching in the fur on their hoods, in their hair. The road swung wide around a jut of hillside to reveal again the rough black walls and pine-shaped towers of Harte. Its windows, patterned and stained with color, were already blazing with torchlight. The road ran into its mouth.

"The doorway into Isig," Danan Isig said. "No one goes in or out of the mountain without my knowledge. The greatest craftsmen of the realm come to train in my home, work with the metals and jewels of Isig. My son Ash teaches them, as Sol used to before he was killed. It was Sol who cut the stars that Yrth set in your harp."

Morgon touched the harp strap. A sense of age, of roots, of beginnings was waking in him at Danan's words. "Why did Yrth put stars on the harp?"

"I don't know. I didn't wonder, then. . . . Yrth worked months on that harp, carving it, cutting the designs for the inlay; he had my craftsmen cut the ivory and set the silver and stones in it. And then he went up into the highest room in the oldest tower of Harte to tune the harp. He stayed seven days and seven nights, while I closed the forges in the yard so that the pounding wouldn't bother him. Finally, he came down and played it for us. There was no more beautiful harp in the world. He said he had taken its voices from the waters and winds of Isig. It held us breathless, the harping and the harpist. . . . When he had finished playing, he stood still a moment, looking down at it. Then he passed the flat of his hand over the strings, and they went mute. When we protested, he laughed and said the harp would choose its own harpist. The next day he left, taking it with him. When he returned to my service a year later, he never mentioned the harp. It was as though we had all dreamed the making of it."

Morgon stopped. His hand twisted in the harp strap while he stared at the distant, darkening trees as though somehow he could shape the wizard out of the twilight. "I wonder—"

Danan said, "What is it?"

"Nothing. I would like to speak to him."

"So would I. He was in my service almost from the Years of Settlement. He came to me from some strange place west of the realm I had never heard of; he would leave Isig for years at a time, exploring other lands, meeting other wizards, other kings . . . every time he returned, he would be a little more powerful, gentler. He had a curiosity like a trader's and a laugh that boomed down into the lower mines. It was he who discovered the cave of the Lost Ones. That was the only time I ever saw him completely serious. He told me I had built my home over a shadow, and that I would be wise to forbid the waking of that shadow. So my miners have been careful never to disturb it, especially since they found Sol dead at its doorway. . . ." He was silent a little, then added, as though he had heard Morgon's unspoken question, "Yrth took me to it once to show me. I don't know who made the door to the cave; it was there before I came, green and black marble. The inner cave was incredibly rich and beautiful, but— there was nothing in it that I could see."

"Nothing."

"Just stones, silence, and a terrible sense of something lying just beyond eyesight, like a dread in the bottom of your heart. I asked Yrth what it was, but he never told me. Something happened there before the settlement of Isig, long before the coming of men to the realm of the High One."

"Perhaps during the wars of the Earth-Masters."

"I think there may be a connection. But what, I don't know; and the High One, if he knows what happened, has never said."

Morgon thought of the beautiful, ruined city on Wind Plain, of the glass shards he had uncovered like a hint of an answer in one of the empty, roofless rooms.

And suddenly, thinking of it, the terrible dread of a simple answer struck him, and he stopped again in the still, icy dusk, the mountain polished smooth and white as a bone in front of him. He whispered, "Beware the unanswered riddle."

"What?"

"No one knows what destroyed the Earth-Masters. Who could have been more powerful than they were, and what shape that power has taken . . ."

"It was thousands of years ago," Danan said. "What could that have to do with us?"

"Nothing. Perhaps. But we've been assuming just that for thousands of years, and the wise man assumes nothing. . . ."

The mountain-king said wonderingly, "What is it you see ahead of us in the darkness that no one else can?"

"I don't know. Something without a name. . . ."

They reached the dark arch of the gates of Harte just as the snow began to fall again. The yard, with its many forges and workshops, was nearly empty; here and there a red-gold light shown through a half-opened door; the shadow of some craftsman at his work spilled across the threshold. Danan led Morgon across the yard into a hall whose rough walls were filigreed with flickering colors of jewels still embedded in the stone. A stream cut a curved path through the floor; a great firebed suspended above it warmed the stones, fire dancing over the dark water. Miners, craftsmen dressed simply in the colors of the mountain, traders in their rich garb, trappers in fur and leather glanced up as Danan entered, and Morgon shifted instinctively to a line of shadow beyond the torch's reach.

Danan said gently, "There's a quiet room in the east tower where you can wash and rest; come down later when it's not so crowded. Most of these men will return to Kyrth after supper; they only work here." He led through a side door out of the hall, up a stairway wind-

ing through the core of a wide tower. He added, "This
is the tower Yrth stayed in. Talies used to visit him
here, and Suth, a couple of times. Suth was a wild one,
hair white as snow even when he was young. He
frightened the miners, but I saw him once changing into
shape after shape to amuse my children." He stopped
on a landing, drew back heavy hangings of white fur in
a doorway. "I'll send someone to make up your fire."
He paused, said a little hesitantly, "If it isn't asking too
much of you, I would love to hear that harp again."

Morgon smiled. "No. It's not asking too much.
Thank you. I'm grateful for your kindness."

He went into the room, sliding the straps from his
shoulder. The walls were hung with fur and tapestry,
but the hearth was swept clean and the room was cold.
Morgon sat down in a chair beside the hearth. The
stones formed a circle of silence about him. He could
hear nothing, no laughter from the hall, no wind outside. A loneliness unlike even the loneliness of his path
through the unclaimed lands touched him. He closed
his eyes, felt weariness deeper than sleep sucking at the
core of him. He rose restlessly, pulling away from it.
Men came in then, bringing wood, water, wine, food;
he watched them build the fire, light torches, set water
to heat. When they were gone, he stood for a long time
at the fire, staring into it. The water began to hiss; he
undressed slowly, washed. He ate something he could
not taste, poured wine, sat without drinking it while the
night locked like a fist around the tower and the strange
dread eddied like a tide deep in his heart.

His eyes closed again. For a while he ran with the
vesta on the surface of his dreams, until he found himself floundering in the snow in his own shape as they
melted away in the distance. Then, the loneliness
poignant, unbearable, he traversed space and time
with a wizard's skill, found himself at Akren. Eliard
and Grim Oakland were talking in front of the fire; he
went towards them eagerly, said Eliard's name. Eliard

turned, and at the blankness in his eyes Morgon saw himself suddenly, his hair lank, his face drawn, the vesta scars vivid on his hands. He said his name. Eliard, shaking his head, said bewilderedly, *You must be mistaken. Morgon isn't a vesta.* Morgon turned to Tristan, who was holding some pointless, rambling discussion with Snog Nutt. She smiled at him eagerly, hopefully, but the hope died quickly and an uneasiness came into her eyes. Snog Nutt said sorrowfully, *He said he would fix my leaking roof, before the rain, but he went away and he never did, and he hasn't come.* He found himself abruptly at Caithnard, pounding on a door; Rood, flinging it open with a whirl of black sleeve, said irritably, *You're too late. Anyway, she's the second most beautiful woman in An; she can't marry a vesta.* Turning, Morgon saw one of the Masters walking down the hall. He ran to catch up. The bowed, hooded head lifted finally at his pleadings; Master Ohm's eyes met his, grave, reproachful, and he stopped, appalled. The Master walked away from him without speaking; he said over and over without response, *I'm sorry, I'm sorry, I'm sorry.*

He found himself on Wind Plain. It was dark; the sea lay heaving, blue-green with unearthly lights on a moonless night; so close he could see the light from Danan's house lay Isig Mountain. Something was gathering itself in the darkness; he could not tell whether it was the wind or the sea; he only knew that an enormity was building itself, huge, nameless, inexorable, sucking into itself all strength, all laws and patterns, all songs, riddles, histories, to explode them into chaos on Wind Plain. He began to run desperately for shelter while the winds howled and the sea half a mile away raised waves so high the spray lashed across his face. He headed for the light of Danan's house. He realized slowly, as he ran, that Harte was broken, empty as an Earth-Masters' city, and that the bone-white light came from deep within Isig. He stopped. A voice split through the mountain out of a cave whose green marble door had not been opened for centuries, cut through the growling, bickering of wind and sea, and said his name.

"Star-Bearer."

10

HE WOKE WITH A START, HIS HEART POUNDING, listening for the echo of the voice that had wakened him; it seemed to linger, a strange voice, neither man's nor woman's, among the stones. Someone was gripping him, saying his name, someone so familiar that Morgon asked unsurprised, "Did you call me?" Then his hands rose, locked on the harpist's arms.

"Deth."

"You were dreaming."

"Yes." The tower walls, the fire, the silence were forming around him again. His hands loosened slowly, dropped. The harpist, a dust of snow on his shoulders and hair, slid the harp from his shoulder, leaned it against the wall.

"I chose to wait for you quietly in Kyrth rather than at Harte; Danan wasn't sure if I was still there, so he didn't tell you." The even, undisturbed voice was soothing. "You took much longer than I expected."

"I got caught in a blizzard." He straightened, running his hands over his face. "Then I met Har . . ." His head lifted abruptly; he stared at the harpist. "You were waiting for me? You expected—Deth, how long have you been here?"

"Two months." He took his coat off; snow spattered into the fire. "I left Herun the day after you did, travelled up the Ose, without stopping, to Kyrth. I asked Danan to keep watch for you, told him where to reach me in Kyrth, and then—waited." He paused a moment. "I was worried."

Morgon watched his face. He whispered, "I had every intention of returning to Hed. You knew that. You couldn't have known I would come here, not after two months, not in dead winter."

"I chose to trust that you would come."

"Why?"

"Because if you had turned your back on your name, on the riddles you must answer—if you had gone back to Hed alone, unprotected, to accept the death you knew must come—then it wouldn't have mattered where I went, whether to Erlenstar Mountain or the bottom of the sea. I have lived for a thousand years, and I can recognize the smell of doom."

Morgon closed his eyes. The word, hanging in the air like a harp note between them, seemed to ease something out of him; his shoulders slumped. "Doom. You see it, too. Deth, I touched the bone of it in Osterland. I killed Suth."

He heard the harpist's voice untuned for the first time. "You did what?"

He opened his eyes. "I'm sorry. I mean that he died because of me. Har saved my life in that blizzard, so I gave him a promise, ignoring the fact that it is unwise to promise things blindly to the wolf-king." He turned a palm upward; the scar shone like a withered moon in the firelight. "I learned the vesta-shape. I ran with the vesta for two months with Suth's son Hugin, who has white hair and purple eyes. I found Suth behind Grim Mountain, an old vesta with one blind eye that he had lost, riddling. He died there."

"How?"

Morgon's hands closed suddenly on the chair arms. "I asked him why he had run from Lungold—I quoted the third stricture of the Founder to him, demanding help when he knew—he knew. . . . He made a choice; he tried to answer me, but he died trying. He pulled me down with him, there at the end of the world where there was nothing but snow and wind and vesta, he died, he was killed, the only wizard seen by men for seven centuries; I was left holding him, holding the last word he ever spoke like a riddle too terrible to answer—"

"What word?"

"Ohm. Ghisteslwchlohm. The Founder of Lungold killed Suth."

Morgon heard the soft, swift draw of the harpist's breath. His eyes were hidden, his face oddly still. He said, "I knew Suth."

"You knew Master Ohm. You knew Ghisteslwchlohm." His grip was rigid on the wood. "Deth, is Master Ohm the Founder of Lungold?"

"I will take you to Erlenstar Mountain. Then, with permission from the High One, if he does not answer that question for you, I will."

Morgon nodded. He said more calmly, "I'm wondering how many other wizards are still alive under Ghisteslwchlohm's power. I'm also wondering why the High One has never acted."

"Perhaps because his business is the land, not the school of wizards of Lungold. Perhaps he has already begun to act in ways you do not recognize."

"I hope so." He took a cup Deth poured for him, swallowed wine. He added after a moment, "Deth, Har gave me five riddles Suth had given him. He suggested I answer them since I had nothing better to do with my life. One of them is: Who will come in the time's ending and what will he bring? I assume that the Star-Bearer is the one who will come; I have come; I don't know what it is I will bring; but what troubles me most is not who, or what, but when. The time's ending. Walking to Harte with Danan I remembered the ruined cities on Wind Plain, on King's Mouth Plain, and how no one really knows what destroyed the Earth-Masters. It happened long before the Years of Settlement; we assumed because the stones had fallen, the weeds grew between them, that a great, terrible war had come and gone, and nothing more of it existed but the empty stones. We also assumed that the wizards were dead. The one thing I know that could destroy us all is the death of the High One. I'm afraid that whatever destroyed the Earth-Masters before the realm was even formed, has been waiting ever since to challenge the last of the Earth-Masters."

"I think it's quite probable," Deth said quietly. He leaned forward, his face etched with fire, and roused the half-log on the hearth. A flurry of sparks burned in the air like fiery snow.

"Has the High One ever explained the destruction of the cities?"

"Not as far as I know. One of the Masters at Caithnard when I was there said he had made a journey to ask the High One that, since it was one of the unanswered riddles on their lists; the High One simply said that the cities were ancient, empty before he mastered the land-law of the realm."

"Which is saying either that he doesn't know, or that he doesn't choose to tell."

"It's unlikely that he doesn't know."

"Then why—" He stopped. "Only the High One could explain the High One. So I will have to ask him."

Deth looked at him. "I have a question of my own," he said slowly. "I asked it in Herun; you chose not to answer it. But now you wear vesta-scars on your hands, you have spoken your own name, and you are putting your mind to this mystery like a Master. I would like to ask it again."

Morgon, thinking back, said, "Oh. That."

"What was it that made you leave Herun to return home?"

"Something Corrig changed into. And the laughter

in his eyes when I killed him." He rose restlessly, went to a window, gazed out at the unrelieved blackness that enclosed Isig.

The harpist said behind him, "What shape?"

"A sword. With three stars on its hilt." He turned abruptly at the silence. "I have thought about it, and the conclusion I have come to is that no one, not even the High One himself, can force me to claim it."

"That's true." Deth's voice was changeless, but there was a faint line between his brows. "Did it occur to you to ask yourself where Corrig might have seen it?"

"No. I'm not interested."

"Morgon. The shape-changers know it belongs to you, that inevitably you will find it, as you found the harp, even though you may not claim it. And when you do, they will be there, waiting."

In the silence, a pitch-laden branch wailed softly. Morgon moved a little at the sound. He said, "I'm nearly at Erlenstar Mountain—that sword could be anywhere . . ."

"Perhaps. But Danan told me once that Yrth made a sword he showed to no one, centuries before he made the harp. Where he put it, no one knows; only one thing is certain: he said he had buried it beneath the place where he forged it."

"Where did—" He stopped. He saw the sword again, recognized the master touch in the flawless designs on its blade, the sure, purposeful shaping of the stars. He put a hand to his eyes, asked, though he already knew the answer, "Where was it forged?"

"Here. In Isig Mountain."

MORGON WENT DOWN WITH DETH THEN, THE HARP over his shoulder, to talk to Danan. The mountain-king, sitting beside the fire with his children and grand-children in the quiet hall, looked up with a smile as they entered.

"Come, sit down. Deth, I wasn't sure if you were still in Kyrth or if you had lost hope and chanced the Pass when I sent for you today. You've been so silent. Morgon, this is my daughter Vert, my son Ash, and these—" he paused to lift a small girl tugging herself onto his knee, "—are their children. They all wanted to hear your harping."

Morgon sat down, a little dazed. A tall, fair man with Danan's eyes, a slender woman with hair the color of pine bark, and a dozen children of varying shapes were looking at him curiously.

The woman, Vert, said despairingly to him, "I'm sorry, but Bere wanted to come, so all of mine had to come, and where my children go, Ash's go, so—I hope you don't mind them." She put her hand on the shoulder of a young boy with blunt, black hair and her grey eyes. "This is Bere."

Another black head appeared suddenly at Morgon's knee: a little girl hardly big enough to walk. She stared up at him, then, going unsteady on her feet, clutched at him drunkenly. She grinned toothlessly at him as he slid his hand down her back to steady her, and his mouth twitched. Ash said, "That one belongs to Vert: Suny. My wife is in Caithnard, and Vert's husband, who is a trader, is making a winter run to Anuin, so we put them all together for the time being. I don't know how we'll ever get them sorted out again."

Morgon, his fingers rubbing up and down between Suny's shoulder blades as she gripped his knee, looked up suddenly. "You all came to hear me play?"

Ash nodded. "Please. If you don't mind. That harp and the making of it are legends in Isig. When I heard you were here with it, I couldn't believe it. I wanted to bring all the craftsmen in Kyrth with me to see it, but my father restrained me."

Morgon untied the harp case. Suny tugged the case strings curiously out of his fingers; Bere whispered, "Suny—" She ignored him; he stepped to Morgon's side, lifted her up patiently and held her. Morgon, aware of the curious, expectant faces watching him, said futiley, "I haven't played in two months." No one answered. The stars, as he uncovered the harp, pulled it free of the case, caught fire; the white moons seemed rimmed with it as the flame's reflection travelled a liquid path down the silver inlay. He touched a string; the note sounded in the silence, pure, sweet, hesitant as a question; he heard someone loose a breath.

Ash's hand moved involuntarily toward the stars, dropped. He breathed, "Who did the inlay?"

"Zec of Hicon, in Herun—I can't remember his full name," Danan said. "He was trained by Sol. Yrth designed the patterns."

"And Sol cut those stars. May I see them?" he pleaded, and Morgon passed the harp to him. Something small, formless had bloomed in the back of his mind at Ash's words; he could not trace it. Bere peered over Ash's head, his lips parted as Ash studied the harp; Suny, reaching wildly for a gleaming harp string, startled him and he straightened, shifting his hold of her.

Vert begged, "Ash, stop counting the facets on the stones; I want to hear it."

Ash handed it reluctantly back to Morgon. Morgon took it as reluctantly, and Vert, her eyes softening with sudden understanding, said, "Play something you love. Play something from Hed."

Morgon righted the harp on his knee. His fingers strayed over the strings aimlessly a moment, then wandered into the gentle, sad chords of a ballad. The rich, beautiful tones only he could sound reassured him; even the simple love-ballad he had heard a hundred times took on an ancient dignity. As he played, he began to smell oak burning in the fire before him, saw the light around him wash over the walls of Akren. The song woke a peace in him that he knew instinctively was in Hed that night: a stillness of land dormant under snow, of animals dreaming placidly in warm places. The peace touched his face, easing, for the moment, the tension and weariness out of it. Then two things pieced together in the back of his mind, effortlessly, inarguably, and he stopped, his fingers motionless on the harp strings.

There was a small, inarticulate protest. Then he heard Deth's voice out of the shadows where he had seated himself, away from the children, "What is it?"

"Sol. He wasn't killed by traders because he was too frightened to hide from them in the Cave of the Lost Ones. He was killed—as my parents were killed, as the Morgol Dhairrhuwyth was killed—by shape-changers. He had gone into the cave and come out again to die on the threshold because of what he had seen. And what he saw in there was Yrth's starred sword."

They were still, even the children, their faces turned to him, unblinking. Then Vert shivered as though a cold wind had touched her, and Ash, all the joy of the harp faded from his face said, "What sword?"

Morgon looked at Danan. The king's lips were parted; he seemed struggling back toward a memory. "That sword . . . I remember. Yrth forged it in secret; he said he had buried it. I never saw it; no one did. That was so long ago, before Sol was born, when we were just opening the upper mines. I never thought about it. But how could you possibly know where it is? Or what it looks like? Or that Sol was killed because of it?"

Morgon's fingers moved from the strings to clasp the wood; his eyes fell to it as though the neat sweep of strings ordered his thoughts. "I know a sword exists with three stars on it, exactly like the stars on this harp; I know the shape-changers have seen it, too. My parents were drowned crossing from Caithnard to Hed bringing this harp to me. The Morgol Dhairrhuwyth was killed travelling through Isig Pass to answer a riddle about three stars. The wizard Suth was killed in Osterland a week ago because he knew too much about those stars and tried to tell me—" Ash's hand reached out to stop him.

"Suth was killed—Suth?"

"Yes."

"But how? Who killed him? I thought he was dead."

Morgon's hands shifted a little. His eyes met Deth's briefly. "That is something I will ask the High One. I think Yrth hid that sword there in the cave of the Lost Ones because he knew it was one place no one would go. And I think Sol was killed not by traders but by either the shape-changers, or—by whoever killed Suth, because he knew too much about those stars. I don't know your mountain, Danan, but I know that a man trying to escape death doesn't run toward it."

There was silence, except for the weave and rustle of flames and a sigh from one of the children asleep on the floor. It was broken unexpectedly by Vert.

"That's what always puzzled me," she said slowly. "Why Sol did run down that way when he knew the mountain so well he could vanish like a dream in passageways no one else could see. You remember, Ash, when we were small—"

"There's one way to find out," Ash said abruptly. He was on his feet; Danan's swift, immediate, "No!" overran Morgon's.

The mountain-king said succinctly, "That, I forbid. I will not lose another land-heir." Ash faced him a moment without moving, his mouth set; then the stubbornness went out of his face. He sat down; Danan added wearily, "Besides, what good would that do us?"

"The sword, if it's there, belongs to Morgon. He'll want it—"

"I don't want it," Morgon said.

"But if it belongs to you . . ." Ash said, "if Yrth made it for you—"

"I don't recall being asked if I wanted a sword. Or a destiny. All I want is to get to Erlenstar Mountain without being killed—which is another reason I'm not interested in going down to that cave. And, being, incidently, the Prince of Hed, I don't want to go armed before the High One."

Ash opened his mouth, and closed it. Danan whispered, "Suth . . ." A baby began to wail, a thin, sad sound; Vert started.

"Under your chair," Ash said. "Kes." He glanced around at the uneasy, uncomprehending faces. "We'd better put them to bed." He retrieved a blinking, bewildered baby from the thick fur at his feet, heaved it like a sack to his shoulder.

Danan said as he rose, "Ash."

Their eyes met again. Ash said gently, "You have my promise. But I think it's time that cave was opened. I didn't know there was a deathtrap in the heart of "Isig." He added to Morgon before he turned to go, "Thank you for playing."

Morgon watched him leave, a child in each arm. The group faded away beyond the light. He looked down at the harp; a twist of bitterness rose in his throat. He stirred, slid the harp mechanically back into the case.

A soft conversation between Deth and Danan checked as he rose; the mountain-king said, "Morgon, Sol—no matter who killed him—has been dead three hundred years. Is there any way I can help you? If you want that sword, I have a small army of miners."

"No." His face was taut, white in the firelight. "Let me argue with my fate a little longer. I have been protesting from Caithnard to Isig, though, and it hasn't done much good."

"I would drain the gold from the veins of Isig to help you."

"I know."

"When I walked with you this afternoon, I didn't realize you bore the vesta-scars. That's a rare thing to see on any man, above all a man of Hed. It must be a marvellous thing to run with the vesta."

"It is." His voice loosened a little at the memory of the calm, endless snow, the silence lying always beneath the wind. Then he saw Suth's face, felt the hands pulling at him as he knelt in the snow, and his face turned sharply; the memories faded.

Danan said gently, "Is that how you plan to get through the Pass?"

"I planned it that way, thinking I would be alone. Now—" He glanced questioningly at Deth.

The harpist said, "It will be difficult for me, but not impossible."

"Can we leave tomorrow?"

"If you wish. But Morgon, I think you should rest here a day or two. Travelling through Isig Pass in midwinter will be tiring even for a vesta, and I suspect you ran your strength dry in Osterland."

"No. I can't wait. I can't."

"Then we'll leave. But get some sleep."

He nodded, then said, his head bowed, to Danan, "I'm sorry."

"For what, Morgon? For stirring my centuries-old grief?"

"That, too. But I'm sorry I couldn't play this harp for you the way it cries out to be played."

"You will."

Morgon took the tower steps slowly, feeling the harp whose weight he had never noticed, dragging at his back. He wondered, as he rounded the final curve, if Yrth had walked up the stairs every night to the top of the tower, or if he had practiced the enviable art of displacement, moving from point to point in the wink of an eye. He reached the landing, drew back the hangings, and found someone standing in front of his fire.

It was Vert's son, Bere. He said without preamble as Morgon jumped, "I'll take you to the cave of the Lost Ones."

Morgon eyed him without answering. The boy was young, perhaps ten or eleven, with broad shoulders and a grave, placid face. He was unembarrassed by Morgon's scrutiny; Morgon stepped in finally, letting the hangings fall closed behind them. He shrugged the harp from his shoulder, set it down.

"Don't tell me you've been there."

"I know where it is. I got lost once, exploring. I kept

going deeper and deeper into the mountain, partly because I kept taking the wrong turnings and partly because I decided as long as I really was lost I might as well see what was down there."

"Weren't you afraid?"

"No. I was hungry. I knew Danan or Ash would find me. I can see in the dark; that's from my mother. So we could go very quietly without light—except in the cave, you'll need one there."

"Why are you so anxious to go there?"

The boy took a step toward him, his brows crooked slightly. "I want to see that sword. I've never seen anything like that harp. Elieu of Hel, the brother of Raith, Lord of Hel, came here two years ago; he is beginning to do work a little like that—the inlay, the designs— but I've never seen anything as beautiful as the work on that harp. I want to see what kind of work Yrth did with the sword. Danan makes swords for lords and kings in An and Ymris, they're very beautiful. I'm training with Ash and Elieu; and Ash says I will be a master craftsman some day. So I have to learn everything I can."

Morgon sat down. He smiled suddenly at the square-shouldered, peaceful artist. "It sounds very reasonable. But you heard what I told Danan about Sol."

"Yes. But I know everyone in this house; no one would try to kill you. And if we went very quietly, no one would even know. You wouldn't have to take the sword—you could just wait at the door for me. Inside, I mean, because—" His mouth set wryly. "I am a little afraid to go in there alone. And you're the only other person I know who would go with me."

The smile faded from Morgon's eyes; he rose abruptly, restlessly. "No. You're wrong. I won't go with you. I gave my reasons to Danan, and you heard them."

Bere was silent a moment, his eyes searching Morgon's face. "I heard them. But, Morgon, this is—this is important. Please. We could just go, quickly, and then just come back—"

"Like Sol came back?"

Bere's shoulders twitched a little. "That was a long time ago—"

"No." He saw the sudden despair in the boy's eyes. "Please. Listen. I have been half a step ahead of death since I left Hed. The people trying to kill me are shapechangers; they may be the miners or the traders who ate with you at Danan's table tonight. They may be here waiting, thinking I will do just that: claim Yrth's sword, and if you and I are caught in the cave by them, they will kill us both. I have too much regard for both my intelligence and my life to be trapped like that."

Bere shook his head, as if shaking Morgon's words away. He took another step forward; the firelight left his face shadowed, pleading. "It's not right just leaving it there, just ignoring it. It belongs to you, it's yours by right, and if it's anything like the harp, no other lord in the realm will have a more beautiful sword."

"I hate swords."

"It's not the sword," Bere said patiently. "It's the craft. It's the art. I'll keep it if you don't want it."

"Bere—"

"It's not right that I can't see it." He paused. "Then I'll have to go alone."

Morgon reached the boy with one quick step, gripped the square, implacable shoulders. "I can't stop you," he said softly. "But I will ask you to wait until I've left Isig, because when they find you dead in that cave, I don't want to see Danan's face."

Bere's head bowed, his shoulders slumped under Morgon's hold; he turned away. "I thought you'd understand," he said, his back to Morgon. "I thought you'd understand what it is to have to do something."

He left. Morgon turned after a moment, wearily. He added wood to the fire and lay down. For a long time, watching the flames, feeling the exhaustion settling into his bones, he could not sleep. Finally he drifted into a darkness where odd images began to form and break like deep slow bubbles from a cauldron.

He saw the high, dark walls of inner Isig, veined with torchlight: silver, gold, iron black; saw, in the secret parts of the mountain, uncut jewels, crystals of fire and ice, mid-night-blue, smokey-yellow cracking through their husks of stone. Arched trails, high passageways wandered through webs of shadow. Rocks thrust downward from ceilings vaulted and lost in blackness, formed by the slow sculpture of forgotten ages. He stood in a silence that had its own voice. He followed like a breath of wind the slow, imperceptible movements of dark streams, thin as glass, that deepened, then hewed through hidden chasms and spilled into vast, measureless lakes, where tiny nameless things lived in a colorless world. At the end of one river he found himself in a chamber of milk-white blue-veined stone. Three steps led upward out of a pool of water to a dais on which two long cases of beaten gold and white jewels stood glittering beneath a torch. A sadness touched him for the dead of Isig: Sol, and Grania, Danan's wife; he stepped into the pool, reached out to a casket. It opened unexpectedly, from within. A face, blurred, unrecognizable, neither man's nor woman's, looked up at him and said his name: *Star-Bearer.*

He found himself in an abrupt shift back in his own chamber, dressing again, while a voice murmuring out of the corridors of Isig called to him, low and insistent as a child's call in the night. He turned to go, then checked, slid the harp over his shoulder. He moved without sound down the empty tower stairs, through the hall where the vast fire had dwindled. He found without faltering the doors of the stone archway beyond the hall that opened into the mountain itself, to the wet, cool shaft that led downward into the mines. Instinctively, without question, he found his way through the main corridors, down passages and stairways, into the mine shaft below. He took a torch from the wall there. A split in the solid rock at the end of the shaft loomed before him; the call trailed out of it and he followed without question. The path beyond was unlit, worn with age. The half-formed heads of growing rock thrust upward underfoot, slippery with the endless drip of water. The ceiling loomed down at him so suddenly he was forced to bend beneath it, then shot upward into impossible heights while the walls nudged against him and he carried the torch high over his head to ease himself through. The silence hung ponderous as the swell of rock overhead; he smelled, in his dream, the faint, clean, acrid scent of liquid stone.

He had no sense of time, of weariness, of cold; only the vague drift of shadows, the endless, complex pattern of passages he followed with an odd certainty. He wound deeper and deeper into the mountain, his torch burning steadily, untouched by wind; sometimes he could see the reflection of it in a pool far beneath the thin ledge he walked. The trails began to level finally; the stones closed about him, edging down from the ceiling, together at the sides. The stones were broken around him, as from some ancient inner turmoil. He had to step over some of them that had shaken free like great teeth from the ceiling. The trail stopped abruptly at a closed door.

He stood looking at it, his shadow splayed behind him on the wall. Someone said his name; he reached out to open it. Then, as though he had reached through the surface of his dream, he shuddered and woke himself. He was standing in front of the door to the cave of the Lost Ones.

He blinked senselessly at it, recognizing the polished green stone teared with black, shot with fire from his torch. Then, as the chill he had not felt in his dream began to seep through his clothes, and he realized the enormous mass of rock, silence, darkness sitting above his head, he took a step backward, a sound beginning to build in his throat. He whirled abruptly; found a darkness that his torch, beating a minute, jagged circle of light about him, could not begin to unravel.

His breath hissed out of him; he ran a few steps forward, stumbled over a broken rock and brought himself up short against the wet wall of rock. He remembered then the endless, chaotic path he had taken in his dream. He swallowed drily, his blood panicked through him, the sound still building in his throat.

Then he heard the voice of his dream, the voice that had led him out of Danan's house, down through the maze of the mountain:

"Star-Bearer."

It came from behind the door, a strange voice, clean, timbreless. The sound stilled the panic in him; he saw clearly as though with a third eye the implications of danger beyond the door, and the implications of a knowledge beyond hope. He stood for a long time, shivering every once in a while from the cold, his eyes on the door, weighing probability against possibility. Thousands of years old, unweathered, originless, the door yielded no answer to his waiting. Finally, he laid one hand flat on the smooth stone. The door swung at his gentle touch to a crack of darkness. He eased forward, torchlight flaring off walls massed with undiscovered beds and veins of jewels. Someone stepped into the light, and he stopped.

He drew a soft, shaking breath. A hand, the bones of it blurred, tapered, touched him, as Suth had done, feeling the reality of him. He whispered, his eyes on the still, molded face, "You are a child."

The pale head lifted, the eyes star-white, met his. "We are the children." The voice was the same, a child's clear, dreaming voice.

"The children?"

"We are all the children. The children of the Earth-Masters."

His lips moved, forming a word without shape. Something that was no longer panic began to grow heavy, unwieldy, in his throat and chest. A vague, gleaming boy's face moved a little under his eyes. He reached out to it suddenly, found it unyielding to his touch.

"We have become stone in the stone. Earth mastered us."

He lifted the torch. Around him, light, vague figures of children were rising out of the shadows, gazing at him curiously, without fear, as though he were something they had dreamed. Faces the light traced were as delicate, molded stone.

"How long—how long have you been here?"

"Since the war."

"The war?"

"Before the Settlement. We have been waiting for you. You woke us."

"You woke me. I didn't know . . . I didn't know—"

"You woke us, and we called. You have the stars." The lean hand moved, touching them. "Three to life, three to the winds, and three to—" He lifted the sword he carried, offered the starred hilt of it to Morgon, "death. That was promised us."

He swallowed the word like a bitterness in his mouth; his fingers closed around the blade. "Who promised it to you?"

"Earth. Wind. The great war destroyed us. So we were promised a man of peace."

"I see." His voice shook. "I see." He stooped, bringing himself to the boy's level. "What is your name?"

The boy was silent a moment, as though he could not answer. The still lines of his face shifted again; he said haltingly, "I was . . . I was Tirnon. My father was Tir, Master of Earth and Wind."

"I was Ilona," a small girl said suddenly. She came to Morgon trustingly, her hair curving like a fall of ice down her shoulders. "My mother was . . . my mother was . . ."

"Trist," a boy behind her said. His eyes held Morgon's as though he read his own name there. "I was Trist. I could take any shape of earth, bird, tree, flower —I knew them. I could shape the vesta, too."

"I was Elore," a slender girl said eagerly. "My mother was Rena—she could speak every language of the earth. She was teaching me the language of the crickets—"

"I was Kara—"

They crowded around him, oblivious of the fire, their voices painless, dreaming. He let them talk, watching incredulously the delicate, lifeless faces; then he said abruptly, his voice cutting into theirs, "What happened? Why are you here?"

There was a silence. Tirnon said simply, "They destroyed us."

"Who?"

"Those from the sea. Edolen. Sec. They destroyed us so that we could not live on earth anymore; we could not master it. My father gave us protection to come here, hidden from the war. We found a dying-place."

Morgon was still. He let the torch drop slowly; shadows eased again over the circle of children. He whispered, "I see. What can I do for you?"

"Free the winds."

"Yes. How?"

"One star will call out of silence the Master of the Winds; one star out of darkness the Master of Darkness; one star out of death the children of the Masters of the Earth. You have called; they have answered."

"Who is—"

"The war is not finished, only silenced for the regathering. You will bear stars of fire and ice to the Ending of the Age of the High One—"

"But we cannot live without the High One—"

"This we have been promised. This will be." The boy seemed no longer to hear his voice, but a voice out of the memory of an age. "You are the Star-Bearer, and you will loose from their order the—"

He stopped abruptly. Morgon broke the silence. "Go on."

Tirnon's head bent. He gripped Morgon's wrist suddenly, his voice taut with anguish, "No."

Morgon lifted his torch. Beyond the fragile planes of faces, the curve of bone, the shape of slender body, the light caught at a shadow that would not yield. In the rags of darkness a dark head lifted; a woman, her face beautiful, quiet, shy, looked at him and smiled.

He rose, the stars leaping fiery about him. Tirnon's head fell on his bent knees; Morgon saw the lines of his body begin to melt together. He turned quickly, pushing through the stone door; it flung him outward and he saw, coming toward him down the trail, carrying lights in the palms of their hands, men of the color and movement of the sea.

He had a moment of utter panic, until he saw out of the corner of his eye, an opening, a slender side path beside him. He flung the torch as far away from him as possible; it blazed like a star towards his pursuers. Then, feeling for the opening, he slipped blind into an unknown path that at every breath and movement rose against him. He felt his way, his hands sliding over wet, smooth skulls of rock, his face and shoulders beaten against the unexpected outcroppings that formed at every twist. Darkness fashioned the trail, fashioned the mold of stones beneath his hands. Behind him the blackness lay unbroken; ahead it pressed against his eyes. He stopped once, appalled at his blindness, and heard above his harsh breathing the relentless silence of Isig. He blundered on, his hands flayed from scraping across unseen rock, blood from a cut on his face catching like tears in his eyelashes, until the stone gave way beneath his feet and he fell into blackness, his cry drowned in water.

He pulled himself back on the raw slab of shore, still clinging without realizing it to the sword, and lay hearing nothing but his breathing like little whimpering sobs. Then, as he began to quiet, he heard a footstep near his face, another's breathing. His breath stopped. Someone touched him.

He rolled to his feet abruptly, backed; a voice whispered, "Morgon, watch out. The water—"

He stopped, his lips caught hard between his teeth, straining to see the pale shadow of a face, but the dark was absolute. Then he recognized the voice.

"Morgon. It's me, Bere. I'm coming toward you. Don't move, or you'll fall in the water again. I'm coming . . ."

It took, as he felt the blood pounding in the back of his throat, all the courage he possessed to stay still, let the darkness come to him. A hand touched him again. Then he felt the sword move in his grip and made a sound.

"It was there. You were right. I knew it. I knew he would have etched the blade. It's . . . I can't see that well; I need—" His voice stopped briefly. "What did you do? You cut your hand, carrying it like that."

"Bere. I can't see you. I can't see anything. There are shape-changers trying to find me—"

"Is that what they are? I saw them. I hid in the rocks, and you ran past me. Do you want me to leave you here and get—"

"No. Can you help me find a way back?"

"I think so. I think if we follow the water it leads toward one of the lower mines. Morgon, I'm glad you came for the sword, but what made you go without telling Danan? And how did you find your way down here? Everyone is looking for you. I went up to talk to you later to see if you'd changed your mind, but you were gone. So I went to Deth's room, to see if you were there, but you weren't, and he heard me and woke up. I told him you were gone, and he dressed and woke Danan, and Danan woke the miners. They're all looking for you. I came ahead. I don't understand—"

"If we get back to Danan's house alive, I'll explain it to you. I'll explain anything—"

"All right. Let me carry the sword for you." The hand at his wrist tugged him forward. "Be careful: there's a low overhang to your left. Bend your head."

They moved quickly through the darkness, silent but for Bere's murmured warnings. Morgon, his body tense against unexpected blows, strained to see one faint brush of stone or glimmer of water, but his eyes found no place to rest. He closed them finally, let his body flow after Bere's. They began to climb; the path wound endlessly upward. The walls moved like living things under his hands, now narrowing, closing until he eased between them sideways, now flowing wide, stretching beyond his reach, then leaping back together again. Finally Bere stopped at some isolated piece of darkness.

"There are steps here. They lead to the mine shaft. Do you want to rest?"

"No. Go on."

The steps were steep, endless. Morgon, shivering with cold, feeling the blood well and drip over his fingers, began to see shades and flares of color behind his closed eyes. He heard Bere's sturdy, tired breathing; the boy said finally with a sigh, "All right. We're at the top." He stopped so suddenly that Morgon bumped into him. "There's light in the shaft. It must be Danan! Come on—"

Morgon opened his eyes. Bere went in front of him through an arch of stones whose walls rippled unexpectedly with wavering light. Bere called softly, "Danan?" And then he pushed back, stumbling against Morgon, the breath hissing sharply out of his throat. A blade, grey-green, raked across the light, struck his head and he fell, the sword ringing beneath him.

Morgon stared down at his limp, motionless body, looking oddly small on the harsh stones. Something unwieldy, uncontrollable, shook through him, welled to an explosion of fury behind his eyes. He ducked a sword thrust that bit at him like a silver snake, pulled the harp strap over his neck and dropped it, then reached for the sword beneath Bere. He plunged through the archway, eluding by a hairsbreadth two blades that whistled through the air behind him, caught a third on its way down, brought it up, high upward to a dull ring and blaze of sparks, then loosed it abruptly and slashed sideways. Blood burst like a sun across one shell-colored face. A blaze of fire ripping down his arm, caught his attention; he whirled. A blade drove toward him; he sent it spinning almost contemptuously across the floor with a single, two-handed stroke; then reversed the ponderous circle of the blade's sweep and the shape-changer, coughing, hunched himself over the line of blood slashing from shoulder to hip. Yet another blade descended at him like a thread of silver that would have split him; he jerked back from it. He brought his sword down like an ax against a stump in a field, and the shape-changer, catching the blade in his shoulder, pulled it out of Morgon's hands as he fell.

The silence settled ponderously about him. He stared down at the stars, shaken slightly with the last breath of the shape-changer; the hilt was webbed with blood. One of the strange lights, fallen and still burning, lay just beyond the shape-changer's outstretched hand. Morgon, looking at it, shuddered suddenly, violently. He turned, extinguishing the light with a step, walked forward until he could go no further and pushed his face against the solid black wall of stone.

11

THE SLASH DOWN HIS ARM TOOK TWO WEEKS TO heal, and he had scars striped across the vestahorns on his left hand from the sword blade. He said nothing when Danan's miners, their torchlight flaring into the cave, found him, the dead shape-changers, and the great sword with its stars winking like blood-red eyes. He had said nothing, though something moved behind his eyes, when Bere, one hand on his head, a line of blood down his face, stumbled blinking into the light. Walking up through the mines, he had heard Danan's questions, but did not answer them. He had not walked long when the darkness of the mountain plummetted down at him, the torches growing small, going blue, and cold, and then black.

He broke the silence finally, lying in his chamber with his arm bound from shoulder to wrist, watching Bere, his square face intent, absolutely content, making sketches of the engravings on the sword. Bere, in response to his request, got Deth and Danan. Morgon told them flatly, precisely, what they wanted to know.

"Children . . ." Danan whispered. "When Yrth took me there, I saw only stones. How did he know what they were?"

"I'll ask him."

"Yrth? You think he is still alive?"

"If he is alive, I'll find him." He paused briefly, his eyes, indrawn, inaccessible. "There is someone else involved in this game beyond the Founder, the shape-changers, the strange names I was given—Edolen, Sec; someone they called the Master of the Winds. Perhaps they meant the High One." He looked at Deth. "The High One is also a Wind-Master?"

"Yes."

"And there is a Master of Darkness, who will no doubt reveal himself when he's ready. The age of the High One is drawing to an end—"

"But how can that be?" Danan protested. "Our lands will die without the High One."

"I don't know how it can be. But I touched the face of the son of a Wind-Master while he spoke to me, and it was of stone. I think if that is possible, anything is possible, including the destruction of the realm. This is not our war—we didn't begin it, we can't end it, we can't avoid it. There is no choice."

Danan drew a breath to speak, but said nothing. Bere's pen had stopped, his face was turned toward them. Danan's breath went out of him slowly. "The ending of the age. . . . How can anyone put an end to a mountain? Morgon, you may be wrong. Those who began this war thousands of years ago did not know they would have to reckon with men who will fight for what they love. These shape-changers can be destroyed; you have proved that."

"Yes. I have. But they don't have to fight us. If they destroy the High One, we are doomed."

"Then why are they trying to kill you? Why have they been attacking you instead of the High One? It makes no sense."

"It does. Every riddle has an answer. When I begin to piece together all the answers to the questions I must ask, then I will have the beginnings of an answer to your question."

Danan shook his head. "How can you do it? Not even the wizards could."

"I'll do it. I have no choice."

Deth said little; when they left, taking Bere with them, Morgon rose painfully, went to one of the windows. It was dusk; the flanks of the mountain were blue-white, motionless with the coming night. He stood watching the great trees weave into shadows. Nothing moved, not an animal or a snow-weighted branch, while the white head of Isig gradually blurred into the black, starless sky.

He heard steps on the stairs; the hangings slid apart, and he said without turning, "When should we leave for Erlenstar Mountain?"

"Morgon—"

He turned then. "That's a note I rarely hear in your voice: protest. We're on the threshold of Erlenstar Mountain, and there are a thousand questions I need answers to—"

"Erlenstar Mountain is Erlenstar Mountain," Deth said quietly, "a place where you may or may not find the answers you want. Be patient. The winds that blow down from the northern wastes through Isig Pass are merciless in deep winter."

"I've stood in those winds before and not even felt them."

"I know. But if you step into that winter before you are strong enough to bear it, you will not live two days beyond Kyrth."

"I'll survive," Morgon said savagely. "That's what I'm best at—surviving by any means, any method. I have great gifts, unusual in a Prince of Hed. Did you see the miners' faces when they walked into that cave and found us all? With all the traders in this house, how long will it be, do you think, before that tale reaches Hed? Not only am I adept at killing, I have a sword with my name on it to do it with, given to me by a stone-faced child, given to him by a wizard who forged it assuming that the man whose name it bore would accept his own destiny. I am trapped. If there is nothing I can do but what I am meant to do, then I will do it, now, as quickly as possible. There is not a breath of wind. If I leave tonight, I could reach Erlenstar Mountain in three days."

"Five," Deth said. "Even the vesta sleep." He moved to the fire, reached for wood. His face, lit as the flames leaped up, revealed hollows and hair-thin lines that had not been there before. "How far could you run with a crippled leg?"

"Do you suggest I wait here to be killed?"

"The shape-changers moved against you here and lost. With Danan's house guarded, the sword taken, the answers the stone-faced children gave you inaccessible, they may prefer to wait for your move."

"And if I don't move?"

"You will. You know that."

"I know," he whispered. He whirled abruptly away from the window. "How can you be so calm? You are never afraid; you are never surprised. You have lived for a thousand years, and you took the Black of Mastery—how much of all this did you come to expect? You were the one to give me my name in Herun." He saw the startled, almost imperceptible wariness in the harpist's eyes, and he felt his mind turn on the question awkwardly, like an old mill groaning into movement. "What did you expect from me? That having put my mind to this game, I would leave anything or anyone unquestioned? You knew Suth—did he give you the riddles he learned of those stars? You knew Yrth; you said you were in Isig when he made my harp. Did he tell you what he had seen in the cave of the Lost Ones? You were born in Lungold: were you there when the School of Wizards was abandoned? Did you study there yourself?"

Deth straightened, meeting Morgon's eyes. "I am not a Lungold wizard. I have never served any man but the High One. I studied awhile at the School of Wizards because I found myself growing old without aging, and I thought perhaps my father had been a wizard. I had no great gifts for wizardry so I left—that is the extent of my acquaintance with the Lungold wizards. I searched for you five weeks in Ymris; I waited two months for you in Kyrth without touching my harp, in case someone realized who I was and who I must be waiting for; I searched Isig Mountain with Danan's miners for you: I saw your face when they found you. Do you think that if there is something I could do for you, I would not do it?"

"Yes." There was a sharp, brittle silence before either of them moved. Morgon reached methodically for the sword Bere had been sketching by the fire, swung it in a wide, blazing half-circle, smashed it in a snap of blue sparks against the stone wall. It gave a deep, flawless, bell-like protest before he dropped it, and he said bitterly, hunched over his stinging hands, "You could answer my questions."

He broke his seclusion in the tower finally, went out into the craftsmen's yard a few days later. His arm was nearly healed; a half-forgotten strength was returning to him. He stood in the broken snow smelling the metal-smiths' fires. The world seemed becalmed under a still, grey-white sky. Danan spoke his name; he turned. The mountain-king, enveloped in fur, put a gentle hand on his shoulder.

"I'm glad to see you better."

He nodded. "It's good to be out. Where is Deth?"

"He rode into Kyrth this morning with Ash. They'll be back at sundown. Morgon, I have been thinking . . . I wanted to give you something that might help you; I racked my brains trying to think what, when it occurred to me that there are times in your journey that you might simply want to disappear from enemies, from friends, from the world, to rest awhile, to think. . . . There's nothing less obvious than a tree in a forest."

"A tree." Something in his mind quickened. "Danan, can you teach me that?"

"You have the gift for shape-changing. Shaping a tree is much easier then shaping the vesta. You must simply learn to be still. You know what kind of stillness is in a stone, or a handful of earth."

"I knew once."

"You know, deep in you." Danan looked up at the sky, then glanced at the bustling, preoccupied workers around him. "It's easy to be still on a day like this. Come. No one will miss us for a while."

Morgon followed him out of Harte, down the winding, quiet road, then into the forests high above Kyrth. Their footprints broke deep into the powdery snow; they brushed pine branches heavy with it, shook soft snow flurries loose that bared webs of wet, dark fir. They walked silently until, turning, they could not see the road, or Kyrth below it, or Harte, only the dark, motionless trees. They stood there listening. The clouds, softly shaped by the wind, rested on the silence; trees were molded to a stillness that formed the whorls of their bark, curve of branch, the heavy, downward sweep of their needles and pinnacle of tip. A hawk floated in the silence, barely rippling it, dove deep into it and vanished. Morgon, after a long while, turned to Danan, feeling suddenly alone, and found beside him a great pine, still and dreaming above Isig.

He did not move. The chill from his motionlessness began to trouble him, then passed as the silence became a tangible thing measuring his breath, his heartbeat, seeping into his thoughts, his bones until he felt hollowed, a shell of winter stillness. The trees circling him seemed to enclose a warmth like the stone houses at Kyrth, against the winter. Listening, he heard suddenly the hum of their veins, drawing life from deep beneath the snow, beneath the hard earth. He felt himself rooted, locked into the rhythms of the mountain; his own rhythms drained away from him, lost beyond memory in the silence that shaped him. Wordless knowₑ ₑ moved through him, of slow measureless age, of fierce winds borne beyond breaking point, of seasons beginning, ending, of a patient, unhurried waiting for something that lay deeper than roots, that lay sleeping in the earth deeper then the core of Isig, something on the verge of waking . . .

The stillness passed. He moved, felt an odd stiffness as though his face were being formed out of bark, his fingers dwindling from fingers of twig. His breath, which he had not noticed for a while, went out of him in a quick, white flash.

Danan said, his voice measured to the unhurried rhythm of the silence, "When you have a moment, practice so you can fade in a thought from man to tree. Sometimes I forget to change back. I watch the mountains fade into twilight and the stars push through the darkness like jewels pushing through stone, and forget myself until Bere comes calling for me, or I hear the movements of Isig beneath me and remember who I am. It's a restful, comfortable thing to be. When I'm too tired to live any longer, I will walk as far as I can up Isig, then stop and become a tree. If this path you take becomes unbearable, you can simply disappear for a while, and no wizard or shape-changer on earth will find you until you are ready."

"Thank you." His voice startled him as though he had forgotten he possessed one.

"You have great power. You took to that as easily as one of my own children."

"It was simple. So simple it seems strange that I never tried it before." He walked beside Danan, following their broken trail back to the road, still feeling the placid winter stillness. Danan's voice, with its own inner peace, scarcely disturbed it.

"I remember once when I was young spending an entire winter as a tree, to see what it was like. I scarcely felt the time passing. Grania sent the miners looking for me; she came herself, too, but I never noticed her, any more than she noticed me. You can survive terrible storms in that shape, if you need to, on your way to

Erlenstar Mountain; even the vesta tire, after a while, running against the wind."

"I'll survive. But what about Deth? Is he a shape-changer?"

"I don't know. I've never asked him." His face wrinkled a little in thought. "I've always suspected he has greater gifts than harping and tact, and yet I can't imagine seeing him turn into a tree. It doesn't sound like something he would do."

Morgon looked at him. "What gifts do you suspect?"

"Nothing in particular; I just wouldn't be very surprised by anything he could do. There is a silence in him that as often as I have talked with him, he has never broken. You probably know him better than anyone."

"No. I know that silence. . . . Sometimes I think it's simply a silence of living, then at other times, it changes into a silence of waiting"

Danan nodded. "Yes. But waiting for what?"

"I don't know," Morgon said softly. "I want to know."

They reached the road. A cart rattled over it filled with skins from trappers in Kyrth. The driver, recognizing them, slowed his horses, and they hoisted themselves onto the tail. Danan said, leaning back against the skins, "I've been curious about Deth since the day he walked into my court one winter, seven hundred years ago, and asked to be taught the ancient songs of Isig in exchange for his harping. He looked much the same as he does now, and his harping . . . even then, it was unearthly."

Morgon turned his head slowly. "Seven hundred years ago?"

"Yes. I remember it was just a few years after I heard about the wizards' disappearance."

"I thought—" He stopped. A cartwheel jogged over a hidden stone in the dark rutted snow. "Then he wasn't in Isig when Yrth made my harp?"

"No," Danan said surprisedly. "How could he have

been? Yrth made the harp about a hundred years before the founding of Lungold, and Lungold is where Deth was born."

Morgon swallowed something in the back of his throat. Snow began to fall again lightly, aimlessly; he looked up at the blank sky with a sudden, desperate impatience. "It's beginning all over again!"

"No. Couldn't you feel it, deep in the earth? The ending . . ."

Morgon sat alone in his chamber that evening without moving, his eyes on the fire. The circle of stones, the circle of the night surrounded him with a familiar implacable silence. He held the harp in his hands but he did not play it; his fingers traced slowly, endlessly, the angles and facets of the stars. He heard Deth's step finally; the shift of the hangings, and he lifted his head, caught the harpist's eyes as he entered, sent the swift, tentative probe of thought past the blurring, fathomless eyes.

He felt a brief sensation of surprise, as though, opening the door of some strange, solitary tower, he had stepped into his own house. Then something snapped back into his own mind like a blaze of white fire; shocked, blinded, he stumbled to his feet, the harp clattering on the floor. He heard nothing for a moment, saw nothing, and then, as the brilliant haze receded behind his eyes, he heard Deth's voice.

"Morgon—I'm sorry. Sit down."

Morgon lifted his head from his hands finally, blinking; flecks of color swam across the room. He took a step, bumped into the wine table; Deth eased him back to his chair.

He whispered, "What was that?"

"A variation of the Great Shout. Morgon, I had forgotten the mind-work you learned from Har; you startled me." He poured wine, held it out. Morgon, his hands closed, rigid, the vibrations of the shout moving like a tide in his head, opened one hand stiffly to take it. He stood up again unsteadily, sent the cup flying across the room, wine splashing out of it, to crack against the wall.

He faced the harpist, asked reasonably, "Why did you lie to me about being in Isig when Yrth made his harp? Danan said it was made before you were born."

There was no surprise, just a flash of understanding in the harpist's eyes. His head bent slightly; he poured more wine and took a sip. He sat down, cradling the cup in his hands.

"Do you think I lied to you?"

Morgon was silent. He said almost surprised, "No. Are you a wizard?"

"No. I am the High One's harpist."

"Then will you explain why you said you were in Isig a hundred years before you were born?"

"Do you want a half-truth or truth?"

"Truth."

"Then you will have to trust me." His voice was suddenly softer than the fire sounds, melting into the silence within the stones. "Beyond logic, beyond reason, beyond hope. Trust me."

Morgon closed his eyes. He sat down, leaned his aching head back. "Did you learn that at Lungold?"

"It was one of the few things I could learn. I was caught accidentally in a mind-shout of the wizard Talies once, when he lost his temper. He taught it to me, in apology."

"Will you teach it to me?"

"Now?"

"No. I can barely think now, let alone shout. Do you use it often?"

"No. It can be dangerous. I simply felt another mind entering mine and reacted. There are simpler ways to disengage; if I had realized it was you, I would never have hurt you." He paused. "I came in to tell you that the High One has set his name into every rock and tree in Isig Pass; the lands beyond Isig are his, and he can feel every footfall like a heartbeat. He will allow no one but us through. Danan suggests we leave when the ice on the Ose begins to break. That should be soon; the weather is turning."

"I know. I felt it. Danan taught me the tree-shape this afternoon." He rose to pick up his wine cup from across the room. He added, pouring wine, "I trust you, with my name and my life. But my life has been torn out of my control, shaped to the answering of riddles. You have given me one tonight; I will answer it."

"That," the harpist said simply, "is why I gave it to you."

A few days later, going up Isig alone to practice shape-changing, Morgon caught again the current of stillness and found in it an unexpected tap of warmth rising deep from the earth, spreading through vein and joint of branch until, himself again, he felt it still in the tips of his fingers, the roots of his hair. A wind breathed across Isig; he looked into it and smelled the earth of Hed.

He found Deth with Danan, talking to one of the craftsmen in the yard. Danan, glancing up as he came to them, smiled and reached into an inner pocket in his cloak. "Morgon, one of the traders came in from Kraal today—they start coming like birds at the beginning of spring. He brought a letter for you."

"From Hed?"

"No. He said he's been carrying it for four months, from Anuin."

"Anuin . . ." Morgon whispered. He pulled his gloves off, broke the seal quickly. He read silently; the men watched him. The soft south wind that had touched him in the mountains rustled the paper in his hands. He did not look up immediately when he was finished; he was trying to remember a face that time and distance had worn into a lovely blur of colors. He raised his head finally.

"She wants to see me." The faces in front of him were, for a moment, indistinguishable. "She told me to stay off ships, coming home. She said to come home."

He heard the boom and crack of the Ose that night

in his dreams and woke to the sound. By morning, webs of broken ice had formed on it like filigree; two days later the river, dark and swollen with melting snow, spun wedges of ice huge as carts past Kyrth, heading eastward toward the sea. The traders began packing their wares at Harte, bound for Kraal and the sea. Danan gave Morgon a packhorse and a sweet-tempered, shaggy-hooved mare bred in Herun. He gave Deth a chain of gold and emerald for his playing during the long, quiet evenings. At dawn one morning, the mountain-king, his two children, and Bere came out to bid farewell to Morgon and Deth. As the sun rose in a blaze of blue, cloudless sky above Isig, they rode through Kyrth, down the little-travelled road that led through Isig Pass to Erlenstar Mountain.

Bare granite peaks glittered around them as the rising sun pushed slabs of light inch by inch down the mountainsides. The road, kept clear three seasons of the year by men who worked for the High One, was rough with fallen stones, trees snapped by wind and snow. It wound beside a river, rose upward to the rim and edge of mountains. Great falls unlocked by the gentle, persistent south wind, murmured in hidden places among the trees, or glittered in frozen silver out-pourings high between the peaks. In the silence, the sound of hoof on bare rock snapped in the air like iron.

They spent the first night camped beside the river. Above them the sky, deep flaming blue during the day, began to stain with night. Their fire flickered back at the huge stars like a reflection. The river lazed beside them, deep and slow; they were silent until Morgon, washing a pot and cups in the river, heard out of the immense darkness a blaze of harp song that ran quick and fiery as the sunlit waters of a falls. He listened, crouched by the river until he felt his hands burn with cold. He went back to the fire. Deth softened the song to match the river's murmur, his face and the polished lines of the harp drawn clear by the fire. Morgon added wood to the fire. The harping stopped; he made a sound of protest.

"My hands are cold," Deth said. "I'm sorry." He reached for the harp case. Morgon, leaning back against a fallen log, gazed back at the cold, aloof faces of stars caught in the webs of pine needles.

"How long will it take us?"

"In good weather it takes ten days. If this weather holds, it shouldn't take us much longer."

"It's beautiful. It's more beautiful than any land I've seen in my life." His eyes moved to the harpist's face, half-hidden under his arm as he lay beside the fire. The quiet mystery of him began to nag at Morgon again. He put aside his questions with an effort and said instead, "You were going to teach me the mind-shout. Can you teach me the Great Shout, too?"

Deth lifted his arm, slid it beneath his head. His face looked open, for once, peaceful. "The Great Shout of the body is unteachable; you simply have to be inspired." He paused, added thoughtfully, "The last time I heard it was at the marriage between Mathom of An and Cyone, Raederle's mother. Cyone shouted a shout that harvested an entire crop of half-ripe nuts and snapped all the harp strings in the hall. Luckily I heard it from a mile away; I was the only harpist able to play that day."

Morgon gave a grunt of laughter. "What was she shouting about?"

"Mathom never told anyone."

"I wonder if Raederle could do that."

"Probably. It was a formidable shout. The body-shout is uncontrollable and very personal; the mind-shout will be more useful to you. It's a gathering in one quick moment all the energy in your mind, concentrated into one sound. Wizards used it to call one another in different kingdoms, if they had to. Both shouts may be used in defense, although the body-shout is unwieldy. If you are unusually moved, however, it is very effective. The mind-shout is generally the more dangerous: if you shout with full force into the mind of a man sitting close to you, he may lose consciousness. So be very careful with it. Try it. Call my name."

"I'm afraid to."

"I'll stop you if it's too strong. It takes time to learn to gather force. Concentrate."

Morgon stilled his mind. The fire smudged before his eyes, thinning into the darkness. The face opposite him became nameless as a tree or a stone. Then he slid past the shell of the face and let his thoughts blaze suddenly with Deth's name. His concentration shattered, he saw the face and the fire and the ghosts of trees form again before him.

Deth said patiently, "Morgon, you sounded as though you were on the other side of a mountain. Try again."

"I don't know what I'm doing—"

"Say my name, as you would naturally, using your mind-voice. Then shout it."

He tried again. This time, forgetting Har's teaching, thrown back against himself, he heard the shout futile in his own mind. He cleared his mind, tried again, and produced a full concentration of inner sound, which seemed to build and explode like a bubble in a cauldron. He winced.

"I'm sorry—did I hurt you?"

Deth smiled. "That was a little better. Try again."

He tried again. By the time the moon rose, he had exhausted his ability to concentrate. Deth sat up, reached for wood.

"You are trying to produce an illusion of sound without sound. It's not easy, but if you can exchange thoughts with a man, you should be able to shout at him."

"What am I doing wrong?"

"Perhaps you're being too cautious. Think of the Great Shouters of An: Cyone of An; Lord Col of Hel and the witch Madir, whose shouting-feud over the land-right to an oak forest their pigs fed in is legendary; Kale, first King of An, who scattered an enormous army from Aum by his shout of despair over its numbers. Forget you are Morgon of Hed and that I am a harpist named Deth. Somewhere deep in you is a wealth of power you are not using. Tap it, and you might make the beginnings of a mind-shout that doesn't sound as if it's coming out of the bottom of a well."

Morgon sighed. He tried to clear his mind, but like leaves there came drifting through it the bright images of Col and Madir throwing shouts at each other that cracked in the blue sky of An like lightning; of Cyone, dressed in purple and gold on her wedding day shouting an immense, mysterious shout of legendary result; of Kale, his face lost in the shadows of faded centuries, shouting with utter despair the hopelessness of his first battle. And Morgon, moved oddly by the tale, shouted Kale's shout and felt it snap away from him clean as an arrow into the eye of a beast.

Deth's face drifted before him again, frozen still above the fire.

Morgon said, feeling oddly peaceful, "Was it better?"

Deth did not answer for a moment. Then he said cautiously, "Yes."

Morgon straightened. "Did I hurt you?"

"A little."

"You should have—why didn't you stop me?"

"I was too surprised." He drew a deep breath. "Yes. That was much better."

The next day the river dropped away from them as they rode, the path rising high above it, tracing the mountainside, the white slope melting downward to halt at the blue-white water. For a while they lost sight of it, riding through the trees. Morgon, watching the slow procession of ancient trees, thought of Danan, and the mountain-king's face seemed to look back at him out of aged, wrinkled bark. Midafternoon brought them back to the cliff edge, where they saw again the brilliant, impatient river and the mountains shrugging off their coats of winter snow.

The packhorse, straying aside, sent a rock below them, bouncing into the river; Morgon turned to tug it back. The bright sun glanced off the peak above them; fingers of light flicked along a row of icicles on the cliff. Morgon glanced up at the slope above their heads, and the bone-white blaze of mountain burned in his eyes.

He looked away, and said to Deth, "If I wanted to harvest a crop of nuts in Hed with the Great Shout, how would I do it?"

Deth, brought out of his own thoughts, said absently, "Provided that the crop of nuts is in a secluded place away from your animals, who would scatter to the twelve winds at a shout like that, you would draw on the same source of energy you used last night. The difficulty lies in producing a sound without considering physical limitations. It requires both sufficient impulse and great abandon, which is why you would do better to wait for a good wind."

Morgon considered. The gentle, rhythmic clop of hooves and the distant voice of the river sounded frail against the silence, which seemed impervious to any shout. He thought back to the previous night, trying to find again the source of inexhaustible energy, private and undefined, that had overwhelmed him to produce the silent shout. The sun, leaping from behind a bend in the road, suddenly showered his path with stars. The unbroken blue of the sky quivered with a great, soundless note. He drew a breath of the hidden sound and loosed a shout.

There was an answering shout from the mountains. For a second he listened to it without surprise. Then he saw Deth stop ahead of him; his face turned back in surprise. He dismounted, wrenched at the packhorse's reins, and Morgon, suddenly placing the sound, slid off his horse and drew it to the wall of the cliff. He crouched flat beside it as the hiss and rattle of stones swept towards them, bounced onto the road and down the slope.

The rumble shook through bare peaks and hidden forests. A boulder half the size of a horse struck the cliff edge above their heads, sailed lightly over them and flung itself down the slope towards the river, crushing a tree as it passed. Then the silence, regathered and locked into place, strained at their ears in triumph.

Morgon, flat against the cliff as though he were holding it up, turned his head cautiously. Deth's eyes met his, expressionless. Then expression came back into them.

He said, "Morgon—"

He stopped. He eased the trembling horses away from the cliff. Morgon soothed his own horse, brought it back on the road. He stood beside it, suddenly too tired to mount, sweat pricking his face in the chill air.

He said after a moment, blankly, "That was stupid."

Deth dropped his face against his horse. Morgon, who had never heard him laugh before, stood amazed in the snow, listening. The sound flung itself back at them from the high crevices until the laughter of stone and man tangled into an unhuman sound that jarred Morgon's ears. He took a step forward, disturbed. As Deth sensed the movement, he quieted. His hands were twisted, locked in his horse's mane; his shoulders were rigid.

Morgon said softly, "Deth—"

The harpist's head lifted. He reached for the reins, mounted slowly without looking at Morgon. Down the slope a great tree, half uprooted, its trunk snapped like a bone, laid its face against the snow. Morgon, staring down at it, swallowed drily. "I'm sorry. I had no business practicing the Great Shout on a mountain of melting snow. I could have killed us both."

"Yes." The harpist checked briefly, as though feeling for his voice. "The Pass seems to be proof against shape-changers, but not against you."

"Is that why you were laughing like that?"

"I don't know what else to do." He looked at Morgon finally. "Are you ready to go on?"

Morgon drew himself on his own horse wearily. The late sun, drifting towards Erlenstar Mountain, was drawing a wake of light down the Pass.

Deth said, "The road descends down to the river in a couple of miles; we can camp then."

Morgon nodded. He added, soothing the neck of his trembling mare, "It didn't sound that loud."

"No. It was a gentle shout. But it was effective. If ever you shout the Great Shout in truth, I think the world will crack."

In eight days they tracked the river to its source: the melting slopes and high snowbound peak of the mountain that overlooked the kingdoms of the High One. They saw the end of the road on the morning of the ninth day; it crossed the Ose and ran into the mouth of Erlenstar. Morgon reined, catching his first glimpse of the threshold of the High One. Lines of huge, ancient trees marked the road, which, cleared of snow across the river, glittered like the inner walls of Harte. The outer door was a crack in the stone face of the mountain, smoothed and molded to an arch. A man walked out of the arch as he watched, came down the fiery road to wait at the bridge.

"Seric," Deth said. "The High One's Watcher. He was trained by the wizards at Lungold. Come."

But he did not move himself. Morgon, a mixture of fear and excitement beginning to gnaw at him, glanced at Deth, waiting. The harpist sat still, his face quiet as always, looking at the door into Erlenstar. Then his head turned. His eyes on Morgon's face held an odd expression, half-searching, half-questioning, as though he were weighing a riddle and an answer in his mind. Then, without resolving one to the other, he moved forward. Morgon followed him down the final length of road, across the bridge where Seric, his long, loose robe seemingly woven from all the colors under the sun, stopped them.

"This is Morgon, Prince of Hed," Deth said, as he dismounted. Seric smiled.

"So Hed has come at last to the High One. You are welcome. He expects you. I'll take your horses."

Morgon walked beside Deth down the flickering path, alive with worn, uncut jewels. The mouth of Erlenstar opened to a wide sweep of inner hallway, a great fire ring in the middle of it. Seric took their horses down one side of it. Deth led Morgon towards arched double doors. They opened softly. Men in the same light, beautiful robes bent their heads to Morgon, closed the doors again behind them.

Light pricked endlessly through the shadows, drawn by the play of fire on jewelled floor, walls, arched dome of rock, as though the High One's house were the center of a star. Deth, his hand light on Morgon's arm, led him forward towards a dais at the other side of the round room. On the third step a high-backed throne carved of a single yellow crystal sat between two torches. Morgon stopped at the bottom of the steps. Deth left his side, went to stand beside the throne. The High One, his robe sun-gold, his white hair drawn back from his brow to free the simple, austere lines of it, lifted his hands from the arms of the throne and brought the tips of his fingers together.

"Morgon of Hed. You are very welcome," he said softly. "How may I help you?"

Morgon's blood shocked through him, then slowed unbearably with the dull pound of his heart. The jewelled walls pulsed around him in silent, flickering beats of light. He looked at Deth. The harpist stood quietly, the midnight eyes watching him dispassionately. He looked back at the High One, but the face remained undisguised by richness: the face of a Master of Caithnard he had known for three years and never known.

His voice came heavy, ragged. "Master Ohm—"

"I am Ohm of Caithnard. I am Ghisteslwchlohm, the Founder of Lungold, and—as you have guessed —it's destroyer. I am the High One."

Morgon shook his head, a weight growing behind

his throat, his eyes. He turned again to Deth, who blurred suddenly in his gaze, yet, blurred, stood with a silence undisturbed and insurmountable as the silence sitting heavy as ice above Isig Pass. "And you—" he whispered.

"I am his harpist."

"No," he whispered. "Oh, no." Then he felt the word well up from some terrible source, tear out of him, and the barred doors of the High One's house split from top to bottom with the force of that shout.

———

THE RIDDLE-MASTER OF HED *is the first of three books about Morgon, Raederle, the world they live in and the end of an age.*

People and Places

AIA wife of Har of Osterland.

AKER, JARL dead trader of Osterland.

AKREN home of the land-rulers of Hed.

ALOIL ancient wizard in the service of the kings of Ymris, preceded the school of wizards of Lungold.

AMORY, WYNDON farmer of Hed; Arin, his daughter.

AN large kingdom; chief city, Anuin; ruler, Mathom.

ANOTH physician at the court of Heureu of Ymris.

ANUIN chief city of An; seat of Mathom.

ASH son and land-heir of Danan Isig.

ASTRIN land-heir of Ymris; brother of Heureu.

ATHOL dead father of Morgon, Eliard and Tristan; a prince of Hed.

AUBER OF AUM descendant of Peven of Aum.

AUM ancient kingdom now one of the three portions of An.

AWN OF AN ancient land-ruler of An; died because he deliberately destroyed part of An to keep it from an enemy.

BERE grandson of Danan Isig: son of Vert.

CAERWEDDIN chief city of Ymris; seat of Heureu; a port city.

CAITHNARD a free-port city between Ymris and An; site of the college maintained by the Riddle-Masters.

COL   ancient lord of Hel.

CORRIG   shape-changer.

CRON   ancient Morgol of Herun; full name Ylcorcronlth. His harper was Tirunedeth.

CROWN CITY   chief city of Herun; ringed by seven circular walls; seat of the Morgol El of Herun.

CYONE   wife of Mathom of An; mother of Raederle and Rood.

DANAN ISIG   Land-ruler and king of Isig.

DETH   harpist of the High One.

DUAC   son of Mathom and land-heir of An.

EARTH-MASTERS   ancient inhabitants of the land; builders of two now-ruined cities, both in Ymris, one on Wind Plain, one on King's Mouth Plain.

EL   morgol (land-ruler) of Herun, full name Elrhiarhodan.

ELIARD   brother of Morgon and land-heir of Hed.

ERIEL MEREMONT   wife of Heureu, land-ruler of Ymris.

ERLENSTAR MOUNTAIN   site of the home of the High One.

GALIL   ancient king of Ymris in the time of Aloil.

GHISTESLWCHLOHM   founder of the school of wizards at Lungold.

GRANIA   dead wife of Danan Isig, mother of Sol.

GRIM MOUNTAIN   site of Yrye, home of Har of Osterland.

HAGIS   dead king of An, grandfather of Mathom.

HAR   land-ruler and king of Osterland, sometimes called the wolf-king.

HARTE   home of Danan Isig, on Isig Mountain.

HED   small farming principality on an island.

HEL   ancient kingdom, now a part of An.

HERUN   kingdom; chief city, Crown City; ruled by the Morgol El.

HEUREU   king and land-ruler of Ymris.

HIGH ONE law-giver and sustainer of life since the passing of the Earth-Masters.

HLURLE trade-port town near Herun.

HUGIN son of Suth the wizard.

IFF OF THE UNPRONOUNCEABLE NAME wizard in service to Herun at the time of Morgol Rhu.

INGRIS OF OSTERLAND refused to take in the disguised Har of Osterland and died as a result.

ILON ancient harper of Har of Osterland.

ISIG kingdom ruled by Danan from his home at Harte; known for its fine metal and jewel work.

ISIG PASS the route from Harte to Erlenstar Mountain.

KALE first King of An, who won a desperate battle with a Great Shout.

KERN OF HED ancient prince of Hed, subject of the only riddle to come from Hed.

KING'S MOUTH PLAIN site of ruined city of the Earth-Masters; name is of a later date.

KOR, RUSTIN trader.

KRAAL trade-city of the far north, located at the spot where the River Ose flows into the sea.

KYRTH trade-city near Harte, home of Danan Isig; on the Ose.

LAERN Riddle-Master at Caithnard; lost his life in a riddle game with Pevin of Aum.

LUNGOLD ancient city founded by Ghisteslwcholm as the site for the school for wizards.

LOOR fishing village in Ymris.

LYRA daughter of the Morgol El of Herun; land-heir of Herun; full name Lyraluthuin.

MADIR ancient witch of An.

MARCHER territory in north Ymris governed in the king's name by the high lord of Marcher.

MASTER, CANNON farmer of Hed.

225

MATHOM   land-ruler and king of An; father of Rood, Raederle and Duac.

MEREMONT   coastal territory of Ymris governed by the high lord of Meremont.

MEROC TOR   high lord and ruler of Tor; subject of Heureu of Ymris.

MORGON   land-ruler and prince of Hed.

NUN   ancient wizardess of Lungold, in service to the lords of Hel.

NUTT, SNOG   pigherder of Hed.

OAKLAND, GRIM   overseer for Morgon of Hed.

OEN OF AN   conqueror of Aum; king of An; built a tower to trap the witch Madir.

OHM   a Riddle-Master of Caithnard.

OSTERLAND   kingdom ruled by Har from Yrye.

PEVEN OF AUM   ancient lord of Aum held captive for five hundred years in a tower by the rulers of An, guarding the ancient crown of Aum.

RAEDERLE   daughter of Mathom of An, promised to the winner of the crown of Peven of Aum.

RAITH   current lord of Hel, under Mathom.

RE OF AUM   offended an ancient lord of Hel, and in trying to insure his safety, allowed the lord of Hel to trap him on his own estate.

RHU   fourth morgol of Herun; built the seven walls surrounding Crown City; died seeking the answer to a riddle; full name Dhairrhuwyth.

ROOD   land-heir of An; son of Mathom; friend of Morgon of Hed.

RORK   high lord of Umber, under Heureu.

RYE, TOBEC   trader.

SERIC   the High One's watcher; trained by the wizards at Lungold.

SOL OF ISIG dead son of Danan of Isig; died at the door of the cave of the Lost Ones at the bottom of Isig Mountain; cut the stones for the stars on the harp Yrth made.

SPRING OAKLAND dead mother of Morgon of Hed; wife of Athol.

STONE, HARL farmer of Hed.

STRAG, ASH trader of Kraal.

SUTH ancient wizard, friend of Har of Osterland.

TALIES ancient wizard.

TEL one of the Riddle-Masters of the college at Caithnard.

TIR Earth-Master; Master of Earth and Wind.

THISTIN OF AUM current lord of Aum, under Mathom.

TIRUNEDETH harper to the Morgol Cron, ancient ruler of Herun.

TOL small fishing-town in Hed; a seaport.

TRISTAN sister of Morgon of Hed.

UMBER midland territory governed by Rork, under Heureu.

UON harpmaker of Hel, three centuries before.

USTIN OF AUM ancient king of Aum who died of sorrow over the conquering of Aum by An.

VERT daughter of Danan Isig.

WIND PLAIN plain in Ymris, site of Wind Tower and a ruined city of the Earth-Masters.

WIND TOWER only complete structure in the ruined city on Wind Plain; top of tower cannot be reached.

WOLD, LATHE great-grandfather of Morgon of Hed.

WOLD, SIL farmer of Hed.

XEL wild cat belonging to Astrin, gift of Danan Isig.

YLON   ancient shape-changer.

YMRIS   kingdom ruled by Heureu from the chief city Caerweddin.

YRTH   most powerful wizard in Lungold after the Founder, sometimes known as the Harpist of Lungold.

YRYE   home of Har of Osterland.

ZEC OF HICON   craftsman who did the inlay work on the harp with three stars.

Patricia A. McKillip discovered the joys of writing when she was fourteen, endured her teenage years in the secret life of her stories, plays and novels, and has been writing ever since—except for a brief detour when she thought she would be a concert pianist.

She was born in Salem, Oregon and has lived in Arizona, California and the England that is the setting for *The House on Parchment Street*. After a number of years in San Jose, where she received an MA in English from San Jose State University, she moved to San Francisco, where she now lives.

Miss McKillip has also written *The Throme of the Erril of Sherill*, *The Forgotten Beasts of Eld*, *The Night Gift*, and *Heir of Sea and Fire*.